GRAVE PAST

A NOVEL

GRAVE PAST

A NOVEL

MARK GILLEO

PRESS

ALSO BY MARK GILLEO

Hunting Rabbits
Out of Tupelo
Terminal Secret
Favors and Lies
Love Thy Neighbor
Sweat

PRESS

2020 Press, LLC.
Copyright © 2025 by Mark Gilleo

Visit the author's website at www.markgilleo.com
ISBN: 978-0-9990472-8-6
ISBN: 978-0-9990472-9-3 (ebook)

First trade edition: December 2025

ACKNOWLEDGMENTS

I WOULD LIKE to thank the following people for their input and/or editing assistance: Tim Davis, Sue Fine, Michele Gates, Dan Lord, Danielle Allen, Audrey Hubbard, Stacey Porcaro, and Nora Smith. Last but not least, I would like to thank my wife, Ivette, for all of her support.

CHAPTER 1

FEW PLACES ARE worse than an elevator to battle a panic attack. For Grace Homan, employment on the seventh floor left her with few alternatives. Her choices were simple. Thirty seconds in the confines of the elevator or three minutes in a dimly lit, twisting stairwell. Sealed office windows complicated an unsavory third option and, although Grace would never admit it, the expression "break glass in case of emergency" had run through her mind more than once.

Grace gasped for air as she pressed the silver button and closed her eyes. Behind its shiny metal doors, the elevator began its descent with an initial drop. Grace struggled to corral her thoughts as she reached for the handrail. She glanced up at the illuminated numbers over the door, breathing deeply as the elevator reached the fourth floor. The walls closed in and the ceiling inched lower. She felt faint and closed her eyes. *Keep it together a little longer.* She tried to override her anxiety with calming thoughts, but her mind raced on without permission, latching onto any nugget of negativity that could be blown out of proportion and instantly replayed on a loop. When the doors opened, Grace exited the elevator and headed for the lobby, passing the security presence at the front desk.

"Early lunch today?" the nearest security guard asked. His blue rent-a-cop shirt was pressed and his faux badge shined.

Grace didn't respond, her hand moving towards her face to conceal her embarrassment, as if her internal meltdown was visible to everyone.

On the sidewalk outside, fresh air came mixed in a cloud of exhaust from the rear of a DC Metro bus.

Head down, Grace walked west to the nearest cross street and turned the corner. She stopped, put her hands on her hips, and counted five deep breaths to no avail. If oxygen alone had been the panacea to her attacks, she would have kept a tank of it next to her desk. And no one would have cared. When you spend your days buried in legal briefs, the occasional hit from an oxygen tank would scarcely be noticed. All manner of things can be overlooked when doing serious work that requires dedication and endurance. Not to mention a law degree from a prestigious university and near-perfect pedigree. Indeed, all manner of things could be overlooked, as long as the work was being done well. Unfortunately for Grace, the increasing frequency of her anxiety attacks was now putting her work in jeopardy.

Exhaling, she continued walking westward. Eyes open wide, pupils dilated, she stared into faces passing in the opposite direction. She wondered if any of them were in a similar mental state. With the buildings around her seeming to lean in, her mind tumbled from one morbid thought to the next. Exasperated, she stepped to the curb, raised her hand, and hailed a cab.

The four-doctor medical suite shared a single waiting room without a receptionist. The room boasted a beige carpet, seating for fifteen, and a window with a view of DuPont Circle. Grace took a seat, grabbed a magazine from a side table, and waved it in front of her flushed face. She was certain the makeup she had applied to her Californian, girl-next-door face needed to be refreshed. She placed the magazine on the chair next to her, removed her glasses, and tied back her blond hair. She grabbed the magazine for the second time, continuing to use it for impromptu ventilation. She closed her deep blue eyes with the hope of wishing her thoughts away. When she opened them, she glanced at the clock on the wall. She wouldn't have to wait much longer.

Dr. Micha Joffee, tall and thin with olive skin and a full head of curly dark hair, appeared at the precipice of the waiting room and the hall that led to the doctors' offices. A woman and her teenage son stepped from the hall, crossed the room, and exited the suite. Dr. Joffee glanced around the room as if searching for his next patient. Locking eyes with Grace, he scowled and pursed his lips. With a flick of his head, punctuated by his bouncing hair, he invited Grace to follow him down the hall.

"Grace, I've told you before that you can't just stop by," Dr. Joffee said, closing his office door and running his fingers through his hair. "That's not the way my office works. I'm sure you understand. I'm sure people can't just drop in on you at your place of business."

"I'm sorry. I'm really sorry."

"I have five minutes before my next patient. Take a seat. What's going on?"

Grace quickly sat down on a sofa that she had come to know better than the one at her home. She looked around the office, eyeing its all-too-familiar decorations. The waist-high Buddha statue in the corner. The relief map of Asia on the wall. A series of framed diplomas behind the desk. The sound of the small waterfall in the corner pushing a stream of water over fake rocks.

Returning her focus back to Dr. Joffee, Grace spoke. "I think the time has come to take you up on the offer for Xanax. I can't go on like this. I have a job to do."

"Okay. But first, tell me what happened today."

"Same thing as usual. Nothing. I met with Judge Cardin to go over the bench memoranda I was preparing. Standard work stuff. Halfway through the meeting, I could feel myself slipping. By the time the meeting was over, I was past the point of no return."

"How long ago was this?"

Grace checked her watch. "Forty-two minutes since the first inkling of trouble."

"And was there anything unusual about this meeting? Were voices raised? Was there a confrontation? A disagreement?"

"No." Grace clenched her teeth. Tears streaked down each cheek as if racing for her jawline. "Tell me what to do, Dr. Joffee. I don't know what to do. And I fully realize how desperate that sounds."

"I can certainly prescribe Xanax. It may help treat your symptoms, but it won't address the cause of the anxiety attacks. That, we still have to figure out." Dr. Joffee paused as if considering his words carefully.

"I'm not sure how much longer I can wait to figure it out. This has been going on for eight months and it's not gotten better."

"I had hoped and, quite frankly, expected improvement by now."

"What else do you have in your bag of tricks?"

"I don't have a bag of tricks. I wish I did."

"There have to be options."

Dr. Joffee quietly sighed and nodded. "We could try alternative therapies."

"Such as?"

Dr. Joffee paused again. "Before I start that discussion in earnest, you should be aware that some alternative therapies are not viewed favorably by medical professionals in my chosen field."

"Meaning?"

"Some are deemed controversial."

"With the exception of a lobotomy, I'm willing to explore controversial alternatives."

"Okay. Keep that in mind going forward." Joffee stepped to his desk, rummaged through a drawer, and turned back around to face Grace on the sofa. He extended his hand, opened it, and offered her a pill from his palm. Grace took the small pill and held it up for inspection. Dr. Joffee stepped to the mini fridge in the corner, removed a small bottle of water, and handed it to Grace.

"Xanax. Point five milligrams. You could even start with half if you prefer. See how you feel. If it sits well with you, I can write you a prescription," Dr. Joffee said. "If anyone asks, I never gave that to you."

"Bottoms up," Grace replied, placing the pill on her tongue, and washing it down with water.

"With your permission, I would like to discuss your case with a colleague of mine. She's a psychiatrist, but with a different specialty."

"A controversial alternative specialty?"

"Indeed."

"Fine by me."

"Let me make a call and see what I can arrange."

"How long will it take?"

"I'll speak with her later today and get back to you."

Dr. Joffee checked the clock on the wall and seemed to do a calculation in his head. "Why don't you have a seat in the waiting area and see how you feel with the Xanax. I'll check on you in a little while. Sit back. Read a magazine. Relax. And breathe."

CHAPTER 2

DR. MELISSA FABRIZIO SAT at the end of the bar, sipping an old-fashioned and reading the screen of her phone. Her straight brown hair tickled the shoulder of her wrinkled business suit. Orange high heels wrapped around the front legs of her bar stool.

Dr. Joffee approached from the side and the two doctors with matching medical degrees embraced. Dr. Fabrizio placed her phone on the bar. Dr. Joffee pulled up a stool and sat down.

"I haven't been to Off the Record in forever," Dr. Fabrizio said, sipping her drink and leaving a lipstick print on the glass.

"It's been a while," Dr. Joffee concurred.

A bartender in a bow tie arrived and Joffee ordered a scotch on the rocks. Turning to face Fabrizio, the light scent of vanilla from her perfume reached his nose.

"I have something to ask, but you have to promise to remain professional."

"When have I ever not been professional?"

Dr. Joffee raised an eyebrow.

"I don't think I like your tone," Fabrizio said, trying to conceal a smirk.

"I have a patient for you to see. For hypnotherapy," Joffee said, cutting to the chase.

"Hypnotherapy? Really? This is a first," Fabrizio replied.

"If you're going to make a big deal out of it, then forget it. I'll find someone else."

"No, I won't. I promise," Fabrizio said, smiling as she stirred her drink with a swizzle stick. "I just never expected it."

"Neither did I. There's a first time for everything."

"What can you tell me about the patient?"

"She's a twenty-seven-year-old female attorney. She moved to DC about a year ago for a new job. The patient is suffering from severe anxiety attacks. Insomnia. Agoraphobia. Claustrophobia."

"A stressed-out attorney? More than a few of those in this town."

"I initially thought so, but now I'm not so sure."

"How long has she been symptomatic?"

"Nine months. But her symptoms have progressed in both intensity and frequency."

"How long have you been treating her?"

"Eight months. She started coming a month after her attacks began."

"Weekly sessions?"

"We started with weekly sessions. It's been twice a week for the last couple of months. Today, she dropped in without an appointment for the third time."

"Medical background?"

"Nothing of note."

"Substance abuse?"

"None."

"Alcohol?"

"Claims she is a moderate drinker."

"Don't we all?" Fabrizio said, raising her drink. "Medication?"

"Various. Zoloft. Started at fifty mg. She's at two hundred a day now. I'm considering a switch to Lexapro. She has a prescription for a beta blocker. Ambien for sleep. I gave her a Xanax today. Just to try it out."

"No one can accuse you of failure to treat the patient."

"It's more medication than I typically prescribe."

"Anything in the patient's family history?"

"The patient states she comes from a good home. Religious parents. Parents are still together after thirty-some years of marriage. No history of family mental illness that she is aware of."

"We both know how family secrets can remain secret. You said she moved to DC a year ago. Where's she from?"

"Raised in Morgan Hill, California, south of San Jose. Went to Stanford on an academic scholarship and then followed that up with Stanford Law."

"So intelligence is not in question."

"Definitely not. She graduated summa cum laude. First in her class. She was probably first in her class in every school she ever attended. After law school, she worked a couple of years in a New York firm and then joined Thomas Cardin as a law clerk."

"Who is Thomas Cardin?"

"Judge for the Federal Court of Appeals for the DC Circuit. Apparently, it's a big deal to be a judge for the DC circuit."

"Did you know that, or did you have to look it up?"

"The patient told me. Then I looked it up."

"That makes me feel better."

"And being a clerk for a judge for the federal court of appeals is also a big deal. It's a very competitive position. It's often a fast track for the clerk to becoming a judge one day."

"So we're not talking about a clerk in the sense of someone who files documents and makes copies."

"Most definitely not. We're talking about a law clerk who helps judges to make important legal decisions. Briefs, bench memoranda, draft opinions for oral arguments."

"Sounds riveting."

"She claims it's very solitary."

"And her symptoms started shortly after she moved to DC and began clerking for the judge."

"That's what she says."

"If you had to guess, what do you think is the cause of her anxiety? The move to a new city? The job? Her boss?"

"I don't know. Eight months of therapy has left me stumped. I don't think it's the job, per se. She moved here from New York where she was putting in eighty hours a week. I actually think she works less now. Not much less, but less. She claims she hasn't been dating since she moved here. So I don't think it's being caused by a bad relationship. She has been besieged by anxiety several times while at work and the attacks are starting to impact her career. I just can't pinpoint a trigger."

Dr. Fabrizio finished her drink and put her empty glass back on the bar. "Okay. If she's willing to see me, I'll make the time."

CHAPTER 3

GRACE SAT DOWN on the sofa and checked the clock on the wall, mentally marking the beginning of her next fifty-minute hour. The sound from the small waterfall in the corner seemed to echo.

Dr. Joffee fell into his worn leather chair on the other side of the table from his patient.

"How are we today, Grace?"

"So far, so good."

"I'm glad to hear it."

"I apologize again for busting in the other day without an appointment."

"It's fine."

"No, it's not. I understand there are protocols to follow and you have other patients. Unfortunately, my ability to remain rational is severely diminished when my anxiety hits."

"Really, it's fine, Grace," Joffee repeated. "The life of a psychiatrist is riddled with unconventional patient behavior."

"If that was supposed to make me feel better, it didn't work."

"Don't want to be lumped in with the masses?"

"Not the unconventional masses. That's why I'm seeing you for treatment."

Joffee chuckled. "Fair enough. I spoke with my colleague about you. Her name is Dr. Fabrizio. If you're still willing to explore an alternative therapy, she's willing to meet with you."

"What exactly is this alternative therapy option?"

"Hypnotherapy."

"You want to hypnotize me?"

"I wouldn't. My colleague would be in charge of the session. But I would be in the room with you the entire time."

"And this Dr. Fabrizio is a medical doctor, correct? She's not a PhD. No offense to PhDs."

"She's a licensed psychiatrist with a full-fledged medical degree. She just happens to also practice hypnotherapy when it presents itself as a viable alternative."

Grace seemed to digest the explanation.

"I understand your concern," Dr. Joffee said. "To be honest, in general, mental health professionals view hypnotherapy with skepticism. But you said you were willing to consider alternatives."

Grace wrung her hands. "What do I have to lose?"

"With any luck, your anxiety."

Grace smiled. "Can we do it here, in this office?"

"If that would make you more comfortable."

"It would."

"I'll arrange it."

⌒

Grace was on her back on the sofa, pillow under her neck. Dr. Fabrizio, brown hair pulled back, sat in Dr. Joffee's leather chair, her knees mere feet from Grace's head. On the other side of the sofa, Dr. Joffee shifted his weight in his desk chair. He wrote the date at the top of the yellow notepad in his lap.

Dr. Fabrizio took a sip of water and cleared her throat. "Grace, any last questions before we get started?"

"No. It sounds pretty straightforward. You're going to hypnotize me and dig around in my past to see if you can find a cause for my anxiety attacks."

"That's right. High level, that's what we're trying to do."

Grace cranked her neck in the direction of Dr. Fabrizio. "What if it doesn't work? What if I can't be hypnotized?"

"That's a possibility. Believe it or not, colleagues from your alma mater, Stanford, developed a hypnotic susceptibility scale. That scale has shown that less than 15 percent of people are unsusceptible to hypnosis."

"Meaning they can't be hypnotized."

"That's correct. But most people fall somewhere in the middle of the scale and exhibit some degree of susceptibility. Statistically speaking, you're more likely to be hypnotized than not. That said, over the years, I've had numerous patients who I couldn't put under."

"Fair enough," Grace said. "Let's give it a whirl."

"Okay. Please know that Dr. Joffee and myself will be here the entire time. We will also be recording both video and audio."

"You're in good hands," Dr. Joffee added.

"Thanks."

"Get comfortable, take a deep breath, and we'll get started."

Dr. Fabrizio began reciting the hypnosis script in a soothing voice, "Your eyes are becoming heavy. It takes effort to keep them open. Soon they are going to slowly close as you relax the muscles around your eyes. You can allow yourself to relax with your eyes shut and let yourself fall into deep relaxation. You feel comfortable warmth all around you. Take deep comfortable breaths as you let yourself relax. You can feel yourself falling deeper into relaxation as you listen to the sound of my voice. Your eyes are shut and your breathing is deep and relaxed. You are at ease."

Dr. Joffee watched as his patient reached a state of relaxation he had never seen in her. Gone was the frantic energy. Her shaking hands and wide-eyed gaze vanquished. The tension on Grace's face seemed to fade with each breath.

Dr. Fabrizio continued with her hypnotherapy script, helping Grace reach a subconscious level of deep relaxation.

"Let that comfortable feeling you have flow all the way to your toes. Every muscle, every cell in your body is relaxing. Every muscle, every cell is comfortable and at peace."

Dr. Fabrizio paused to watch Grace's chest rise and fall in a slow, steady rhythm.

"Good. Keep listening to the sound of my voice as you continue to relax every muscle. All is well. Now, see yourself at the top of a long staircase. You have no fear. Slowly, you take your first step and begin descending the stairs, each step bringing you down into a state of deeper relaxation. You have no anxiety. Each step is welcomed. Slowly, you reach the bottom of the stairs…."

Dr. Fabrizio broke her gaze from the patient and looked over at Dr. Joffee. She nodded slightly, as if indicating the patient had achieved full hypnosis. Dr. Joffee checked his watch. The time for the hypnotic induction had taken nearly ten minutes.

Dr. Fabrizio spoke again, "Now allow yourself to wander back. Your mind gently floating back in time. You can still hear my voice, but you are relaxed and comfortable as your mind drifts back to events and memories and experiences from your past. You can hear my voice and you, too, can speak. Your mind is moving through the memories of long ago."

Another five minutes passed, Dr. Fabrizio repeating herself throughout with only slight variation in her verbal guidance.

"Yes," Grace suddenly replied, her voice softer than what it had been prior to hypnosis.

Dr. Fabrizio and Dr. Joffee locked eyes for a second. Then Dr. Fabrizio turned her attention back to the patient.

"Good. All is well. Can you tell me what you see?"

"I see people."

"Where you are?"

"I'm sitting in a crowd. Everyone is in a chair," Grace replied.

"What are you wearing?"

"A black gown. Everyone is dressed in black. I also have a gold sash around my neck. It's hot."

"What year is it?"

"The top of the hat on the person in front of me says it's 2016."

"Can you describe what's around you? What else do you see?"

"Buildings. Lots of buildings and green grass. A banner over the stage says Stanford University."

"Are you a student?"

"Yes. A law student."

"How do you feel?"

"I'm happy. But it's hot. Everyone is sweating because we're wearing black in the sun."

"Do you recognize anyone around you?"

"Yes. The guy next to me is named Sheridan. He died after graduation. In a small plane accident."

"Were you friends with Sheridan?"

"We had classes together. He and his girlfriend were both killed. I don't remember her name."

"That's okay. That's okay."

"They're calling the names of people who are graduating. The next group begins with people whose last names start with H. I'm in the next group. When my name is called, I stand up and walk across the stage."

"What happens next?"

"There's a big party. At a fancy house overlooking the ocean. We stay awake until morning."

"Are you still happy?"

"Yes. But the police come to the house. I don't know why."

"Do you talk to the police?"

"No. The owner of the house does. Then we all leave. I sleep all day. I wake up happy."

"Okay, Grace. That's good. Now let's go back further. Allow your mind to move on to your next memory. Allow yourself to drift back to memories that may be important to you."

Grace remained silent as Dr. Fabrizio nudged her further into her past.

"Grace, can you tell me what you see. How do you feel?"

"My name is not Grace. My name is Mary."

"Mary?"

"Yes."

Dr. Joffee flashed a look of confoundment.

"Where are you Mary?" Dr. Fabrizio asked.

"I'm outside."

"What's the weather like?"

"It's hot."

"And your name is not Grace?"

"Grace is not here. My name is Mary."

Dr. Joffee raised his eyebrows as if at a loss to comprehend what he was witnessing. Dr. Fabrizio noticed his reaction and patted her hands in the air in a calming motion.

"Okay, Mary. Can you tell me what you see around you?"

"I see trees. A small field. I see water. A body of water."

"How old are you, Mary?"

"I'm not sure. I'm drinking and smoking. I think I'm in high school."

"Who are you with?"

"I'm with friends, and friends of friends. There's a boy I like."

"What's his name?"

"I recognize him. It's Thomas."

Dr. Joffee excitedly flipped the top sheet on his yellow notepad and scribbled across the empty page. He held the paper up for Dr. Fabrizio to read. Dr. Fabrizio acknowledged the note with a nod.

"Is the Thomas you see Judge Thomas Cardin?" Dr. Fabrizio asked, seeking confirmation.

"He's not a judge yet. We are sitting next to each other, talking."

"What are you talking about?"

"Just chatting. We are drinking and smoking and talking and laughing. It's a nice day."

"How do you feel?"

"I feel good."

"Are you happy?"

"Yes. Thomas says he wants to show me something."

"What is it?"

"I don't know," Grace answers, her voice changing tone. "But he wants to be alone with me to show it."

Grace's head began to sway back and forth. Her breathing quickened and then her head jerked violently. "*Nooooo!*" she shrieked. Her scream pierced the air of the medical suite. Her voice turned into a gargle, followed by a second, blood-curdling howl. The cry of a wounded animal.

"What's happening, Mary?" Dr. Fabrizio asked in a calming tone.

A bubbling gasp escaped Grace's lips, followed by a whisper, "I can't breathe." The two psychiatrists watched as Grace's chest ceased moving. The veins in her neck bulged.

"What's going on?" Dr. Joffee asked Dr. Fabrizio.

"I don't know. She's experiencing something traumatic."

"Bring her out of it. End the session."

"We could let her work it out. We may discover what's causing her condition."

The patient moaned. Tears streaked down her face, her flesh flush, her lips turning blue. Suddenly, she sucked air back into her lungs and her eyes widened. "I'm dying," she said. "He killed me."

"Who did he kill?"

"Me. Mary. He killed Mary." Grace began to weep harder, still struggling for air.

"Bring her out of it. The session is over," Dr. Joffee said firmly, repeating his previous order.

"Done," Dr. Fabrizio replied.

Speaking to Grace, she said, "I'm going to count backward from five and when I do, you will wake, refreshed."

❦

Grace Homan sat upright on the sofa, looking at her therapist of the last eight months. She seemed to realize from his expression that the alternative therapy session had produced results.

"How do you feel?" Dr. Fabrizio asked.

"Swampy," Grace replied. She touched the perspiration on her shirt near her armpit. "Like I went for a jog."

"I assure you that you never left the couch," Dr. Joffee said. "Do you have any recollection of the session that just concluded?" he asked.

"No."

"Nothing at all?"

"No. Am I supposed to?"

Dr. Fabrizio answered, "Not always. In many cases, a patient will remember their hypnotherapy session, but it's not a hard rule."

"So how did it go?" Grace asked. "You're both staring at me as if I said something surprising. What happened? Did my head spin around?"

"Your head didn't spin around, but you did take us by surprise," Dr. Joffee responded.

"How exactly did I do that?"

"I think it'd be better if you reviewed a video of the session. We can let you watch it by yourself, or we can watch it with you. Then we can discuss it."

"Okay," Grace answered, her voice fading. "Let's watch it together."

❦

When the recording of the session ended, Joffee reached down and paused the laptop sitting on the table.

Grace looked back and forth at the two psychiatrists, her mind registering what she'd just seen in the recording of her own hypnotherapy session.

"What the hell was that?" she asked, her voice cracking.

"We're not sure," Dr. Joffee replied.

"*You're* not sure?"

"It was a first for me," Dr. Fabrizio admitted.

"A first for us," Dr. Joffee added.

Grace glared at Dr. Fabrizio. "I thought this was your specialty."

"Hypnotherapy is. This was different. This seems as if it could have been a recollection from a past life," Fabrizio answered. "It's rare."

"Past-life regression? Meaning that under hypnosis I told you of a past life?"

"Perhaps. You clearly claimed to be someone named Mary."

Grace sat frozen, unsure of what to think and unconvinced of what she'd seen.

"You just watched the video, Grace. What do you think happened?" Dr. Joffee asked.

Grace's upper lip began to quiver. "I don't know and a big part of me doesn't want to know."

"You don't?" Dr. Joffee asked.

"No, I don't," she confirmed. "Could I get another bottle of water?"

Dr. Joffee retrieved a bottle from the fridge and passed it to his patient. Grace took a sip, the bottle shaking in her hand.

"In the house I grew up in, you didn't play with Ouija boards or tarot cards. You didn't talk about ghosts, and you sure as hell didn't discuss past lives," Grace said.

"Grace, it's possible what you revealed during the session is the cause for your current mental condition," Dr. Joffee offered.

"I'm going to have to disagree. Believing what I heard on that recording might contribute to a further decline in my mental condition."

Dr. Fabrizio interjected, "I can appreciate your concern. But you may want to reconsider."

"Reconsider what?"

"With your permission, we could explore what you revealed more deeply. It may prove helpful. It could be the key to resolving some of your issues."

"You mean you want to try again?"

"That's correct," Dr. Fabrizio said.

"Not going to happen. You do not have my permission. We can all consider this hypnotherapy experiment over."

"It could help," Dr. Fabrizio said one last time.

Grace took another sip of water. "I don't think either of you appreciate the position that recording puts me in. If someone finds out I'm taking a half-dozen different meds for mental stability, my career could be in jeopardy. If anyone were to catch wind that I thought my boss, a highly respected judge, killed me in my previous life, well… I'd be practicing pro bono law in rural Montana."

CHAPTER 4

THE TWO DOCTORS sat on the sofa, an open wine bottle standing on the side table next to half-empty glasses. Dr. Fabrizio's blouse was half buttoned, her cleavage on display. Joffee's hairy legs extended from a pair of plaid boxers. The rest of their collective clothing was on the bedroom floor, lying where it had fallen.

"Any other thoughts on what transpired today with our patient?" Joffee asked.

"Such as?"

"I'm willing to consider all possibilities."

"Have you heard of confabulation?"

"Yes. It's a memory distortion."

"Not exactly. It's a disturbance defined as the production of distorted, fabricated, or misinterpreted memories. In true cases of confabulation, it is done without any intention to purposely deceive."

"Sounds difficult to prove."

"I'm hoping your patient will come around to a second session. It may be the only way we get answers to what happened today."

"She seemed adamant about not participating in another session."

"She did. And without a change of heart, I'm not sure how we move forward."

Fabrizio's laptop was on the coffee table in front of the sofa, and

Joffee eyed the keyboard. He sat up straight, took a sip of wine, and said, "Maybe we don't move forward. Maybe we should move backward."

"What do you have in mind?" Fabrizio asked.

Joffee flicked his head in the direction of the coffee table. "Can I borrow your computer?"

"That depends on what you want it for."

"Have some faith. I was thinking we should take a few minutes and poke around into Judge Thomas Cardin's past."

"You mean you want to validate your patient's hypnotherapy session?"

"Or perhaps invalidate it. For the patient's sake."

Fabrizio reached for her computer, entered her password, and passed the laptop to Joffee. Joffee began tapping on the keys while Fabrizio grabbed her wine glass and moved closer.

"Here we go," Joffee said, staring at the computer screen. "Judge Thomas Cardin's public bio."

"What does it say?"

"Thomas Cardin went to The Hammond School in Columbia, South Carolina. It's private. He graduated in 1987. Then he went to Duke for undergrad and law school."

"A Blue Devil."

"Let's hope he's not a red one, too," Joffee retorted.

"Your patient said her name was Mary and that she was in high school when Thomas killed her."

"She didn't say that Thomas was in high school. He could have been older, or younger."

"When you were in high school, who did you hang out with?"

"Point taken. Let's see if anyone named Mary was murdered in Columbia while Thomas Cardin was in high school. It shouldn't be hard to figure out." Joffee typed again and the search results produced several promising leads. Joffee pointed to the screen. "Do you see that? The fourth result."

"Click it," Fabrizio said.

Joffee eyed the page, a scanned copy of an original article from *The State*, South Carolina's flagship newspaper.

"Fuck me," Joffee whispered.

"I already did," Fabrizio replied, her body pressing into his.

"In 1986, during the summer after Thomas Cardin's junior year of high school, a local girl went missing. Want to guess what her name was?"

"You're not going to tell me it was Mary, are you?"

Joffee touched his finger to the screen. "Mary Spears." His eyes darted to the end of the two-columned article. Without waiting for Fabrizio to catch up, Joffee continued with his summary. "Here we go. A man named Odin Rowe was convicted of Mary Spears's murder, as well as the murder of two students at the University of South Carolina in the fall of that same year. The article says Odin Rowe got three life-terms. Not eligible for parole. The body of Mary Spears was never found."

"Does it say how this Odin Rowe character murdered his victims?" Fabrizio asked.

Joffee nodded. "It says he strangled them."

"And Grace indicated during her hypnosis session that she couldn't breathe when Thomas Cardin killed her," Fabrizio said.

"She did."

"I just got goosebumps."

Silence fell over the room as they both finished their wine and topped off their glasses.

Joffee returned to the computer screen and continued clicking, scrolling, and reading. "There's no mention of Thomas Cardin involved with any of the murders," Joffee finally said.

"Can I have a look?"

Joffee handed the laptop back to its rightful owner. He sipped wine and stared straight ahead as Dr. Fabrizio scanned articles.

"You're right. There's no mention of Thomas Cardin in any of the stories related to the girl named Mary who went missing."

"It was a long time ago. I'm not sure how many newspapers articles were digitized."

Fabrizio typed another query. "The Cardin family seems to have quite a presence in Columbia. Attorneys. Professors. Construction."

Joffee leaned back into the sofa cushions and sighed. "I don't know what to make of it."

"Me either."

"It's hard to comprehend, really. Is it even remotely possible that this Judge Cardin killed a girl forty years ago and now that girl is reincarnated and working for the judge as a clerk?"

"I've read some interesting stories of past life regression."

"Honestly, I'd feel better if my patient was a burnout or drug abuser. Hell, I'd even take a schizophrenic at this point. But she isn't any of those. She's an intelligent, successful woman who has been suffering from debilitating anxiety and panic attacks since she moved to DC."

"Which is around the same time she started working for the judge."

Joffee nodded. "If I don't believe what I saw in the therapy session today, then what was it? Is my patient pulling our leg? If she is, for what? She's demanding secrecy. She has nothing to gain and everything to lose."

Another moment of silence followed. "In your professional opinion, do you think the patient exhibited any traits of being delusional?" Joffee asked.

"I don't think she's delusional."

"Then I want to know what happened."

"Know what, exactly?"

"If he did it. If Judge Thomas Cardin killed a girl named Mary when he was in high school."

Dr. Joffee felt Dr. Fabrizio run her fingers through his thick curls as she said, "I'm sure you don't want to hear this from me, but looking into a decades-old murder may be crossing the line as far as professional behavior goes."

"I need to know," Dr. Joffee said, eyes misting. "When I look at Grace Homan, I see my sister."

"I understand," Fabrizio answered. "If you're really interested in pursuing this, you should talk to someone who knows more than I do about the subject."

"Who do you have in mind?"

"One of the doctors I went through residency with is now in academia. Dr. Chuck Pando. I haven't talked to him in years. Last I heard he was down at UVA and had been dabbling in these types of cases."

"A hippie doc who specializes in past lives?"

"He's not a hippie."

"Can you set something up?"

"I'll see what I can do. But before you go down this rabbit hole, I'm curious to know how far you're planning to take this. Are you going to close your practice and start playing detective?"

"No. I'm going to hire one."

CHAPTER 5

ENTERING THE BACKDOOR of an establishment where its occupants are armed can be dangerous. Sweating from the summer heat, Dan Lord glanced down the alley in both directions. Slowly, he twisted the knob and pushed the door inward. Faint light escaped from an opening at the far end of the room. He quietly shuffled through the darkness, sidestepping several oil paintings perched on easels. Pausing, he strained to listen to the muted conversations on the other side of the wall. At the opening of the doorway, Dan eyed the light switch. Reaching out, he cast the next room into darkness with a flick of his finger. He quickly entered the darkened room and stepped to the side, his back against the wall. The screen of a mobile phone came to life and a hand reached out to reilluminate the room.

"Surprise!" Dan yelled, ruining the punchline to his own party.

"Don't shoot," the baritone voice of Detective Earl Wallace boomed.

Detective Emily Fields, sitting in the corner of the room, released her grip on the butt of her still-holstered weapon.

Detective Earl Wallace, thirty-year veteran of the DC Metropolitan Police Department, stood and embraced Dan in a bear hug. "Happy birthday, Dan. I told them a surprise party was a bad idea. Anyone who's been to your office upstairs knows better. All that security. You're not the type of person people should throw a surprise party for."

"Guess that makes you the smart one."

Detective Emily Fields, Wallace's recently transferred partner from the suburbs, approached Dan for her own embrace. Dan immediately noticed a cut over Fields's eyebrow. "What happened there? Someone get the better of you?"

"It was my fault. I mistimed my defense on a kali stick," Fields replied.

"That'll hurt."

"It did. But paybacks are a bitch. I should sell tickets to our next training session."

"If you do, put me down for one."

"Will do. We can talk later. I'm going to help Lucia finish setting up."

Next to offer a birthday wish was Steve Ryker, a.k.a. Stryker, a bail bondsman who had employed Dan's services during the lean years of COVID. Dressed in an unseasonable pair of leather pants, Stryker offered a hug-handshake combo. "Happy birthday, Dan. I'm always surprised when you make it through another year."

"The feeling is mutual."

"And I'm glad you've moved on from your explosives phase. I sleep better at night being out of that line of business."

"Keep that conversation between the two of us," Dan said.

"I have a surprise for you," Stryker said.

"That's the point of a surprise party."

A man in jeans and a white T-shirt approached from Stryker's rear. "Tobias made it out. Just for your party," Stryker said.

Dan flashed a broad smile as he shook hands with Tobias. "I'm flattered that you came."

"It wasn't an easy decision. But my girlfriend has me taking meds. She grinds them up and adds them to my protein shake. Little does she know how often I add a dose of Viagra into the evening mix."

Dan ignored the medical update. "You still keeping a headcount of the people you know who have passed away?"

Tobias leaned in and whispered. "Yes, but I don't mention it anymore. I'm much better these days. Much more even-keeled."

"Good."

"I've been working on some AI solutions that you may be interested in. You should come out to the house and have a look."

"I'd love to. Even though AI is probably the beginning of the end."

"I think we'll be okay as long as we keep AI away from robots and quantum computing."

"I understand the robot reference, but you may need to educate me when it comes to quantum computing."

"At your service. Any time."

"How is Peso?" Dan asked in reference to a Rottweiler he'd given Tobias earlier in the year.

"She's good. Better than good. But she's shit for protection. Licks everyone and everything. Wants to play with the deer while they eat my plants."

"Just put her on the front porch. Her size alone should be enough of a deterrent."

"She prefers the tempered climate of the indoors. She's soft."

"That's odd, considering her previous owner's background."

"I agree. In no way does she act like an assassin's dog," Tobias said.

Lucia Messi, Dan's tenant, art gallery owner, and resident artist, interrupted and handed Dan a bottle of vodka. "A man who identified himself as a retired KGB agent dropped that off earlier today."

"That would be Alex."

"He looked vaguely familiar. He said to wish you a happy birthday."

"I don't think I ever opened the last bottle he gave me."

"I'll put it to the side and you can decide what to do with it."

Lucia stepped to a table filled with booze, opened a bottle of champagne, and poured glasses. Clearing her throat, she offered a toast to the small gathering. "Happy birthday to Dan. Here's to another year of happiness, fewer injuries, and no explosions on the premises."

The crowd in the art gallery raised their drinks and, one by one,

Dan touched glasses with everyone in attendance. Swapping out champagne for red wine, Dan found a seat next to Detective Wallace.

"What's the word on the mean streets of DC?" Dan asked.

"Carjacking is the sport of the season. We're averaging four a day. They're forming a carjacking task force, and both yours truly and my stick-fighting partner have been assigned to it."

"Sounds like fun. Do you get to drive around in bait cars?"

"It's been suggested."

"Let me know if you do. I'd be interested in riding with you for a shift or two."

"I'm sure that would never get approved," Wallace replied. "Listen, there's something I need to know. Are you and Emily, I mean Detective Fields, an item or not? She won't tell me."

"I can't kiss and tell."

"I don't care about kissing. I want to know if the two of you are bumping uglies. I couldn't tell from the birthday hug."

"We made a deal. She decides who she wants to share our relationship status with. I'll follow her lead."

"I'll take that as affirmative."

Dan shrugged. "Your prerogative. Doesn't mean it's true, but it's your prerogative."

"Speaking of truth, I finished my polygraph examiner course."

"A real detective doesn't need a polygraph to spot a lie."

"Law enforcement requires more than a hunch. I'm staring down mandatory retirement for detective work, but as a polygraph examiner, mandatory retirement doesn't apply."

"My offer to have you join me on the private investigator front still stands. Partners. Fifty-fifty after expenses."

"I appreciate it. Who knows? Maybe someday."

"How long is the training to be a polygraph examiner? It seems like you just started."

"Time flies. Four hundred hours of instruction and then field work with another examiner."

"You're aware that polygraphs are only accurate because people believe they're accurate, right?"

"Then lucky for me most people believe they are."

"Touché."

"What's going on in the private detective, shady legal adviser world?"

"I'm in between cases. Considering my options. Sue asked for help on a case. I might pursue it."

"Ex-CIA, former intern, Sue?"

"One and the same. She opened her own PI firm. Runs it out of her apartment in Northeast, DC."

"She finished trapsing around the world looking for your mother?"

"For the time being."

"The two of you have a complicated relationship."

"Some of the best friendships start off a little rocky."

"Amen to that," Wallace said, raising his glass with a nod. "After all, you and I became friends at a strip club."

"A strip club in the middle of the afternoon. Nothing more jolting than coming out of a strip club and seeing sunlight."

"I can think of a few things more jolting."

"Yeah, you're right. So can I. Another surprise birthday party."

"Only if you make it to another birthday. We've all learned you have a remarkable track record of finding cases that put you in peril."

"I don't find cases. They find me."

As if by magic, Dan's phone began to vibrate.

CHAPTER 6

DAN LORD STOOD in front of the window checking his phone when Dr. Joffee appeared at the door to the waiting room. "Dan Lord?"

Dan put his phone in his pocket, crossed the room, and extended his hand. "That's me. Dr. Joffee, I presume."

Joffee nodded. "Pleasure to meet you."

"Shall I call you 'Doctor'?"

"If you want. You can also call me Micha. Or Joffee. And my friends have been calling me Joff since, well, forever. Take your pick."

"I'll see what comes natural."

"Fair enough. Come on back," Joffee said, holding open the door. Seconds later, Dan followed Dr. Joffee into his office. Joffee motioned toward the sofa. Dan sank into the middle cushion, imagining the countless patients who had flopped onto the same couch for treatment.

Joffee sat in his leather chair. "First of all, thank you for agreeing to meet me here. I'm between patients for the next hour. I don't get a lot of time away during business hours."

"No problem. My schedule is fluid. Besides, I had a thing or two to take care of in DC today. It wasn't out of the way."

"I'm jealous when people tell me they have work flexibility. Seeing patients remotely is not the best option in my line of work. I miss out on a lot of body language."

"I can see how that would be true."

"You come highly recommended, Mr. Lord. I've had two patients who've mentioned using you as their private investigator."

"My services are almost exclusively referrals. I prefer it that way."

"As I've heard. You'll understand if I can't mention the patients' names who provided referrals. That would be a blatant HIPAA violation without their consent. But suffice it to say both were married to prominent individuals in this city and you helped them out of bad situations."

"I appreciate your candor and confidentiality. And just so we understand each other, I don't take every case that comes my way."

"No, of course not. But, as I said, you come highly recommended."

"That's nice to hear."

"Can you tell me a little about yourself?"

"Well, as you know, I'm a lawyer and a private investigator. Growing up, I moved around a lot. My mother worked for the government and my dad had a job that traveled well wherever my mother was stationed. My brother and I grew up in embassy housing in Asia, Europe, and South America. I studied a few martial arts. Dojos and books were my things."

"Sounds interesting."

"It was."

"And the combination of your occupations is a plus."

"Plus. Minus. Depends. Either can get you into or out of trouble."

"I imagine."

"So, what's on your mind, Doc?"

"I have a rather unusual case I want to discuss."

"Intriguing segue."

"Have you ever heard of a judge named Thomas Cardin?"

"I have. He's a judge on the DC circuit court."

Joffee seemed surprised. "Is that something all attorneys know?"

"No. But I had a run in with another judge on that circuit the year before last."

"How did that turn out?"

"We reached an understanding. But it was painful."

"I assume you're speaking metaphorically."

"I wish. I took a knee to the groin."

"Oh, I see," Joffee replied, cocking his head with a look of curiosity.

"What is it about this judge that interests you?" Dan asked.

"I'm not sure how this is going to sound but here it goes. I'd like to hire you to find out if Judge Thomas Cardin killed someone. Potentially."

"Potentially hire me, or potentially the judge killed someone?"

"Both."

Dan paused. "You're serious?"

"I am. I heard an unconfirmed rumor that Judge Thomas Cardin may have killed a woman several decades ago."

"Decades?"

"In 1986 to be exact."

Dan whistled. "That is a while ago."

"Is that a problem?"

"Not in and of itself. Though, I can think of a handful of complications with a case that old."

"I've considered some complications myself."

"Am I correct in assuming that one of your patients divulged this information regarding the judge?"

"Why would you assume that?"

"Seems logical."

"Hypothetically, let's say 'yes.'"

"During therapy?"

"Correct again. Hypothetically."

"Is this patient aware that you're looking to hire someone to investigate information provided during medical treatment?"

"Hypothetically, the patient would not be aware. But there is no HIPAA violation if I don't divulge the patient's name."

"Legally, there would be no HIPAA violation. There could be other issues."

"My patient is not involved in this case in any way. I'm your client."

"So you're paying for this investigation?"

"Yes. I'm the financially responsible party."

"My current rate is $450 an hour."

"That's more than I charge."

"Have you ever been shot on the job?"

"I haven't."

"Consider it a risk premium."

"Your going rate is fine. Frankly, I don't foresee this being a lengthy investigation."

Dan's eyes slowly danced across the wall of framed degrees and accolades behind the doctor's desk. "I'll have to think about it. Let me get back to you."

"I understand your position. But before you make a final decision on whether or not to take the case, I was hoping you would agree to a one-day trial of sorts."

"One day? No case is solved in a day."

"That's not what I meant."

"Then I'm afraid you've lost me."

"I'd like you to meet with someone and listen to what he has to say. He's a specialist in his field. A professor and medical doctor at UVA. Based upon that conversation, you can determine if this case is something you want to get involved in."

"A one-day trial?"

"One day. All expenses paid. I'll cover your hourly rate, as well as your transportation expense, meals, and a hotel for the night."

Dan nodded. "I'll go for it. UVA is my alma mater. I love Charlottesville. And I have a classmate who opened a brewery in town. I've been meaning to visit."

"Super. Add all-the-beer-you-can-drink to the offer."

"Who in their right mind would turn that down?"

"I'm not the best source to ask about people in their right mind."

CHAPTER 7

CHARLOTTESVILLE, SEAT OF the University of Virginia, sprawled across the landscape in the shadows of Thomas Jefferson's former residence, Monticello. As the founding father of UVA, Jefferson's home overlooked the campus, which still flaunted its paternal roots with Jeffersonian architecture and historical plaques.

Dan parked in the Fourteenth Street Garage near the UVA Medical Center and strolled toward the edge of the campus. The roof of the rotunda glistened in the sun as Dan disappeared into Pinn Hall, a modern addition to the historical facades of the university. Dan took the stairs to the second floor. At the end of the corridor, he pushed his way through a set of double doors. A blue sign on the wall indicated he had entered UVA's Division of Perceptual Studies. A voice emanated from a small cubicle in the corner. A service bell sat on a table with a handwritten sign that read "Ring Me."

Dan reached out and announced his arrival with his index finger.

A young blond woman in a UVA sweatshirt popped out from the cubicle.

"Can I help you?"

"Yes. I'm here to meet Dr. Pando. My name is Dan Lord."

"Dan Lord?" the woman confirmed.

"That's me."

She pointed at a hall on the far side of the room. "Head left. Corner office. His door is usually open."

Dan followed the girl's directions and a moment later knocked gently on the frame of an open door.

"Come in," Dr. Pando said, prying his eyes off the computer screen before standing. "You must be Dan."

"That's right."

"Chuck Pando," the man said, standing, exposing a basketball-sized belly on an otherwise normal frame.

The two men shook hands, and Dr. Pando watched as Dan's eyes danced around the room's interior. Sagging bookshelves lined one-half of the large office. Rows of filing cabinets filled the back wall.

"Let me officially welcome you to the University of Virginia Medical School, Psychiatry and Neurobehavioral Sciences, Division of Perceptual Studies," Dr. Pando said.

"You must have trouble fitting all of that on a business card."

"We use small font," Dr. Pando replied with a wink. "We're commonly referred to as DOPS."

"I can handle that."

"I hear you're interested in a quick lesson on what we do here."

"I think my client, Dr. Joffee, is interested in my reaction to whatever you do here."

"Very well. Let me start with a question."

"Shoot."

"Where do you stand on reincarnation?"

"Reincarnation?"

"That's right. It's a probing first question. I like to ask since it lets me know what I'm up against. I'll be the first to admit, there's nothing I love more than converting skeptics."

"I lived in various locations around the world growing up, so there isn't much I haven't been exposed to with regard to different religions, including reincarnation. But for the sake of this discussion let's say I'm open-minded, with a dose of lapsed-Catholic skepticism. Why don't you give me the rundown and we'll take it from there?"

"Have a seat," Pando offered and both men sat down at a small table. "In many ways UVA and this department is credited with being the first in the nation to examine behavioral and perceptual studies not readily explained by science or medicine. These research efforts began here at UVA in the early sixties with a psychiatrist by the name of Dr. Ian Stevenson."

"I'm not familiar with him."

"He was the founder of DOPS and performed extensive research into past-life regression, out-of-body experiences, near-death experiences, and related visions."

"When you say extensive research, what kind of numbers are we talking about?"

"Over three thousand cases spanning four decades."

Dan considered the number. "Seventy-five cases a year, give or take."

"Yes. But if you're trying to equate frequency with validity, that may be misleading."

"I'm just giving the numbers a quick sniff test."

"How did they smell?"

"No scent."

"Good. Among the topics studied here, Dr. Joffee requested that I provide you with a thorough review of past-life regression. To that end, I'd like to share a couple of quick examples I provide to my students. All of the cases have been vetted for authenticity."

"Perfect."

"The first is the case of Manoj, a three-year-old boy from Goa, India. Without any prodding, and to the shock of his parents, young Manoj began telling the story of how he had been killed in a previous life by an axe blow to the head. The boy also recalled his former name and the village where he lived in his previous incarnation."

"Interesting."

"It gets better. Manoj's parents eventually took their son back to the village where Manoj claimed he had previously lived. It was roughly a thousand miles from where the boy was born. For Manoj's family, it was quite a journey in both distance and expense. Once at the village, the boy identified the location of his own grave, the murder weapon, and his killer. Later, when the remains were exhumed, the bones indicated the deceased had died as a result of a blow to the head. The time of death was two years prior to Manoj's birth."

"The boy was reincarnated and remembered specific details of his death in his previous life?"

"In layman's terms, that's correct. Whether or not that's enough to convince you, I don't know. But perhaps the final tidbit of the story will help you decide where to lay your belief. When Manoj and his family confronted his alleged killer, the man admitted to the crime as described by the boy. He's spending the rest of his life behind bars."

"And all of this is verified?"

"It is. By a well-known doctor. And an attorney. In addition to official court and prison records."

Dan remained stoic. "No offense, but the story would be more palatable if it wasn't about a boy in India."

"You mean you have a geographical bias?"

"Foreign countries come with foreign cultures and foreign beliefs. It can be a hurdle to believability."

"How about the case of a girl from Santa Fe, New Mexico?"

"Lay it on me."

"In the late nineties, a four-year-old girl from Santa Fe told her parents that she died in a hotel fire in Boston twenty years earlier. She told them her name had been James."

"James?"

"That's right. Over time, much like in Manoj's case, the girl convinced her parents to investigate. When they did, they discovered a hotel fire fitting the description of the one their daughter frequently talked about. Her parents then asked their daughter to describe this

'James' she often referred to. The daughter was able to provide a very detailed description. Later, the daughter was shown a photo array of the hotel victims without any names attached and she immediately pointed to James Rather, a salesman who died in the incident."

"Hmmm. Any reason both of your examples deal with children?"

"Dr. Stevenson did extensive research on children. He found them to be far less likely to have been influenced by books, movies, stories, what have you."

"But children also have more active imaginations."

"That, they do. No argument there," Dr. Pando said. "If the age of the subjects is throwing you off, how about a case that deals with adults?"

"Maybe one more will win me over."

"Okay. Try this on for size. Six or seven years ago, a retired fire chief and EMT who was on vacation became ill at ease while visiting Antietam Battlefield in Maryland."

"Antietam, as in the Civil War?"

"That's correct. In this case, the retired first responder who visited the Antietam battlefield as a tourist was so struck by ill feelings that he became obsessed with the battle. Over the next several months, his obsession began to have an impact on his health. He couldn't sleep and developed stomach issues. He went to his general physician who referred the man to a therapist. Time passed, but his obsession with Antietam would not abate. Hypnotherapy was suggested as a possible solution and over the course of several sessions, the man seemed to have a breakthrough. Under hypnosis, he recalled serving as a soldier in the battle of Antietam. Armed with this knowledge, he traveled to the Library of Congress. During his research, he found himself gleaning a photography collection of injured soldiers and battlefield doctors. As a career first responder, he seemed to have a connection to the topic. In the course of his research, he stumbled upon a photograph of an injured Civil War soldier on a gurney who looked very similar to himself."

"How similar?"

"I smell skepticism lingering in the air."

"There's nothing wrong with your nose."

"I can have the photographs pulled for you if you want to see them for yourself."

"I'd love to."

"There's actually more to the story, but you might want to chew the first bite before I give you the whole sandwich."

"Interesting analogy."

A knock on the door interrupted the conversation. Dr. Pando stepped toward the door, exchanged whispers with a young man, and then turned back toward Dan.

"What else do I need to know about past-life regression?" Dan asked.

"I'm glad to hear you're still curious because we have something special planned this afternoon. I was hoping the timing would work out and I was just informed that it has."

"What is it?"

"A live session. You're invited to observe from behind a two-way mirror. I will be there with several colleagues, along with a few PhD students and graduate assistants from the Psychology Department. We're on the schedule for three o'clock." Dr. Pando checked his watch. "In the meantime, I'll have someone round up copies of the photographs I mentioned."

"Thanks," Dan replied.

"I'll meet you back here in an hour."

CHAPTER 8

THE ROOM BEHIND the two-way mirror boasted three rows of observers in stadium seating. A dozen people filled half of the available seats. Along one wall, a table was topped with sodas, water, chips, and a large bowl of M&Ms. A second table ran along the width of the room, beneath the bottom edge of the two-way mirror.

Dan took a handful of M&M's and found a seat next to Dr. Pando at the end of the first row of chairs. A button on the doctor's shirt had gone missing and Dan could see a patch of pale flesh on Dr. Pando's protruding midriff.

"What's the lowdown?" Dan asked, throwing an M&M into his mouth.

"Past-life regression with xenoglossy thrown in for good measure."

"Xenoglossy? From the Greek meaning foreign and tongue?"

"Bonus points for you. It's the ability of someone to speak a language they have never been exposed to. A language they have never studied. A language they have no reason to speak."

"It's a good Scrabble word."

"Our xenoglossy subject today is Liam Kelly. He's a four-year-old from outside of Boise, Idaho. His parents are farmers. They're also very worried about their son."

"What did he do?"

"It's not what he did, it's what he can do. Liam speaks Aramaic. Specifically, Western Neo-Aramaic."

"I am familiar with term Aramaic. But I'm adding 'Western Neo-Aramaic' to today's growing list of things I've never heard before."

"Western Neo-Aramaic is rare. In fact, only three villages in western Syria still speak it. And since the most recent war in Syria, and the displacement of many residents, the number of Western Neo-Aramaic speakers has plummeted even further. We believe there are less than a thousand speakers of the language alive today."

"I assume the boy and his parents have never been to Syria."

"They have not. The parents are quite religious. Fundamental Christians to be exact. Due to their beliefs, when their son first started speaking to them in Aramaic, they thought he was possessed. They immediately called for their pastor. The next day, members of their church attempted to perform an exorcism. To no avail. The parents then contacted an organization in California, which, in turn, referred them to this office. A week later, we received an audio recording of the boy speaking what sounded like Aramaic, according to the dean of the Foreign Language Department here at UVA. From there, we sent a copy of the audio overseas for verification."

Dr. Pando paused as a string of visitors filed into the room on the other side of the two-way mirror. A young boy with blond hair in a bowl cut led the procession.

"That's Liam, his parents, and their minister," Dr. Pando said.

"Have you met them before?"

"I have. I flew out to Boise last spring. I also spent an hour with them last evening. Unyielding religious beliefs aside, they're good people. A solid family. This morning, they were still on the fence about going through with today's session. But they came around. Fortunately for us."

Two middle-aged men of seemingly Middle Eastern descent entered the room next. The older man was frail, with short white hair and thick glasses. The younger of the two men wore a brown suit that almost matched the color of his skin.

"Who are they?" Dan asked.

Pando answered, "The older gentleman is named Nizar. He is fluent in Western Neo-Aramaic. It's his mother tongue. He's from a rural area of western Syria."

"I assume he's going to be the other half of the conversation we're going to witness."

"He is. The hiccup in this session is that Nizar doesn't speak English very well. He speaks Western Neo-Aramaic and standard Arabic."

"And the second man?"

"He is a linguistics professor from Damascus. He speaks nine languages fluently."

"Is Western Neo-Aramaic one of the nine?"

"It is not. But the professor also speaks Arabic. So if a translation is needed, we can translate from Aramaic to Arabic to English."

"What do you mean 'if a translation is needed'?"

"Liam will try to translate for us, but he's only four. With a four-year-old's vocabulary."

"So there's some limitation."

Dr. Pando grunted and Dan thought he heard a muffled fart. "Perhaps. We're going to hear what Liam has to say first. Then later, we can have the elderly gentleman and the linguistics professor validate Liam's translations."

"What could go wrong?" Dan asked sarcastically. "A four-year-old translating via the telephone game using Western Neo-Aramaic, Arabic, and English?"

"Dan, don't take this the wrong way, but I think you've sold yourself short as a skeptic."

"Did I say something inaccurate?"

"We're all going to find out together if this works. Regardless, consider what you're about to witness. In all likelihood, there are only two people in the eastern United States at this very moment who speak

Western Neo-Aramaic. And they're both in that room," Dr. Pando said, pointing at the glass.

"What are they going to discuss?"

Dr. Pando smiled. "Whatever a four-year-old wants to talk about."

≪

Liam and Nizar sat across from each other at the table. Liam's parents sat next to him, his mother on his left, his father to his right. The professor from Damascus sat next to Nizar. At the far end of the table, out of the way, the minister from Boise sat with consternation on his face. A camera stood in the far corner of the room, a second rested on the table on the audience side of the two-way mirror.

"Go ahead, son," Liam's father said, patting the young boy on the shoulder and nodding his head in the direction of Nizar. "This gentleman would love to have a conversation with you in your special language."

Liam stared at Nizar, his gaze tracing the man's boney hands and arms, up to his hair, over the wrinkles on his forehead, and coming to rest on the thick lenses of his glasses.

Liam finally spoke and Nizar smiled. Nizar responded and Liam's eyes opened wide.

"What did he say?" Liam's father asked.

"He said his name is Nizar. And he said it was nice to meet me."

Liam dove back into the nascent conversation, growing more animated with each passing sentence.

Moments later, Nizar turned toward the linguistic professor and spoke in Arabic. The linguistic professor then translated to the room. "Nizar asked Liam where he learned to speak Aramaic and the boy said Bakh'a, Syria. It's the same town Nizar is from."

Further conversation ensued with the audience at rapt attention. At times, the two spoke so quickly that they seemed to overrun each other's words.

"Take it easy, son," Liam's father said, hand again on his son's shoulder.

"Okay," Liam replied. "Did you know Nizar is eighty-one? I told him that I knew him before."

"You've met him?" Liam's father asked incredulously.

"I didn't *meet* him. I said I *know* him. Nizar is my nephew."

Liam's father looked over at the linguistic professor from Damascus and nodded, as if asking for confirmation. The professor leaned into Nizar and spoke quietly in Arabic. Nizar nodded and responded. A moment later the professor relayed the conversation. "Indeed, Nizar says the boy was his uncle."

Liam engaged Nizar again, both parties rattling off questions and answers with native fluency. At the end of a long dialogue, tears began running down Nizar's face. Liam stood from his chair, walked around the table, and rubbed his hand on the older man's back, whispering into the man's ear. Nizar lowered his head into his hands, covered his face, and sobbed.

"What did you say to him?" Liam's mother asked.

"Nizar asked me if I remembered my nickname for him when he was a boy."

"And?"

"I remember. I used to call him Ziso."

"Did he recognize that name?"

"Of course. Don't be silly. I'm his uncle, Talmai."

On the other side of the two-way mirror, Dan turned to Dr. Pando. "What's the population of the village where Nizar is from?"

"Several hundred."

Dan gazed back through the glass as Nizar dabbed his eyes with a tissue.

"What did you think?" Dr. Pando asked.

"Very convincing. Then again, that's the hallmark of a good parlor trick."

"I assure you there was no sleight of hand or subterfuge with what you witnessed."

"I believe you. Or, at the very least, if it was a parlor trick, I don't think you were in on it."

"Why would you say that?"

"It would be overkill to set something like this up for my benefit. I've got no skin in this game."

"Everything you witnessed was on the up and up."

Dan thought for a moment. "I have a question that's so obvious, I'm almost embarrassed to ask."

"Shoot."

"Unless I missed something, Liam was never placed under hypnosis."

"That's correct, the boy wasn't hypnotized."

"And in the previous examples of children with past lives, Manoj and the girl from Santa Fe, they weren't hypnotized. How's that? What did I miss?"

"Children don't need to be under hypnosis to recall a previous life."

"Say again?"

"Hypnotherapy for past-life regression is almost exclusively the domain of adults. Dr. Stevensen figured this out early on. That's another reason why he concentrated primarily on children."

"But the Civil War soldier turned fireman was hypnotized?"

"That's correct."

"How does your field of expertise explain the difference in the phenomenon?"

"We don't know the mechanism behind this discrepancy. Generally speaking, for some reason, children who reveal past lives can do so without hypnotherapy. But there's a catch."

"There always is."

"Children who are able to recall past lives generally lose their ability to do so by the time they are five or six years old."

"And then what happens?"

"One of two things occur. Those memories can only be recalled during hypnosis, or they are lost forever."

Dan considered the information he had just been given. "And Liam is four. Which is why you wanted to get this session recorded. Before he potentially forgets everything."

"We wanted to record this session for several reasons. One reason is Liam's age. We wanted to document his xenoglossy before he loses it."

"I imagine you also wanted to record the conversation before there's no one else alive for Liam to speak Western Neo-Aramaic with."

"It crossed my mind."

⋟

A young man came into the room and handed Dr. Pando a manila envelope. Dr. Pando removed several photographs and flipped through them. He rotated a large photograph, tilted his head, and handed the stack to Dan.

"Those are the photos of the firefighter and his injured, Civil War soldier counterpart."

Dan took his time examining the photographs and settled on two clear images for comparison.

"What do you think?"

"They're almost identical."

"I told you the photographic evidence was impressive."

Dan brought the photo closer. "The left side of the soldier's head is wrapped in bloody bandages."

"He was injured. He lost a majority of his ear. According to the medical log, he later succumbed to his injuries. Likely from an infection. You can see the damage more clearly in some of the other photos without the bandages."

Dan compared the men in the photographs and then focused on a photo of the fire chief.

"What's going on here?" Dan asked, holding up another photo of the same image.

"That's the fire chief's ear."

"It's also mangled?"

"It is. From birth. But for the fire chief, the mangled ear is merely unsightly. His hearing is fine."

"I don't know what to make of that."

"It's more common than you think."

"What is?"

"In many cases of reincarnation, a subject displays scars or birthmarks from their previous life. Often times these scars or birthmarks appear in the location where the reincarnated subject was seriously injured in their previous life. In many instances, these marks are connected to the injury that caused their death."

"Are you kidding me, Doc? People carry injury markings on their body from a previous life?"

Pando shrugged. "It happens."

"What about the boy, Manoj? Did he have a scar on his head?"

"He did not."

"How do you explain that?"

"The scenario I've described is not a given. It happens, but not always."

Dan sat in silence for a long minute, flipping back and forth between the photos. "Can I keep these?"

"They're yours. I have more photos from this file that are equally surprising. Apparently, one of my PhD students checked them out for research. Not exactly protocol, but it happens. When I get them back, I'll make sure you get copies."

⤐

Dan sat on the step of the rotunda at UVA, looking south across the lawn. Both sides of the expanse were lined with drafty two-hundred-year-old dorm rooms with fireplaces and no toilets. In the grass between the wings of dorm rooms, a small group of summer students with laptops sat on folding chairs. A frisbee intermittently buzzed overhead.

Dan called Dr. Joffee, who answered on the third ring.

"How was your day?" Joffee asked.

"Interesting."

"So, you understand why I asked you to indulge me in a one-day trial?"

"I do."

"I hope some of your questions were answered, preemptively."

"Some of them were. And now I have a question for you."

"I thought you might."

"It's a question regarding your patient."

"Understood."

"Based on today's dog and pony show, I'm going to assume your patient was more involved in the murder that was supposedly perpetrated by Judge Cardin than you originally let on. I think your patient not only conveyed that Judge Cardin may have killed someone in 1986, but that your patient was the one the judge killed."

"That's very perceptive, Mr. Lord."

"No other explanation makes sense, given today's information session. Now, I'm trying to connect the dots."

"I see."

"Out of curiosity, did your patient reveal how they were killed?"

"Based on what we witnessed during their hypnotherapy session, it seemed like strangulation. Respiratory failure. At the very least, respiratory impairment of some sort."

"Respiratory impairment?"

"Yes."

Dan opened the folder that Dr. Pando had given him and stared at the photograph of the Confederate soldier turned modern-day firefighter.

"You still there?" Joffee asked.

"Any chance you would know if your patient has any pronounced scars or noticeable birthmarks?"

"As a psychiatrist, I don't see the amount of skin that other medical doctors may encounter. That said, I'm fairly sure the patient doesn't have any noticeable skin anomalies on their face or hands. I would have noticed."

"Can you contact your patient and inquire about any birthmarks or scars on their body. Something they would have had since birth?"

"I could. Can you tell me why?"

"Let's say it could be a tiebreaker for whether or not I take the case."

"I'll get back to you," Dr. Joffee replied.

❧

Ten minutes later, still on the steps of the rotunda, Dan answered his phone.

"What's the word, Doc?"

"I called the patient, and they called back. The patient stated they have a birthmark that starts from the base of their neck and runs along their right clavicle. They confided that they make an effort to keep it concealed with clothing."

"So the patient is female," Dan stated.

"I never said that."

"You didn't have to. A woman would be more concerned with hiding a scar than a man would."

"I never said it was a woman," Dr. Joffee reiterated. "Now can you tell me why you wanted to know?"

"Because apparently, reincarnated individuals sometimes carry birthmarks or scars from one life to the next."

"I was not aware."

"According to Dr. Pando, in addition to a scar or birthmark being passed from one life to the next, it can be an indicator of how that person died in a previous incarnation. And if we're going to consider the possibility of reincarnation, we should probably consider all aspects of it," Dan said.

"I see your point," Joffee replied. He let out an audible sigh before continuing, "I need to tell you there's been a secondary development that may be pertinent to this conversation. It could help decide whether or not you want to take the case. When I spoke with the patient to ask about any birthmarks or scars, they informed me of some upcoming changes in their employment. Apparently, sometime in the next seventy-two hours, Judge Thomas Cardin is going to be nominated for the vacant seat on the Supreme Court."

"You're kidding."

"That's what my patient says. It's not public yet, but the announcement is coming."

"That's not good news."

"I didn't think it was either."

"Things are going to heat up with a nomination to the Supreme Court. We can expect Senate hearings and due diligence on the judge's past decisions, both in the court and outside the court. We need to find out whatever there is to know before Judge Thomas Cardin becomes Supreme Court Justice Cardin. Once he's appointed, no one in their right mind would accuse him of a thirty-some-year-old murder. At least not without a body, DNA evidence, and a long list of reliable witnesses. Any investigation of your patient's claim against the judge will face heavy scrutiny."

"Does that mean you're taking the case?"

Dan mentally parsed a list of pros and cons. "I'll take the case. I wouldn't be able to look myself in the mirror if a murderer managed to make his way onto the Supreme Court when I could have stopped it."

"Then we have a deal."

"We do."

Dan paused. "Let me ask another question. Do you have any idea where Judge Cardin allegedly killed your patient?"

"We didn't pose that question to the patient under hypnosis. But Judge Thomas Cardin grew up in Columbia, South Carolina. He graduated from high school in 1987. And in the summer after his junior year, 1986, a girl in town named Mary Spears went missing."

"Sounds thin."

"Under hypnosis, my patient claimed her name was Mary when Thomas Cardin killed her."

A long pause followed before Dan spoke again. "Sounds like I'm going to South Carolina."

CHAPTER 9

THE HEADQUARTERS FOR the City of Columbia Police Department shared a block with the Richland County courthouse and Zion Baptist Church. All three buildings boasted tall white columns. A mile from the University of South Carolina's main campus, the law-and-prayer block stood on a plateau of level ground as it rose from the banks of the Congaree River.

Dan stepped from his Uber and the Southern heat engulfed him. He gave his bag a tug in the direction of the building and the wheels on his suitcase clicked over the seams in the sidewalk. In the air-conditioned lobby of the police HQ, he stopped at the security booth manned by a uniformed officer.

"My name is Dan Lord. I'm here to see Captain Collins."

"Just a moment," the officer replied, simultaneously picking up his phone and pushing a clipboard through the pass-through in the security glass. A second later the officer hung up. "Sign in and he'll be right with you."

Dan scribbled his name and returned the clipboard. He strolled over to the bulletin board next to the elevator and perused the station's most wanted list. Classic mugshots of criminals wanted for myriad crimes dotted the board. Bank robbery, assault, murder, check fraud, meth production. The common ills of humanity found where the masses congregate.

As Dan reached the end of the mugshots, a man with a buzz cut, a pressed uniform, and a strong jawline came around the corner. The officer in the security booth sent the man in Dan's direction with a point of his finger.

"See anyone you recognize?" the man asked as he approached from Dan's rear.

Dan turned away from the wall. "Captain Collins?"

"All day long."

"Thanks for meeting with me," Dan said as the two men shook hands.

"My pleasure. Hope your trip down went well."

"It was uneventful, which is the best you can hope for. The heat took me by surprise. The DC area has hot and humid summers, but not like this. And it's still before noon. I might have to wait until midnight to go for a jog."

"Columbia's official city motto is 'Famously Hot.'"

"That's not a nickname a city would embrace without a very good reason."

"Some folks say summer temps around here can be measured on the Scoville scale."

"I may use that."

"Be my guest. Just give me credit," Captain Collins said. "You mentioned on the phone that you're an attorney and a private investigator."

"That's right."

"I'm curious. Which are you today?"

"Let's go with attorney."

"Noted," Captain Collins said. "Out of professional courtesy, I reached out to the prosecutor who handled the case way back when. I left a message with his office. He's older now. Mostly retired."

"Thank you for greasing the wheel."

"Proper manners can still get you places in the South."

"I'll keep that in mind."

"Follow me. I have someone for you to meet."

Collins led his guest to the elevator, and the two men chit-chatted as they rode the elevator to the fourth floor. A sea of gray cubicles and glass walls greeted them as the elevator opened. Dan followed Collins to a corner office and stepped inside. Two large windows stretched from floor to ceiling. A table filled the middle of the room. At the end of the table, surrounded by files, was an older man with a white mustache.

"Dan Lord, let me introduce Detective Roy Huff."

The gentleman with the white mustache stood and extended his hand. Dan noticed the old detective's grip was powerful, his fingers rough. Veins bulged in his forearm. Dan estimated the man to be in his mid-seventies, with the strength of someone half his age.

"Pleasure to meet you," Dan said.

Captain Collins continued introductions. "Huff here was the lead detective on the murder case you're interested in. He knows everything there is to know. Never been a better detective in Columbia law enforcement. And he's a helluva fisherman."

"I'm retired," Detective Huff added in a gravelly voice.

Collins nodded as if to confirm the detective's employment status. "But he's agreed to come out of retirement to meet with you. I'll let the two of you get acquainted. Let me know if there's anything you need."

"Captain Collins tells me you came all the way from DC to ask questions about a forty-year-old murder case." Detective Huff's white mustache hopped on each syllable as he spoke.

"That's right. Thank you for entertaining the request. Sounds like I'm intruding on your time off."

"Not a problem. I got my fishing in early this morning. Nothing will bite again until the temperature drops this evening."

"I've never had much luck fishing. Next time, I'll blame it on the temperature."

Dan felt Huff measuring him up, a glare of assessment the retired detective had likely perfected in a long career of dealing with criminal deceit.

"What kind of fishing have you tried?" Huff asked.

"All kinds. Didn't matter. I spent most of the day just holding the rod."

Detective Huff winked. "Whether or not you catch anything, it's still fishing."

"That's what they say."

"If you're in town for a few days, I can show you some proper river fishing."

"Let's see how it goes."

"Fair enough," Huff replied, never taking his eyes off Dan. "You know, I gotta admit I'm curious why someone from DC is interested in a murder case from the eighties. Particularly a murder case that has been solved. Maybe if you told me what exactly it is you're investigating, I could pinpoint what you need. Save us both some time."

"I'm not at liberty to say. My client, a medical doctor, claims a patient mentioned something that led him to look into the disappearance of Mary Spears. He found out what he could online, but didn't get as far as he had hoped. He's still looking for an answer or two."

"A medical doctor?"

"That's correct."

"Interesting."

"My client seems motivated to get answers," Dan added. He looked around at the stack of files and the large legal box on the table. "Are these the case files?"

"They are. We duplicated everything for you. All of it is in hard copy. Pretty standard for a case as old as this one. Eventually, I imagine older documents will be scanned into the electronic case system. But let's face it, there aren't many people interested in records from four decades ago for a crime that was solved."

"I understand," Dan replied.

Huff motioned for his guest to take a seat at the table. Dan settled into a chair, and Huff slid a manila folder from the top of the box in Dan's direction. Dan began reading through the file as Detective Huff recounted the highlights aloud from memory.

"Mary Anne Spears. Birth date, March 2, 1969. Disappeared July 10, 1986. Five foot seven. One hundred and thirty pounds. Red hair. Freckles. Last seen near Lake Katherine. She was riding her bike home after a day of swimming and going to the movies. She had friends who lived on Lake Katherine. She lived in the Shandon neighborhood."

Dan reached for his suitcase and rolled it next to his chair. He slipped his hand into the pocket on the side of the case. "I picked up a map at the airport. How far apart are those two locations you just mentioned?" he asked, unfolding the map.

Huff took a moment to get his bearings, viewing the map upside down. He pointed twice, once for Lake Katherine and once for Shandon. "The distance is a little over two miles."

"Not next door."

"Like I said, she was on a bike. Back then, kids were kept on longer leashes. The streets were safer. Or at least people thought they were. A lot of folks changed their minds after that year."

Dan lowered his eyes to the map again. "So, Mary disappeared somewhere on her way home and was never seen again."

"She was seen at least one more time. By Odin Rowe. A murderer who confessed to killing her. Nasty character. Said he killed her the same night she went missing."

"What led you to the suspect?"

"Mary Spears vanished without a trace in July. In the fall of that year, Odin Rowe was arrested for the murder of two university students. Both strangled to death. One in September. One in October. He confessed to those two murders as well as to killing Mary Spears."

"Anything unusual about his confession?"

"Like what?"

"Consistency in his statements? Coercion by law enforcement?"

Huff frowned. "No."

"Then you probably got your man."

"I'd like to think so. And the good people of Columbia like to think so."

"But you never found a body," Dan stated plainly, measuring Detective Huff's reaction.

"That's right. Mary Spears's remains were never located."

"What about the killer's other victims? The other two students who were murdered?"

"Found where they were slain. One in the brush down by the walking path near the river. The other was found behind the university's nursing school."

"Any unanswered questions about those two crimes?"

"Nope. The MO was the same. Odin Rowe was seen near the first crime scene hours before the body was found by a jogger. A graduate student spotted him walking away from the nursing school the night he killed his second victim. He was arrested and identified in two separate lineups by several witnesses. And then, of course, he confessed. Makes for a nice prosecution package."

"Sounds like it. What did this Odin Rowe say about the night Mary was killed?"

"He said a lot."

"Such as…?"

Detective Huff grabbed another folder from the stack and slid it across the table. "That's the transcript of the confession in its entirety."

Dan started reading the top page.

"Take a few minutes to get acquainted with the specifics of the case. You want a coffee?" Huff offered.

"That would be great. Black is fine."

≪

"Interesting read so far?" Detective Huff asked, finishing his coffee before it had cooled.

"The file shows the circuit solicitor on the Odin Rowe case was Nathaniel Cardin."

"That's right. I believe up north y'all call them district attorneys."

"Most states do," Dan replied. "Is Nathaniel Cardin related to Judge Thomas Cardin?"

"He is. Nathaniel Cardin Senior is Thomas Cardin's father."

"That's interesting."

"Why is that?" Huff asked.

"Just thinking aloud. The files also say that Odin Rowe claimed he killed Mary Spears and buried her body in Belser Arboretum. Where's that?" Dan asked.

Detective Huff pointed at the location on the map still on the table. "On her way home, more or less. The arboretum is ten acres of wooded land donated for use as a park and environmental preservation. Biology classes from the university go out there regularly. Gets a lot of foot traffic."

"And nothing was found to corroborate the killer's confession that he buried the body?"

"Nope."

"How do you explain that?"

"The passage of time. Odin provided his confession in late October and Mary Spears went missing in the beginning of July. Over three months had passed. Rowe claimed he buried the body with a shovel he found on the arboretum premises. There was a groundskeeper's shed in one of the back corners. Had a bunch of tools in it: saws, clippers, a mower, a few shovels, what have you. Exactly what you would expect to find in a groundskeeper's shed."

"Was it locked?"

"There was no lock on the shed in 1986. But most of the property was fenced."

"Any gates in the fence that are open at night?"

"It had a couple of gates, but they were typically locked afterhours. No reason to think they weren't locked all night."

"How tall is the fence?"

"Six foot in a lot of places. The south side of the arboretum property backs up to a few residential homes. The owners of those properties decide what kind of fence they want to have in their backyard."

"Did any residents on the south side of the arboretum report anything odd the night Mary Spears went missing?"

"No."

"Was Odin Rowe a big guy?"

"A little bigger than average."

"Big enough to get a hundred-and-thirty-pound girl over a six-foot fence if he needed to?"

"With the proper motivation."

"Such as?"

"To bury a body."

"So, depending on where he entered the arboretum, he had to get Mary Spears over the fence, find a shovel, then bury her body in a location so deep that it's never been found."

"That's right."

"No other evidence? No clothes? Hair? Blood? Nothing?"

"Nope. This was before DNA testing. But we had people walk shoulder to shoulder throughout the property on multiple occasions. Ran the dogs through and never found anything."

"How do you explain the lack of physical evidence?"

"Didn't have to. Odin Rowe admitted that he had been smoking dope and drinking the day Mary Spears went missing. And three months had passed. He said he couldn't remember exactly where he buried the body. And if you dump a body around here in the summer and you don't bury it properly, it's going to be discovered right quick. Given that, we believe it was buried."

"By one man with one shovel? Who had been drinking all day and smoking dope? It would be quite a feat."

"We considered the difficulty of the task. Probably took him all night."

"No one reported any suspicious odors over the course of that summer?"

"No. And like I said, the arboretum gets its fair share of visitors,"

"So, you just chalked it up to Odin Rowe not remembering where he dumped the body?"

"That's what he said. That's all we know."

Dan stared at the map on the table. "Fair warning. You're not going to like my next question."

"Probably not."

"How certain are you this Odin Rowe character actually murdered Mary Spears?"

Detective Huff squinted. "Highly confident."

"Without a doubt?"

"Look, we had two murders and a missing girl in the span of a couple months. That's the kind of thing that can rattle a town. Especially a town with a major university in the middle of it. It's the kind of thing that's bad for a school's reputation. Bad for business. Hell, it's bad for everyone."

"Doesn't mean he did it."

"He confessed and the murders stopped. That's what I call a satisfactory ending."

"Let's suppose, hypothetically, that Odin Rowe didn't kill Mary Spears."

"I'm not sure I want to."

"Who else was a likely suspect?"

"We didn't have one."

"Humor me."

"As a detective, it's hard to dismiss the simple fact that folks are more likely to be killed by someone they know."

"Which, in this case, means who?"

"One of Mary Spears's friends. A large group of kids hung out together back then. From two different high schools. About a dozen kids in total. They used to pass time out at the lake most days during the summer. Just being teenagers. They were all with Mary Spears the day she died."

"Anyone in that group of particular of interest?" Dan asked, with a name in mind.

"Not as far as the case is concerned."

Dan nodded again. "What can you tell me about these friends?"

"Upper-middle class. From nearby neighborhoods. Most came from good homes with good parents. Churchgoers. Business owners. Professors. Lawyers. A lot of stay-at-home moms."

"Did you question them?"

"I questioned *everybody*. All the friends described a similar scene. A typical end to a long summer day. They'd gone to an early matinee and then spent the afternoon swimming in Lake Katherine. The sun was setting when the group of friends disbanded. About half of them specifically remember seeing Mary leaving. The other half couldn't specifically recall her departure."

Dan flipped to the next page in the folder.

Huff pointed at the top of the page. "That is the beginning of the witness statements."

Dan ran his fingers through several pages and then moved back to the top sheet in the file.

"In addition to Mary's friends, we interviewed half the city," Huff said. "Everyone with a pulse. I reckon I personally knocked on over a thousand doors that summer and fall. And we investigated hundreds of tips that came into a special hotline."

Dan dropped his eyes to the file. "It says here that one of the last people to see Mary Spears alive was Thomas Cardin."

The retired detective reengaged his discerning glare. "That's right. He was the last kid to see Mary. He claimed he walked with Mary to the end of the neighborhood, then he watched her get on her bike and ride off."

"So, Thomas Cardin was the last one to see Mary leave the neighborhood, but Odin Rowe was the last one to see her alive?"

"That's right."

"And no one brought up a conflict of interest between the circuit solicitor, the county's chief prosecutor, Nathaniel Cardin Senior, and his son, Thomas?"

"No. They didn't."

Dan mulled over the confidence of the detective's statement. "Did you know Thomas Cardin?"

"Not personally. He was considerably younger."

"And you're sure Thomas Cardin was never a suspect in Mary Spears's disappearance?"

"No more than any of her other friends."

"Had Thomas Cardin been drinking that day?"

"He had. They all had."

"Were Thomas Cardin and Mary Spears more than friends?"

"They may have gotten together at some point. Hooked up in one fashion or another. But a lot of those kids fooled around with each other back in the day."

A pause fell over the two men. Dan stared down at the open file on the table.

"Why do I get the feeling that you being from DC has everything to do with Thomas Cardin?" Huff asked.

Dan answered without looking up, "Probably because you're a detective."

Huff reached for his cup on the table and stared at the empty bottom. "Let's take a ride."

❧

Huff started his silver four-door and pulled the car out of the parking lot, nudging his way into light traffic.

"Is this your first time in Columbia?" he asked, taking his eyes off the road to glance at Dan in the passenger seat.

"The first time I've stopped. I've driven through a few times over the years."

"How long are you staying?"

"Depends on what I get accomplished. A couple of nights."

"Columbia is a nice town. If you can get past the heat."

"Captain Collins told me the city's official motto earlier. It makes a statement."

The car approached the western edge of the main campus for the University of South Carolina and Huff gave a brief tour from behind the wheel. "It's summer. Most students are gone. Probably a few thousand still around, but it's quiet compared to the fall and spring."

At a red light, a college-aged couple passed in front of the car. The young man proudly sported a black-and-garnet cap that read: *Cocks Soccer*.

"Nice cap," Dan said, without elaborating on the pun.

Huff pointed at a spread of manicured lawn surrounded by buildings from the 1800s. "That area over there is called the Horseshoe. It's the oldest part of the campus. Pope John Paul II gave a speech there in 1987."

"The Pope came to South Carolina?"

"Rumor has it they made his Holiness an honorary Gamecock," Detective Huff added.

"I hope he didn't forget to pick up one of those soccer caps as a souvenir."

Huff laughed. "They do have a good time with their mascot here. So do our rival schools. It cuts both ways."

The short tour continued across the campus through an area known as Five Points, a mix of cheap eats and bars with sticky floors geared toward the student population. Ten minutes east, the detective turned into a subdivision named Lake Katherine, per the signage on a brick wall near the main road. Mature homes on lots dotted with old shade trees lined both sides of the street.

Huff pulled the car over in front of a colonial with a two-car garage. Water was visible in the distance behind the house, the sunlight reflecting off the surface. "This is the Cardin family residence," Huff said, pointing with his nose.

"And I assume that's the eponymous Lake Katherine behind the house," Dan said.

"It is."

"And this is the last place Mary Spears was seen alive?"

"That's right. She would have biked down this street on her way home. Most likely she would have gone in the same direction we just came from."

"Do members of the Cardin family still live here?"

"Nathaniel Cardin Senior spends half his time here and the other half in the Lowcountry."

"And Mrs. Cardin?"

"She was killed in an accident."

"What kind of accident?"

"A car crash. The Cardins were on their way back from the Carolina Cup horse races. Hit by a drunk driver. Mrs. Cardin was killed instantly. Mr. Cardin suffered serious injuries. Been walking with a cane ever since. Everyone in town knows the story. Nowadays, the rumor is that Nathaniel Cardin Senior has dementia to some degree."

"Sounds like everyone knows everyone's business."

"It's the South," Huff replied. "You want to see the arboretum and the house where Mary Spears lived?"

"If you have the time. I can always rent a car and find it myself."

"No problem at all. Pretty much everything in Columbia is ten minutes away. Fifteen if there's traffic."

"What about the Spears family? Do they still live in Columbia?"

"The mother does. The father left a few years after..."

Dan rubbed his chin. "Where is Odin Rowe?"

"He's incarcerated at Lee Correctional Institution in Bishopville. An hour down the road."

"If I wanted to pay him a visit, do you think it can be arranged?"

"I know most of the LCI guards real well. I can get you on the visitor list pretty easy. But that doesn't mean that Rowe will agree to meet with you."

"Can't catch a fish without casting a few lines."

"I appreciate the fishing analogy. When do you want to go?"

"How about tomorrow?"

"Let me make a phone call or two."

CHAPTER 10

"NOT A LOT to see between Columbia and Bishopville," Detective Huff said, wrist resting on the top of the steering wheel, fingers dangling.

Dan turned his attention out the passenger window as the scenery whizzed by. Flat terrain offered minimal variation, the roadside and highway median dotted with thin groves of southern pines.

Huff motioned toward the temperature reading on the dash of the car. "Another hot one today."

"A hundred degrees before noon," Dan confirmed.

As promised, an hour outside Columbia, Detective Huff steered the car toward the exit for Bishopville. Near the end of the ramp, the parking lot of the local Waffle House was full. The same could not be said for the four-stall carwash and the Piggly-Wiggly a quarter mile farther down the road. Huff turned left, and two blocks of shuttered storefronts concluded the tour of the town.

"You said there's not a lot to see between Columbia and Bishopville," Dan said. "There's not a lot to see in Bishopville proper, either."

"Never was. The town's known for being home to South Carolina's version of Big Foot—the Lizard Man of Scape Ore Swamp."

"Get the hell out of here."

"It's no joke. I believe there's still a million-dollar bounty on the Lizard Man."

"Anything factual on this Southern Godzilla?"

"They had a few mauled cars and a dozen reports from citizens who claimed to have seen a seven-foot half-reptile, half-human creature with glowing red eyes."

"I'm sure there's a rational explanation."

"Don't bet on it," Huff replied. "Beyond the Lizard Man, Bishopville was known as a farming community. Now most of the area is supported by employment at the prison."

A right turn onto Wisacky Highway sent the car onto bubbling blacktop surrounded by fields of soybeans and groundnuts. Dan knew they were close to their destination when he saw a sign warning drivers not to pick up any hitchhikers.

"Helpful sign," Dan said aloud. "I guess people should be extra cautious of any hitchhikers wearing digs issued by the Department of Corrections."

"That about sums it up."

The car veered right at the prison entrance and pulled into a spot near the main administrative building. Dan stepped from the car and peered up at layers of looping razor wire lining a two-story fence. Armed guards manned the towers standing in hundred-yard intervals. Buildings stretched out in four directions from the center nexus, bars on the windows visible from the parking lot. A small group of inmates sat against a wall in the shade under the watchful eye of a man with a shotgun.

"It might be better if I speak with Odin Rowe alone," Dan said.

"Fine by me. Odin and I have said all we need to say to each other for this lifetime." Huff then offered advice on Dan's impending prison visit, "Listen to the guards' instructions once we're inside. This place has a history of violence. Tons of riots. When they happen, it gets ugly. Inside this facility, the guys on death row have a better chance of being killed by another prisoner than by lethal injection."

"Sounds like prison."

"Just giving a heads up. There are some tough characters inside these walls and I'm sure they'd be happy to add an attorney to their hostage list."

"Thanks for the warning."

❧

Entry to the prison required fifteen minutes of paperwork, a briefing in procedural guidelines, a trip through a metal detector, and a thorough pat down. Detective Huff hobnobbed with several correction officers on the far side of the processing room as Dan completed his entry proceedings.

"This way," a wide-shouldered guard said to Dan as he slipped his shoes back on.

"I'll be waiting here for you," Huff said as Dan disappeared through a security door.

Dan followed the guard down a gray hall and into a room with "Visitation" painted on the door in block print. The guard motioned toward an empty chair and Dan sat at booth number three, as instructed.

"The prisoner will be here in a moment," the guard said, stepping back into the hall. "I'll be right outside."

Dan eyed the thick glass in front of him and the dial-less phone resting in a cradle on the wall of the partition. A loud buzz snapped Dan to attention, and the door on the other side of the glass opened. A pair of uniformed guards led a man in an off-white prison jumper to his seat. The inmate's hands were cuffed to a chain around his waist and his slow shuffle across the floor gave Dan the impression that the man's feet were also shackled. A guard stood on each side of the prisoner as he sat down. The larger of the two guards unlocked the inmate's handcuffs from the chain around his waist and then opened the cuffs. Both guards stepped away from the prisoner, vanishing into the corners of the room beyond Dan's line of sight.

Odin Rowe leaned forward in his chair and glared at Dan through the glass.

Dan reached for the phone and Rowe slowly followed suit.

"What the fuck do you want?" Rowe asked in a gravelly voice, running his free hand over his short white hair. Dan noticed the prisoner's left eye drifting down and away from his nose, creating an off-center stare. Dark tattoos on the back of the inmate's hand stood out against the backdrop of pale skin. A broken front tooth flashed through an unsettling smirk.

"My name is Dan Lord. I'm an attorney."

"Not my attorney."

"No one is saying I'm your lawyer. I'm here working on another case. For another client."

"Well, I ain't no fucking snitch, if that's what you're getting at."

"Actually, I was hoping to ask you a few questions about why you're in here."

Rowe inhaled through his nose and swallowed from the back of his throat. "You want to talk to *me* about *my* crimes for one of *your* clients."

"Yes."

Rowe's face faded to a grimace. "You think I'm going to help some motherfucker I've never met before? For no good reason?"

"What's the harm?"

Rowe scowled again, his good eye dancing across Dan's face while his lazy eye fell behind. "Is your client another inmate in this shithole?"

"No."

"Then I don't see how I'm going to help. I've been on R&R here for three and a half decades now. Not sure I can help anyone with anything beyond these walls."

"I just want to hear about the case that sent you here. From your perspective."

"Come on. You're a lawyer. You can read. Get the court records."

"I already have them. And I met with the detective who was assigned to investigate the murders you confessed to."

"Detective Huff?"

"Yes."

"Then you don't need me for nothing."

"But I'd rather hear you tell me the story."

"What do I get out of it? Did you bring me anything?" Rowe asked, almost snarling.

"What do you need? I'll see what I can do."

"Hell, I don't *need* anything. I got a roof over my head and three squares a day. What more does a man need? But I *want* things. I got a long list of wants."

"Like what?"

"Women. A vacation. Better entertainment. A fucking cigarette. Did you know they outlawed cigarettes in here a few years back? No one knows why. If you ask me, I think inmates *should* smoke. Kill us off early. Save everyone money in the long run. Make us nicer people to boot."

"I don't think they'll let me bring in cigarettes."

Rowe grunted. "Then what else you got?"

"Consider my visit a form of entertainment."

"For who?"

"For both of us."

"You say you're a lawyer, but you don't look like one."

"I get that a lot."

"How much does an attorney make an hour these days?"

"Four hundred and fifty an hour is my standard rate."

"Goddamn. Then that's my going rate too. Four hundred and fifty an hour."

"For what?"

"A fee for talking with me. A consultation fee."

"Seriously?"

"Why not? Good lawyers cost money. You know that."

"You're not a lawyer."

"No, but from where I'm sitting, I *am* the only person who can answer your questions. And that puts me in the driver's seat."

"Fine. Four hundred and fifty an hour."

"With an hour minimum."

"Fine."

"Good. Now run yourself over to the administration building and add money to my JPay."

"What's JPay?"

"A prison bank account. Bring back a receipt and we'll have ourselves a chat."

✍

Fifteen minutes later, Dan returned to his chair and picked up the phone. He pressed the deposit receipt against the glass, and Odin Rowe leaned in to read the details.

"Ask what you wanna ask," Rowe said.

"I want to know about the events of the summer of 1986. Police records indicate that you confessed to the murder of Mary Spears. Is that correct?"

"I did." Rowe lowered his head to his hand, bit off a piece of fingernail, and spat it on the floor.

"And was your confession coerced in any way by the police department or law enforcement?"

"Nope. I gave that confession with my state-appointed lawyer sitting next to me."

"What did you think of your lawyer?"

"You know how it is. The public defenders' office only offers the cream of the crop."

"Are you still in touch with your attorney?"

"Nope. Can't talk to the dead."

"When did he pass?"

"A year or two after I ended up in here. Hell, even if he were alive, he'd be pushing eighty. Might not even remember me."

Dan nodded. "Can you tell me what you were doing the day Mary Spears went missing?"

"I went fishing and shooting with a buddy of mine. Drank most of the day. Smoked some weed. We fished until we finished off the beer, then headed out past Sandy Run to do some target practice."

"How much did you have to drink?"

"All of it. I don't know exactly. Wasn't counting."

"A six-pack? A twelve-pack?"

"Two guys on a hot summer day? Shit, we probably knocked back a case or more. Bought a couple of twelve-packs that morning, but still had some beer in the cooler from the night before. They were warm, but they chilled up with ice. Good enough to drink."

"And after you finished target practice, then what?"

"My buddy drove me home. Dropped me off around four or five. I was living with a couple of roommates at the time, but they were out of town. Over in Atlanta for the weekend. I headed for the fridge, didn't like what I saw, and then walked over to Henry's Pizza."

"How far away is Henry's?"

"Couple of blocks. I hear it's not there no more. It's called Za something or other now. One of the guys in the next cell block got five years for robbing it and pistol whipping the manager."

"What did you do at Henry's Pizza?"

"What do you think I did?"

"I assume you ate dinner. Do you remember what you had?"

"A small pizza with black olives and Italian sausage."

"Is that what you always got?"

"It was one of my favorites. You know, I haven't had a decent pizza this century. Even plain cheese would be fine right about now. Maybe you could smuggle in a slice or two for me."

"I'll see what I can do. Did you have anything to drink with your pizza at Henry's?"

"I killed off three Miller Lites. Drafts ran seventy-five cents back then."

"Anything else?"

"Played a couple of Aerosmith songs on the jukebox."

"Is it safe to assume you were fairly impaired by this point. After drinking and smoking all day."

"I wasn't sober."

"And how did you meet up with Mary Spears?"

"I was walking home, and she came by on a bicycle. I chatted her up."

"What was she wearing?"

"Shorts and a T-shirt, but she had a pink bikini on underneath. And she was wearing red sneakers. Almost matched the color of her hair."

"Then what happened?"

"I asked her if she wanted to get high."

"And what did she say?"

"She agreed. So we walked her bike over to the trails near the arboretum. I rolled a joint. We got high and talked for a while. Fooled around a bit. Then she changed her mind. Things got out of hand and I killed her. Buried her in the arboretum."

"How did you kill her?"

Odin Rowe raised his tattooed hands. "With the only weapons I had on me."

"Where did you bury her?"

"I told the police where."

"But they never found a body."

"Nope."

"And they never found Mary Spears's bike."

"Columbia is a college town. Bicycles used to go missing all the time. Get repainted, resold, used, and dumped. You can imagine. Don't reckon that's changed much."

Dan leaned back in the chair. "What if I told you that I represent a doctor in DC who has a patient who claims you didn't kill Mary Spears?" Dan asked.

Rowe snarled. "I would call them a liar."

"What if my client's patient claims they were present when Mary Spears was killed and that they can identify her killer?"

"I'd say you found a patient who needs more meds."

"I'll pass that along. The police report says you buried Mary with a shovel you got from a gardener's shed."

"Damn, you read every word of my file."

"I did. Is the police report correct? Did you bury Mary with a shovel."

"That's right."

"What kind of shovel was it?"

"One that moves dirt."

"Did it have a point, or was it straight across the bottom?"

"Straight."

"A shovel good for scooping stuff off a flat surface?"

"I guess. What's your point?"

"I'm curious as to why you can remember the shovel, the type of beer you drank, the band on the jukebox, the type of pizza, the victim's sneakers, and yet you couldn't tell the police where you buried the body."

"I guess that last joint pushed me over the edge."

"Maybe. Tell me this, have you ever heard the name Thomas Cardin?"

"Of course. Most people from these parts know the Cardins."

"Which Cardin did you know?"

"I knew Nate Cardin."

"What about Thomas Cardin? Did you know him?"

"I knew the name and the face. Not sure we ever spoke."

"Tell me about the other girls you confessed to killing in the fall of that same year."

"I can't tell you much about them. They were what people call 'crimes of opportunity.'"

"You say that as if it's a valid reason."

"It is what it is."

"Unprovoked first-degree murder is what it is."

Rowe grunted. "I think this visit is over."

"I have a few more questions."

"Looks like you'll be taking them with you when you leave."

✧

Huff and Dan exited the administrative building and walked back toward the car in the lot.

"What did you learn?" Detective Huff asked, the sun beating down.

"One thing for certain. Everyone is better off with Rowe behind bars."

"No doubt."

"But I'm not convinced he killed Mary Spears."

"Please don't go around saying that."

"Rowe had very specific memories of the night Mary Spears went missing. But he couldn't remember where he buried the body. Something about it doesn't add up."

"Need I remind you, during his confession, he admitted to being drunk and high at the time of the murder."

"That's what he said. In fact, everything in his file and case document seemed to be true. He didn't refute anything that I brought up."

"Hard to refute a true confession."

"Maybe."

"With all due respect, Dan, don't you think it's time you tell me what really brought you here?"

"My client has a patient who claims they know who really killed Mary Spears."

"Is that right?"

"Yes. This patient says it was Thomas Cardin."

"Thomas Cardin?!"

"That's what the patient says."

"And how does the patient know this?"

"The patient claims they were there."

"An eyewitness?"

"Of sorts."

"And what's the patient's name?"

"I can't divulge that."

"Come on, you can't drop that bombshell and leave it. I scratched your back, you scratch mine."

"No can do. Sorry."

Detective Huff unlocked the car doors and both men entered the vehicle. Huff turned the ignition, rolled down the windows to let the hot air escape, and turned the A/C on full blast. He turned toward Dan and the two locked eyes.

"Let me give you a word of warning. Stirring up Mary Spears's murder isn't going to be popular around here with anyone. Casting suspicion on Thomas Cardin and his family will only make it worse. Not to mention the legal shitstorm that could come as a result. Defamation. Libel. Slander."

"What if Rowe didn't murder Mary Spears. What if you got the wrong guy?"

"Between you and me, I don't really care if Odin Rowe didn't do it."

"That would mean that a killer is still loose on the streets, walking free."

"If it was Thomas Cardin, as you seem to be implying, he hasn't murdered anyone else in nearly forty years. Given that, unless we unearth evidence that contradicts Rowe's testimony, I'm happy letting everyone believe that Odin Rowe killed Mary Spears. Very happy. Odin Rowe is a killer. He confessed. I think the population of Columbia sleeps better at night believing he was responsible for three murders."

"Do you sleep better at night?"

"I'm a retired detective. Who says I sleep at all?"

CHAPTER 11

DAN EYED THE name board in the lobby of the six-story office building on Main Street, two blocks from the state courthouse. He confirmed his intended destination and stepped into the elevator. On the fifth floor, he entered the office of Vista Accounting. A middle-aged woman sat behind a reception desk. On the wall behind the desk, the company name was displayed in silver letters.

"Good afternoon," the receptionist said.

"Good afternoon. I called a little while ago. I wanted to meet with Gerald Winters."

"You must be Mr. Lord. I'll find him for you. Please grab a seat. There's coffee and water in the corner if you're interested."

Moments later, Gerald Winters came into the reception area and extended his hand.

"Gerald Winters. Pleasure to meet you."

"Thanks for your time."

Something about the man's Southern drawl and bushy beard gave Dan the impression that his host could leave at a moment's notice with a bottle of fox urine in one hand and a hunting rifle in the other.

"Let's head back to my office."

Dan followed his host down the hall. Entering the office, Gerald motioned for Dan to sit at a small table with a window view. On the far wall was a trio of mounted deer heads. *Bingo*, Dan thought.

"Where did you get those deer?"

"Up in Pickens County. Not far from Pumpkintown."

Dan suppressed a slew of West Virginia jokes. "What's a reasonable distance to shoot a deer from?"

"That all depends. Most deer shots are less than a hundred yards. Fifty or less is preferred." Gerald pointed to the deer head on the left. "That one was from about one hundred and twenty yards. Out of a deer stand. But this is South Carolina; just about any country boy can put a bullet on target from a few hundred yards."

"Well, the deer heads are a nice touch. They add to the ambiance. Nice building. Beautiful office space."

"Thank you. Columbia is going through a revitalization of its old downtown. This building was gutted and refurbished a couple of years ago. There are probably a half-dozen old buildings on the street in the midst of renovations. The street still has a lot of old shops as well."

"I saw a wig store down the block. Didn't look like it had been updated yet."

"Every good Southern town has a wig store."

"I wasn't aware that was a requirement."

"Then you haven't spent much time in the South."

"I grew up in a lot of places. The South wasn't one of them."

"You mentioned on the phone that you're an attorney and wanted to talk about the Mary Spears case."

"That's right. And to be transparent, I'm an attorney and a licensed private investigator."

Gerald took a deep breath. "It's been a long time since anyone wanted to talk about Mary."

"That's what I'm finding."

"Why am I on your list?"

"I've been doing research, reading through the details of Mary's case, including your statements to the police regarding Odin Rowe."

"Another name I haven't thought of in a while."

"Sorry to dredge it up. I just have a few questions. It shouldn't take long."

Gerald clasped his hands. "Fire away."

"What do you remember about the summer Mary went missing?"

"Enough. Too much. I was a teenager. Mary's murder changed a lot of things in this city."

"Were the two of you friends?"

"We weren't friends, but she only lived a few blocks over. I knew her enough to say 'hey Mary' when I saw her. Her mom still lives in the same house and my parents never moved, so there's some remaining connection."

"According to the statements you made to the police, you worked at the pizza parlor the summer Mary went missing."

"I worked there every summer in high school. Every year until I went off to college."

"And you said you were working the night that Mary disappeared."

"I was."

"You also said that you were certain Odin Rowe was there that evening."

"I did. He was."

"Is that still your recollection? I know that three months had passed between the night Mary Spears went missing and the time that Odin Rowe was arrested. Three months is a long time to remember exactly what you did on any given night."

"What can I say? I worked there every Friday night during the summer. Most weekend nights. The only weekends I didn't work were when my family went up to the Outer Banks for summer vacation. We usually did that at the end of July or the first week of August. Not to mention Odin Rowe was a regular."

"That's what the files say. I'm trying to confirm you weren't guessing Odin Rowe was there that night just because he was a regular."

"Nope. He was there."

"How can you be sure?"

"I remember it because it was the first weekend Henry's Pizza reopened after the place got a new drive-through window."

"Come again?"

"A guy from high school drove through the window of the pizza shop on prom night. Weeks before Mary went missing. The car took out some windows and a few booths. The owner put drywall up and cordoned off the damaged area of the shop. He got clearance from the department of health to reopen and petitioned the city for special permission to temporarily put picnic tables outside to make up for the inside seating they lost. The night Mary went missing was the first weekend we had the picnic tables. It was the first night it was opened again."

"That was not mentioned in the police report on Mary's disappearance."

"I don't know what to tell you. Henry's Pizza becoming a temporary drive-through wasn't a secret."

"Anything else in your memory that confirms he was there that night?"

"Just the picnic tables. Mary went missing the night Henry's reopened and by Sunday, we had plastered those picnic tables with Missing Person posters. All the employees helped. And the tables were spanking new. A couple days later, those posters were on every telephone pole in the city. It was an eventful period of time. Hard to forget."

"Any chance you remember what kind of pizza Odin Rowe ordered the night Mary went missing?"

"I'm sure I don't."

"Could it have been black olives and sausage?"

"It could have been anything except anchovies with pineapple. I probably would have remembered that combo. Even after all these years."

"Do you recall if Rowe was drunk or high the night Mary went missing?"

"He was usually drunk or high when he came in. And if he wasn't, he was usually drunk by the time he left."

"Can you draw a diagram of what the shop looked like and where these picnic tables were?"

"Sure," Gerald answered. He grabbed a piece of paper off his desk, turned it over, and quickly sketched on the backside. He circled a seat near the corner of the counter. "This was Rowe's usual seat," Gerald explained. He drew two more circles and continued his explanation, "This area was damaged by the car. And this is where the picnic tables were."

"Where was the bathroom?"

Gerald pointed. "You could still use the bathroom during repairs, but you had to walk around the back of the restaurant and enter from the kitchen side."

"Thanks," Dan said, pausing to think. "Did you know the Cardin family?"

Gerald nodded slowly. "I knew the Cardins. Nate transferred into my high school during my sophomore year. His brother, Thomas, went to Hammond. It's a private school."

"Seems a bit unusual to have your kids go to different schools."

"Nate was also at Hammond, but he was thrown out for smoking pot on school grounds. Apparently, he'd been warned a few times."

"Do you know this? Or is it rumor?"

"I wasn't there when he was expelled, if that's what you mean. But he was going to Hammond one year, and the next year he was in the public high school with me."

"What about Thomas? Was he ever in trouble?"

"Not that I knew about."

"How about any other stories or rumors?"

"The summer Mary went missing and the fall of that year there was nothing but stories and rumors in this town."

"Anything relevant to Mary's disappearance?"

"Nothing concrete. Just stupid stuff people say without thinking it over first."

"Such as?"

"There was a rumor that Mary Spears was seen getting into a car the night she disappeared. Another rumor that she drowned in Lake Katherine and that her friends covered it up because they'd all been drinking and doing drugs."

"Did you believe either of those stories?"

"Anything is possible, I guess. I didn't think that back then. At the time, it all seemed impossible. Like a bad dream. But as you get older, the news makes you realize there's no limit to how despicable humans can be."

"Sobering thought. Why do you think they never found Mary Spears's body?"

Gerald grimaced. "That, Mr. Lord, is the million-dollar question. Everyone in town wondered why they didn't find her body in the arboretum. The authorities dug that place up for weeks and didn't find anything. Some people in this town didn't care that a body wasn't found. But a lot of folks thought finding a body was the key to really closing the case. Closing the case in our hearts and minds."

"Can you think of anybody else around here that I could talk to about Mary?"

"I'd tell you to talk to Mary's mother, but I can't guarantee how she'd react to you showing up on her doorstep. She's a bit of a recluse. My dad thinks she's lost a couple of marbles. She's also become a hoarder."

"Southern town rumors?"

"She's got No Trespassing signs in the yard. She never recovered after she lost Mary."

"What about Mary's father?"

"Not sure. He left town a few years after that summer. I heard they got divorced."

"Can you think of anyone else who worked at the pizza shop who may have something to say about Mary?"

"There are a few of us townies around here from back in the day. Gordon Blueford worked there most weekends, but he was almost always in the kitchen. Most of the other kids who worked at the pizza place were students from the university. They worked for a while and moved on. Graduated. What have you. Mind you, we're talking about a long time ago. I'm not sure I could recall anyone's name."

"Is this Gordon Blueford who worked in the kitchen still around?"

"He is. He's a handyman now. Does a bit of everything. He also runs a martial arts school in town. It's not far from the football stadium. Let me jot down his number for you."

"A dojo? What kind of martial art does he teach?"

"BJJ. Brazilian jujitsu. He was a state wrestling champion in high school. I think BJJ was a natural segue."

"Do you think Blueford would be willing to talk to me?"

Gerald shrugged but didn't answer. He handed Dan a Post-it note with Blueford's number on it. "I'm curious about one thing. Why do you care about this case, if you don't mind me asking?"

"Keep your eyes on the news."

CHAPTER 12

PATRICIA FLYNN FLIPPED her auburn hair over her shoulder and finished her drink. She ran her finger around the rim of her glass as she read the news caption running across the bottom of the flat-screen behind the bar. She continued reading the moving print as she waited for the bartender's next attempt to quench her insatiable thirst. From the reflection in the mirror behind the bar, she knew she was the only one watching the TV. She didn't care. It was her job. As the eponymous driving force behind *The Washington Gazette* column known as Pixie on Politics, she was paid to stay on top of the news.

When the image on the screen focused on the steps of the Supreme Court, Pixie's curiosity piqued further. When a sentence across the bottom of the screen announced the nomination for the next United States Supreme Court justice, Pixie cursed. She fully understood what the announcement meant. Work was going to get busy.

The bartender in a bow tie approached, and Pixie tapped her finger next to the two empty tumblers on the bar. "Another round," she said as her potential beau for the night returned from the men's room and slid in next to her.

"This is my last for the evening," Pixie said with a smile, flashing perfect teeth at the young man whom she'd spent the past hour exchanging exaggerations with as their drink tally climbed. She hadn't asked his age, but estimated he was in his mid-twenties, an age that placed the dimpled think tanker squarely within Pixie's expanding strike zone. She was counting on youth translating into stamina. She could teach him technique, if needed.

"You never answered me as to why they call you Pixie," the young man said, twirling a cufflink that peeked out from a sleeve on his sixteen-hundred-dollar suit.

"I actually started calling myself Pixie when I was younger and the name stuck. By the time I was in the fifth grade, even my parents stopped calling me Patricia."

"Hippie parents?"

"Irish. Born in Dublin."

"Big drinkers?" the young man asked, as if he was trying to make a connection between her parents and Pixie's apparent tolerance of the sauce.

"You could say that 'going out on the piss' was an expression I grew up with."

Pixie pushed a freshly filled tumbler in the direction of her friend. "Let's finish these and get out of here."

"Your place or mine?" the young man asked.

"Mine," Pixie responded, downing her drink in one large gulp. She stood, ran her hand across the small of the man's back, and whispered into his ear. "Pay the bill, and I'll get us an Uber."

The shrinking headquarters of *The Washington Gazette* resided in a concrete-and-glass building on K Street. Nestled among lobbyists and attorneys, the once-proud newspaper was now relegated to a single floor of a building it previously owned outright. Unlike *The Post*, two blocks away, *The Gazette* was still waiting for a sugar daddy to sweep in and save it before the paper slipped into the irrelevancy pile of past DC rags.

Pixie pushed open the glass door to the corner office with her hip, balancing a laptop and legal pad in one hand and a large coffee in the other.

"What's the good word, Pixie?" Ellen Stern barked from behind a desk with a view of the traffic below. With forty years of journalistic experience, Ellen Stern was the engine that ran the third-most popular paper in the nation's capital. White hair with dark streaks framed a face wrinkled by years of deadlines, late nights, and Marlboro Lights. Not one to wait for a reply, Ellen dropped her edition of the morning paper on her desk for affect.

"I assume you're aware that Thomas Cardin was nominated as the next US Supreme Court justice last night."

Pixie took a sip of her coffee. "I am."

"Good. I want a high-level write-up on the new nominee by the end of the day. I want the rest of his background by tomorrow night. Everything you can find."

"I'm all over it," Pixie said.

"You'd better be. Because if Pixie on Politics isn't all over it, then either Pixie needs to change her name or her employer."

"I already started poking around."

"I like the attitude. Especially with those bloodshot eyes screaming you should still be in bed."

"Hay fever."

"Pixie, darling, you don't have to explain anything to me. I woke this morning with an allergic reaction to a delectable Pinot from Sonoma. Advil helped."

Pixie smiled and pain emanated from her temples. "Anything in particular you're looking for?"

"We don't know what we don't know, so let's start with the basics— education, family ties, political lean. Then we can work down from there, start digging into his judicial decisions. I put a call in to Thomas Cardin's office to arrange an interview. I'm waiting to hear back."

"Thanks."

Ellen Stern reached down and lifted a piece of paper with a square barcode on it. "Here's your boarding pass. You're on the 12:15 out of Reagan. You land in Columbia, South Carolina, a little after two. I couldn't officially get on his schedule, but I thought you could try to get a face-to-face with Thomas Cardin's father. He's semi-retired. He was an attorney in Columbia for years."

"So law runs in the family?"

"It does. When you're done in Columbia, drive up to Duke and speak with the retired dean of the law school there. Cardin is the first graduate of Duke Law to be nominated for the Supreme Court. There's bound to be a lot of university interest in the nomination."

"You've been busy," Pixie replied, scribbling on her legal pad.

"You're back tomorrow night on a flight out of Raleigh. Push it to the next morning if you need to."

"A quick thirty hours."

"Make them count. Try to avoid hay fever for the next couple of days."

CHAPTER 13

PIXIE FINISHED HER search of real estate records for Richland County and then punched an address into her phone. Ten minutes later, she pulled her rental car into the Lake Katherine neighborhood as her phone announced she was approaching her destination. A landscaping truck unloaded a trio of mowers as she parked her car. With a business card and legal pad in hand, she climbed the front steps and into the shade of the porch. She rang the doorbell, added an old-fashioned knock, and waited. She repeated her ring-and-knock routine, and when no one answered, she retreated down the walkway, roaring lawnmowers on each side.

Undeterred, Pixie headed next door. As she reached for the doorbell, the front door swung open, revealing a man with a toddler wrapped around his leg.

"My son saw you coming up the walk," the man said.

"Hi. My name is Patricia Flynn. I work for *The Washington Gazette*. I was interested in speaking with the owner of the house regarding the Cardins next door. As you know, one of the children who grew up there is Thomas Cardin, the recent nominee to the Supreme Court."

"I heard. I'm pretty sure everyone in town did. Unfortunately, I don't think I'm going to be able to help you out. We've only lived here for about a year."

"Real estate records indicate the house is owned by Eleanor Watson. Any chance you know her?"

"She's a friend of my mother. Eleanor still owns the house, but she's in assisted living over in Cayce."

"Do you know her personally?"

"I do. She's been my mother's friend forever. She lived here from the time the house was built until a couple of years ago. Spent ten years here alone after her husband passed. Then she fell and broke her hip and shoulder. Her next tumble cracked her skull."

"So she moved into a retirement home," Pixie confirmed.

"Both of her kids moved north years ago and have families of their own. From what I understand, Eleanor was not interested in moving any place colder than here. So they decided she'd be better off in an assisted living facility. She's in the Palmetto Wren. It's the nicest place in the Columbia area. Probably the nicest old folks' home in the entire state."

The man looked down at the child clutching his leg. "I hope my son puts me someplace as swanky when the time comes."

Pixie looked down at the toddler. "Cute kid."

"Thanks."

"You're well-informed."

"Like I said, my mother and Eleanor have been friends for a while."

"Did you ever spend time in this neighborhood when you were younger? Maybe come over with your mother when she visited Eleanor?"

"A few times over the years."

"Did you ever meet Thomas Cardin?"

"We've met. Many years ago. He was older than me by at least ten years. We swam in the lake with some other kids. Not sure I can give you any insight into his legal mind, if that's where you're heading."

"Any lasting memories of him?"

"He was friendly enough. His brother seemed to be on the

wild side. The first fistfight I ever saw in person was between the Cardin brothers."

"Who won?"

"They both got in their licks."

"I understand his father still lives next door."

"Part-time. He's mostly retired. He splits his time between Columbia and the Lowcountry. But when he's here, it's just him and his housekeeper in that big house."

"How is he, health-wise?"

"He uses a cane. His left leg was damaged in a car accident. The same accident that killed Mrs. Cardin."

"Do you ever talk to him?"

"I say hi when I see him, but we don't converse."

The boy attached to the man's leg began chanting for a snack and Pixie smiled. "Thank you so much for your time."

"Sure thing."

Before stepping off the porch, Pixie turned back toward the closing door. "Can I ask something else? Do you think the owner of your home, Eleanor Watson, would mind talking to me about her neighbor?"

"I don't think she'd mind at all."

"Any idea how her memory is?"

"Sharp as a tack, from what I hear."

The Palmetto Wren assisted living center was perched on a hill overlooking the Congaree River, five minutes south of downtown. A post office and library provided the only entertainment within walking distance. For other needs, a shuttle bus left every two hours and ran a circular route through Main Street and past the hospital. On Fridays, the bus added a stop at Blueline Spirits and Wine.

Pixie approached the front entrance, prepared for the ubiquitous stench of a senior living facility. To her surprise, Palmetto Wren smelled of a delicious floral potpourri. The smiling staff, the leather chairs in the lobby, and the yoga class in the activity room further confirmed that the Palmetto Wren was top-notch.

Pixie approached the reception desk. "Hi, my name is Patricia Flynn. I called a little while ago. I'm a reporter for *The Washington Gazette*. I wanted to meet with Eleanor Watson, if possible."

The woman checked the computer screen. "Yep. I have you here in the system. Eleanor is expecting you. Just sign in."

"Excellent."

"Visiting hours are until eight, unless you're family."

"I'm not. But I don't expect to be here that long."

"Then you don't know Eleanor," the woman said before disappearing behind the desk. A moment later, she reappeared from a doorway to the left. "She's a character, Eleanor. Smart as a whip. Loves to tell stories."

Pixie followed the employee in purple scrubs down the hall as they spoke.

"How does she like it here?"

"She seems to be happy. Didn't care for it at first, but she's adjusted. She keeps an eye on things. Helps others. Plays chess with the men and knits with the women...

"Here we are," the woman said, entering an open door on the right.

Eleanor Watson was pouring water into a small plant on the dresser and didn't seem to notice she had visitors. The staff member cleared her throat. "Eleanor, this is Patricia Flynn. She's the reporter who called earlier. She wanted to visit with you and ask you some questions."

"Ah, yes, Pixie on Politics. Come in, dear, come in," Eleanor said.

Pixie entered and as her escort left the room, the staff employee offered Pixie departure instructions. "Stop by the front desk and sign out before you leave."

"Yes, ma'am," Pixie replied.

"Please, dear, have a seat," Eleanor said, motioning toward a tiny table with two chairs.

"Thank you."

"I'll pour some iced tea, and we can chat."

"I'm surprised you've heard of my column," Pixie said, sitting.

"I hadn't. I Googled you after you called," Eleanor admitted. She pointed to a closed laptop on the dresser next to her freshly watered plant.

"I love to Google things. Such a blessing, really. If I had a question when I was a kid, my parents sent me to an old dictionary or a Funk and Wagnall Encyclopedia. And if those two couldn't answer my question, I was off to the library. Rain or shine. Usually rain. Uphill both ways. You know the story. Nowadays, everyone has access to just about every library in the world without having to leave the room. Or even get out of bed."

"Things have changed."

"Yes sirree, they have. Oh, the things I've seen. Hopefully I'll stick around a little longer to see a few more. Between you and me, I wouldn't mind if they figure out teleporting before I'm done with my time here on earth."

"Teleporting?"

"Sure. *Star Trek* stuff. Why not? Travel anywhere in the blink of an eye. Just make sure there are no flies in the little room with me. I saw how that worked out in a movie."

Pixie laughed. Indeed there was nothing wrong with Eleanor's faculties. "I was wondering if you would be willing to talk about Thomas Cardin, our recent Supreme Court nominee?"

"Honey, we can discuss anything you want."

"I went to your house in Lake Katherine earlier and I met your tenant. Nice gentleman with a little boy."

"They actually have three kids, but the little one stays at home most days. The father can work from the house. He's a computer programmer of some sort."

"How long were you neighbors with the Cardins?"

"I lived there when both of their boys were brought home from the hospital."

"What can you tell me about Thomas Cardin or the Cardin family?"

"Thomas was a sweet, well-behaved child. Turned into a fine young man. He did well in school, obviously. Was helpful in the neighborhood. Volunteered. A good kid. Which is not to say he didn't have a little mischievousness in him, but he was a good kid."

"What kind of mischievousness?"

"He toilet papered a few houses. Went skinny-dipping."

"You saw Judge Thomas skinny dipping?"

"When you live on a lake, you see a lot of people skinny dipping. At least that's how it was back in the day."

"The tenant at your house said that Thomas's brother was a little rowdier."

"Nate? Yes, he was. My husband and I used to sit on the back porch and watch Nate get up to no good. He would sit out there on the Cardin's little boat dock after dark with his friends. We would find empty beer cans and cigarette butts in our yard."

"Was Thomas ever out there with his brother?"

"Not usually with his brother. But I saw Thomas down at the boat dock at night on occasion with his friends. Sometimes just him and a girl."

"A girlfriend?"

"I sure hope so, if you know what I mean."

"I don't."

"I'm talking about blowjobs, Pixie."

"Blowjobs?"

"I don't know what people are calling them these days, but that's what we saw. My husband saw it too. Gave him some ideas, I'll tell you."

"Okay, then," Pixie replied, scribbling in her notebook.

"Were the Cardin brothers close?"

"As different as night and day. Nate was a few years older. He was a partier. Fell into drugs. In the end, I think his parents were heartbroken by his behavior. He moved out of the house after high school. Didn't see him much after that. Probably only saw him two or three times after his mother died."

"Where is Thomas Cardin's brother now?"

"Nate died years back. A life of drugs finally caught up with him."

"How old was he?"

"Probably late thirties or early forties when he passed. He was one of those types who looked old before his time. The booze and drugs didn't do him any favors."

"I understand that Mrs. Cardin died in a car accident."

"She did. A big accident out on the highway. The Cardins were hit by a drunk driver. Mrs. Cardin died of her injuries. Mr. Cardin was pretty banged up. They put him together with screws and plates and what have you. Been walking with a cane ever since. Yes sirree, that accident was big news around these parts."

"Why was that big news?"

"Because he was a Cardin and Mrs. Cardin's maiden name was Peterman. Those are two of the most successful families to ever grace this city."

Pixie jotted down the maiden name of Judge Cardin's wife for additional research.

"How about Thomas Cardin's friends? Or girlfriends?"

"He had lots of friends. A whole bunch of them hung out together for years. Until the summer that Spears girl went missing. Things were never the same after that."

"Who is the Spears girl?"

"Mary Spears."

"Never heard of her."

"Because you're not from around here. Mary Spears was one of the kids who hung out by the lake. Disappeared one summer evening on her way home. They never found her."

"And this Mary was friends with Thomas Cardin?"

"She was."

"And you said she disappeared?"

"Vanished off the streets. July 1986. A few months later, two girls were murdered on the campus of the university. The man who murdered the students also confessed to killing Mary Spears."

"Do you recall the man's name?"

"Of course. His name is Odin Rowe. No one who lived in Columbia back then will ever forget it."

Pixie looked down at her handwritten notes and considered follow-up questions.

"What else do you know about this Odin Rowe?"

"He was a local kid. Painted houses for a while. Got into a fair bit of trouble."

"What kind?"

"Drugs. Stealing. Breaking into cars. Vandalizing. That kind of stuff."

"Nothing to indicate he was going to be a murderer?"

"Wasn't until he was arrested for killing those girls that people had any inclination what he was capable of. Shocked a lot of people in Lake Katherine, including the Cardins."

"Was Odin Rowe friends with the Cardins?"

"I don't think so. But, like I said, there were a lot of kids running around the lake back then. Different groups. Different ages. Different cliques."

Pixie again took notes. "I won't beat around the bush with my next question, so I'm coming straight out with it."

"Go ahead, dear."

"Was Thomas Cardin, nominee to the Supreme Court, friends with a convicted killer?"

"Not as far as I know."

"What happened to Odin Rowe?"

"I'm pretty sure he's still alive. He was sentenced to life in prison. I figure if he was dead, I would have heard about it."

"Somehow, I don't doubt it."

ॐ

Pixie sat in her car checking prison records when her phone rang.

"Pixie here."

"What did we learn today?" Ellen Stern, *The Washington Gazette* editor, asked from her office in DC.

"A neighbor told me that Judge Cardin's father has a house in the Lowcountry where he spends half his time. I'm still trying to work out a face-to-face interview. We've been playing phone tag."

"Helpful neighbors are nice. Don't see that much these days."

"This helpful neighbor also told me something interesting about Thomas Cardin."

"Anything we can publish? *The Post* already has a write-up on their website. It's light on specifics, but I imagine it'll be in the printed paper tomorrow."

"I'm working on it. I'll have something before I go to bed."

"Give me a nugget to tide me over."

"I'm planning to visit an incarcerated murderer who may have known Thomas Cardin."

"What murderer? Who?"

"A killer named Odin Rowe. Ever heard of him?"

"Nope."

"Me neither. He may have been hanging around Judge Cardin when a friend of the judge went missing."

"Sounds like an interesting tangent, but don't take your eye off the ball."

"I won't. But I figured it was worth an hour in the car to see if a Supreme Court nominee has connections to a convicted serial killer."

"No argument there. Keep me posted."

CHAPTER 14

ODIN ROWE SAT down in front of the thick security glass. A prison guard stood behind him near the door, arms crossed. Another stood in the far corner, his glare concealed by tinted glasses. Rowe stared at Pixie through the glass, licked his lips, and reached for the phone on the wall of the partition.

"Well, my, my, my. I don't know what I did to deserve this, but *thaaaaank* you."

"Good afternoon," Pixie replied into her phone.

"Right back at you. I wish someone would've mentioned my visitor was a hot piece of ass. I would have gotten spruced up for you."

Odin wiped at the spittle gathered in the corner of his mouth then smiled wide enough for Pixie to see his broken front tooth.

"My name is Patricia Flynn. I'm a reporter for *The Washington Gazette*. People call me Pixie"

"A reporter?"

"That's right."

Rowe whistled. "Shit. Must be a lot going on in Washington. You're my second visitor from DC this week."

"Is that right? Who was the other one?"

"An attorney. And he paid me for my time."

"Did he?"

"Made a deposit into my prison account. Got paid lawyer money. Four hundred and fifty dollars an hour."

"I don't know if I can afford to pay you. Journalism salaries aren't what people think."

"I wouldn't charge you. You've already given me enough, just being here."

"Time away from your cell?"

"No, not exactly." Rowe dropped his gaze to Pixie's torso. "Anyone ever say you've got a great rack?"

"Excuse me?"

"You have nice tits," Rowe said, his tongue flicking out to touch his upper lip.

The prison guard in the corner interjected. "Watch it, Rowe."

"Very charming," Pixie said. "I guess you haven't heard of the Me Too movement."

"You're gonna have to forgive me. I don't get a lot of female visitors."

"And commenting on their tits is a surefire method to keep it that way."

"Well, if I offended you, I'm sorry. Maybe you're not the girl for me, after all."

"Probably not."

"So, tell me, what does a beautiful reporter with a nice rack from the big city want with an inmate who has been behind bars for nearly forty years? You doing a story on Southern incarceration?"

"No. I wanted to ask you a few questions about the Cardin family."

"Well, damn. I reckon this has something to do with Thomas Cardin getting on the Supreme Court."

"You've heard the news?" Pixie replied, ignoring the inaccuracy of his statement.

"Of course. We have TV in here. Cable too. Shit, we even have a ninety-six-inch flatscreen in the common area."

"I'm sure the taxpayers of South Carolina would love to know that."

"Fuck 'em. So what can I do for you, Pixie from DC?"

"Just doing some background on Judge Cardin and his family. If you're willing to talk."

"Hell, I'll talk to you all day long."

"That's very accommodating. What can you tell me about Thomas Cardin?"

"Can't say too much about him. Didn't know him real well. He was a couple years younger than me. I knew his older brother."

"Nate?"

"Yeah."

"I met a neighbor of the Cardin's who said you might have been friends with Nate."

"We partied a couple of times."

"What do you mean by partied?"

"Ran into him from time to time. Drank beer at the same parties. Talked shit. Threw horseshoes. Roughhoused with rival high school kids. That kind of thing."

"Did Thomas Cardin ever get involved in any of these shenanigans?"

"Not with me."

"Are you sure about that?"

"Yeah, I'm sure. What neighbor have you been talking to?"

"An elderly woman who used to live next door to the Cardins."

"Maybe this old woman got Nate and Thomas confused."

"It's possible, but not likely. You realize if a nominee for the Supreme Court was friends with a serial killer like yourself, it would be a story."

"Now, slow down. Let me say on one thing," Rowe said. "I never liked the term serial killer."

"Why's that?"

"Seems like an overstatement. You can't lump me together with those guys who killed two or three dozen people."

"What's the magic number to earn the title of 'serial killer'?"

"I'd have to think about it."

"You can get back to me."

"I'd have to put you on my schedule. I don't have a phone in my cell."

"Sounds like a punishment. Kind of like prison."

"I like your spunk, Pixie. You have any other questions?"

"I'm not sure you answered my first question."

"You asked me if I knew the Cardins, and I gave you my answer. But there's something you probably don't understand, coming from the big city and all. Everyone in Columbia knew the Cardins. Doesn't make me special."

"It doesn't mean you answered honestly either."

"It don't matter. No one believes what I say. Comes with the territory of being labeled a killer."

"I can understand that."

"Do you want to ask about the girls I killed?"

"Do I need to? You confessed, so I figured you did it."

"I did."

"Then I don't need to hear anything else about it. But we can talk about other things related to the Cardins. Unless you have somewhere else you'd like to be."

"Lunch is just around the corner."

"Something good?"

"Probably not. But lunch is lunch. If I'm gonna miss lunch, I'm going to need something in return."

"You said this conversation was free of charge."

"I changed my mind."

"I already told you journalists are poor."

"There's more ways to pay than money."

"Like what?"

Rowe again lowered his gaze to Pixie's breasts then raised his eyebrows. He moved his good eye from her right breast to her left with unabashed focus.

Pixie watched Rowe as if he were a primate in the zoo.

Rowe whispered. "Black or white? C or D? Front clasp or back? I'm dying to know. Just a peek."

"You must be kidding."

"I think it's called quid pro quo. I'm not asking for much. One button," he said, using the reflection in the security glass to check the guards in the room.

Pixie switched hands with the phone and in one quick motion undid the top button of her blouse with her free hand.

Rowe's eyes fell to the top edge of her cleavage. "Go ahead with your questions."

"You mentioned a lawyer from DC came to visit you. What did he want to know?"

"I've been wondering about that myself. Unlike you, he was interested in what landed me behind bars. He had my court files and was asking me questions about what transpired all them years ago. Said he was working for a doctor who had a patient he was trying to help."

"Did he give you a name?"

"Lord. An attorney named Lord from DC. Easy to remember."

"And he came asking these questions a couple of days ago?"

"The day before yesterday."

Pixie thought about the timing. "What did you tell him?"

"I answered his questions about the night Mary Spears went missing."

"Were those honest answers?"

Rowe smiled. "Like I said. Does it really matter? I'm in here for life. No one cares what I say."

"I do."

"Pixie, Pixie, Pixie. We both know that's not true."

The two held a stare for a long second before Pixie broke the silence. "Thank you for your time, Mr. Rowe."

Pixie hung up the phone and watched as Odin Rowe stood from his seat on the other side of the glass. Rowe then tapped on the translucent divider with his handset. Pixie picked her phone back up and placed it to her ear.

"One more thing," Rowe said.

"What's that?"

"Take care of those tits."

CHAPTER 15

DAN PULLED INTO the parking lot between two rows of warehouses. He scanned the names on the buildings until he spotted the sign for a dojo located next to a plumbing supply store.

Dan climbed from his car, crossed the hot asphalt, and stepped into the shade of a small awning. Pulling on the door handle, the chill of air-conditioning greeted him as he stepped inside. Instinctively, Dan bowed toward the mat. Lifting his gaze, he noted the practice weapons, strike pads, and headgear that filled a wall of cubbyholes to the right. Heavy bags hung in a line over the rear of the mat.

"Hello?" Dan called out.

A younger man stepped from a side office wearing white gi pants and a skin-tight shirt. Tattoos ran up both arms. Dan estimated the man was in his late twenties. Thirty tops.

"How can I help you?" he asked, eyeing Dan from head to toe.

"I was looking for the owner. Gordon Blueford. I tried calling and left him a message. I figured I'd try my luck here."

"He can be hard to reach. Are you interested in training?"

"Are you the instructor?"

"I'm one of them. Blueford sensei teaches the higher ranks a couple times a week. I teach most of the other classes. We have a lot of new students every fall when the university starts up. The number dwindles as the year goes on. Summer is quiet. Are you sure you don't want to train?"

"Not today."

"There's no time like the present. We offer a free trial class. I can hook you up with a gi. It's clean."

"BJJ isn't for me."

"Have you tried?"

"Not BJJ."

"Any other martial art?"

"A bit."

"Like what? Tae Kwon Do? Karate? Judo? Muay Thai?"

"Yes."

"And you've never tried BJJ?"

"That's right."

"That's too bad. I'm sure you've heard that BJJ is the most effective martial art in the world."

"In a one-on-one confrontation with no weapons, you could be right."

"Maybe I can convince you otherwise."

"I doubt it. The problem with thinking that one martial art is better than all others is rules. Formal martial arts have too many."

"How about we throw on some headgear and go a few rounds without rules?"

"I appreciate your enthusiasm, but I'll pass."

"Are you sure? It'll be fun. I had a private lesson cancel and classes don't start until six. I'm chomping at the bit."

Dan glanced over at the clock on the wall.

"Come on, I'll go easy on you. We're about the same size. Seems like a fair match."

"I'll pass, but thanks."

"Fair enough," the younger man relented. "Let me make a call to Blueford sensei for you."

"That would be great."

Dan stood by the front door, listening to the muted voice of the instructor speaking on the phone in the dojo's office.

A minute later, the instructor returned. "Blueford Sensei is working at a bar in town, fixing some stuff. The place is called The Happy Cock. He said if you can find your way there before he leaves, he'll talk to you."

"The Happy Cock?"

"That's right."

"You guys love to throw around the C-word."

"Yes, we do."

"Thanks for the help."

CHAPTER 16

A BAR NAMED The Happy Cock would have trouble staying in business anywhere other than Columbia, South Carolina. Its sign, a large red-and-yellow rooster with flashing neon talons, marked the well-known establishment. Standing next to an old train station, the decor—exposed brick and aged wood floors—was similar to a thousand other bars across the country that had exploded on the scene with the craft beer craze.

For Pixie on Politics, the name alone was enough to draw her inside. Bypassing the empty hostess stand, Pixie found a stool at the bar with a view of a TV. She ordered a beer, glanced around the room, and smiled at the four young men seated at a table behind her. Sipping her beer, Pixie eavesdropped on the quartet as they switched from English to what she assumed was German. The group of four continued to switch back and forth between the two languages until Pixie reached the bottom of her glass. When her second drink arrived, she stood, turned around, and smiled at the evening's potential.

"Do you guys mind if I join you?" she asked.

The men, all seemingly in their early twenties, quickly cleared a spot at the table and Pixie sat.

"Are you guys exchange students?" Pixie asked.

"No, we're graduate students here."

"And you all speak German?"

"We do. The University of South Carolina has a top-ranked international business program."

"South Carolina and international business? That's not a combo I would've imagined."

"It's one of the great educational mysteries. We do a full-time MBA with three hours of foreign language classes a day. Students can choose between Spanish, French, German, Portuguese, Japanese, Russian, and Chinese."

"Fascinating."

"This place is only two blocks from the international business building. There's no telling what language you might hear in this bar on any given night."

"Unfortunately, I won't be in town long enough to find out."

The four men raised their glasses, offered a toast in German, and drained their mugs. Pixie quickly followed suit.

"Shall we order another round?" the young man next to Pixie asked.

Pixie dropped her non-drinking hand to the young man's thigh and ran her nails over his knee. "I think we should."

∽

A bucket drummer was setting up his drums on the sidewalk outside as Dan came through the front door of The Happy Cock. Heading in the direction of the bar, he noticed the raucous group speaking a hodgepodge of German and English over a table of beer. Reaching the bar, Dan motioned for the bartender.

"What can I get you?"

"I'm here to see Gordon Blueford."

The bartender pointed to an alcove away from the main bar. "He's back there. Working on some drywall. I think he's almost done."

"Thanks. Do you know if he drinks?"

"Mr. Blueford? You bet. He's a bourbon guy."

"Can you send a couple of drinks over? A good bourbon and a middle-of-the-road draft beer."

"Will do."

Dan walked toward alcove away from the main bar.

Gordon Blueford looked up from his toolbox, light gleaming off his bald head. "You must be Dan."

"And you must be Gordon Blueford."

"Call me Blue. Gerald Winters warned me you'd be reaching out."

"I called and left a message."

"No offense, but an attorney who's also a private investigator isn't at the top of my list of people to call back."

"Apparently. I hope you don't mind that I stopped by your dojo."

"No sweat."

Dan glanced at the spackled hole in the wall and the spread of tools on the table. As Dan checked the worksite, Blue seemed to measure Dan. "Gerald tells me you came into town to ask about Mary Spears."

"I did."

"Why?"

"A case I'm working on."

"I'll give you a bit of free advice."

"I'll take it."

"Let that sleeping dog lie."

"Why?"

"Because nothing good comes from stirring a pot of old stew no one wants to eat."

"I'll only take a minute of your time."

"You already have."

"A couple more and I will be gone."

Blue squinted and nodded before taking a seat at the table and gesturing for Dan to join him.

"Were you working at the pizza shop the night that Mary went missing?"

"I was."

"And did you see Odin Rowe there that night?"

"I can't say for certain. I worked in the kitchen flipping dough. Same thing I told the police all those years ago."

"Did you ever hear anything about Thomas Cardin and Mary Spears being an item? Dating?"

"No. But I wasn't really friends with either of them. I knew they hung around in the same group."

"That's my understanding."

"Given that Thomas Cardin was recently nominated for the Supreme Court, you've got me wondering if that's the reason you're asking these questions."

"Yes and no," Dan answered. "Let me ask you this, why do you think they never found Mary Spears's body?"

"That's an easy one. Because her body wasn't where they looked."

"You don't think she was in the arboretum?"

"I don't."

"Why would you say that?"

"If people really believed she was buried in the arboretum, why hasn't anyone gone back and looked in the last thirty years? Are you telling me we don't have technology to search better than we could in the 1980s?"

"I'm sure we do."

"So, why not? Seems like law enforcement searches for old bodies for all kinds of reasons. Shit, they're still looking for Jimmy Hoffa."

"If she's not buried in the arboretum, where's her body?"

"Don't know. But I'm sure she isn't in the arboretum. And I'm certain more than a few people know she's not. They've probably known for a long time."

"Who are these people you're referring to?"

"I don't know, but if you ask me, that's the question you should be trying to answer."

The bartender delivered a beer and a bourbon to the table. Blue reached for the glass of bourbon and nodded in gratitude. Dan grabbed his beer, nodded in return, and took a slug.

"You know, I was going to tell you to be careful about poking into Mary's disappearance. Sooner or later, you might ask the wrong person the wrong question. They could take offense. But I get the feeling that maybe you're not the worrying kind."

"I try to keep it to a minimum," Dan replied.

"That's either smart or foolhardy," Blue said.

"That's about what I figure, as well," Dan said. "Thanks for your time."

"Thanks for the drink."

Dan paid the bill at the bar and headed for the exit. As he was leaving, he held open the door for an auburn-haired vixen with a young man on her arm. For a brief moment, Dan thought the woman looked familiar. On the sidewalk, Dan watched as the woman headed in the opposite direction. Steps from the corner, the woman looked back over her shoulder at Dan.

Dan took a long walk around the block on his way back to the hotel. A man in tattered clothes and worn flipflops sat on a bench in the designated smoking area near the front entrance. Between drags from his cigarette, the man looked up as Dan approached.

"Hey, man. Any chance your name is Dan?"

Dan stopped. "Who's asking?"

"I'm asking. I was told to give Dan Lord a message. Is that you? You fit the description."

"Who gave you my description?"

"A white dude. Never seen him before."

"When was this?"

"About an hour ago." The man pointed across the street. "I was digging through the trash can at the bus stop over there."

"And this white guy just appeared and asked you to give me a message?"

"Pretty much. He kinda snuck up on me from behind."

"What else can you tell me about this white guy?" Dan asked.

"Nothing."

"Nothing as in you don't recall or nothing as in you were paid to forget."

"I'm a cheap date. What can I tell you?"

"How much did you get paid?"

"A hundred. A lot of money for me."

Dan pulled out his wallet, counted a hundred dollars, and held it out for the man.

"What's that for?"

"Another hundred to tell me what kind of car the guy was driving."

"I didn't say he was driving."

"You didn't have to."

The man stared at the money.

"Yes or no?" Dan asked.

The man took the cash from Dan's fingers. "I can't say for certain, but I might have seen the guy climb into a white pickup truck after he walked away from the bus stop."

"A white pickup truck? I imagine that's a popular vehicle around here."

"I reckon."

Dan glanced around suspiciously. "Okay, so what's the message you're supposed to give me?"

"Go home before you get hurt."

⋙

In his room, Dan used his cell phone to call the front desk of the hotel. A girl with a Southern accent answered with glee.

"Hi. I was wondering if you could tell me if one of my friends is staying at your hotel?" Dan asked.

"Sure, what's the name?"

"Dan Lord."

"Give me one second," the woman replied. "Yes, we have a guest by that name staying at our property."

"Can you tell me what room he's in?"

"I'm afraid I can't do that. It's a violation of our privacy policy."

"Can you connect me to his room without telling me the room number?"

"Yes, I can. Please hold and I will forward your call."

Dan waited for the phone in his room to start ringing and then disconnected the call on his mobile phone.

Staring out the window at the lights of the city, Dan replayed the message from the homeless man in front of the hotel. *"Go home before you get hurt…"*

Then Dan smiled. *Progress.*

CHAPTER 17

PIXIE WOKE UP on a Murphy bed under a black-and-red flag with a rooster on it. She listened to the young man next to her snore with the resonance of someone twice his age. A hairy leg protruded from the covers. Naked, she moved to the edge of the bed and looked around. She spotted her underwear on the floor next to an open closet, stood, and slipped them back on. She silently shuffled around the one-room efficiency, plucking her clothes, item by item, from a table, a chair, and the kitchen counter.

Dressed, Pixie checked her purse for her phone and ID. With a final look around, she quietly slipped out the door and into the hall. On the front steps of the building, the morning sun burned her eyes as she ordered an Uber. An hour later, hair wet from a shower, Pixie stepped through the lobby of the Columbia courthouse. She could still taste the drinks from last evening, especially the nightcap, a vodka and sambuca concoction that coated the tongue. Temples pulsating, Pixie made her way to court records on the fourth floor. At the records window, Pixie lowered her sunglasses and peeked over the lenses.

"Good morning, young lady. How can I help you?" an elderly man in suspenders asked.

Pixie tried to smile. "Hi. I wanted to get a copy of some files. Court records."

The elderly man pointed at the menu on the wall. "Those are the records we keep and the prices to make copies."

Pixie glanced at the list, tried to focus her red eyes, and gave up. "I'm looking for court records on Odin Rowe. He's a convicted killer from the 1980s."

"Odin Rowe needs no introduction around these parts. At least not for old-timers like myself."

"I met him yesterday, believe it or not. Memorable character."

"On behalf of all South Carolinians, I apologize for that experience. He doesn't represent the good people of this state."

Pixie looked down at her blouse in a brief flashback. "Thanks. How long will it take to get copies?"

"Let me run them down. Grab a seat and let me see what I can find."

⮑

Pixie sat on a hall bench between the records alcove and the restrooms, sipping a Mountain Dew from a can. She checked her phone and pecked at her laptop's keyboard, building the skeleton of a story-in-progress.

"Miss," a voice called out.

Pixie stopped typing, put her laptop on the bench, and approached the records counter.

"I've run into a bit of a snafu," the elderly man said. "I can't seem to locate the court records for Odin Rowe."

"They're missing?"

"I'd prefer to say they're temporarily misplaced."

"Since when?"

"Hard to say for certain. I wasn't here for couple of days, so I can't tell you."

"How often do files go missing?"

"Almost never. I'm sure they'll turn up. Somebody probably put them back in the wrong place. It may take me a day or two, but I'll find them."

"Can I leave my number with you? Hopefully you can call me when you find something."

"I sure will."

CHAPTER 18

CARDIN AND CARDIN, LLP occupied the top three floors of an office building at the intersection of Lady and Main in historic downtown Columbia. Heavily tinted windows stretched vertically, covering most of the building's exterior surface in an attempt to keep out the sun and heat.

Pixie rode the elevator to the sixth floor and stepped out. A woman behind a desk directly across from the bank of elevators stood as Pixie approached. After a brief exchange, Pixie was shown to a meeting room with a view of the dome of the State Capitol. Five generations of Cardins stared down at her from portraits on the wall.

A middle-aged man in a suit entered the room and held open the door. An elderly man with a cane shuffled in, the walking aid thumping lightly on the floor. The elderly man sat with an audible exhalation. The younger man moved to the corner and lowered himself into a chair several feet away from the table.

Pixie stood and extended her hand to the elderly gentleman. "Thank you for your time today. My name is Patricia Flynn. Some people call me Pixie. Most people, actually."

"My name is Nathaniel Cardin Senior," the elderly man said with a smile. Pointing toward the portraits on the wall, Cardin Senior continued, "I'm the fourth one on the right. You'll have to excuse the lack of resemblance. The picture was commissioned many years ago. Age has a funny way of doing that."

"It does."

"The man in the corner is Arthur. He's my legal aid, part-time driver, and overall life manager."

Arthur nodded his head.

"He's going to be present during the interview. He's the strong quiet type."

"That's fine." Pixie smiled at Arthur. "As you know, I work for *The Washington Gazette*. It's the third largest paper in Washington, DC. I'm responsible for a column that's called Pixie on Politics."

"Are you familiar with Pixie Stix? It was a candy," Cardin Senior asked.

"I've heard of it," Pixie said, noting that Arthur seemed to shake his head.

"But I digress," the elder partner of the law firm added. "What kind of questions can I answer for you?"

"I'm interested in speaking with you about your son."

"I had two sons."

"I was hoping to speak with you about Thomas Cardin. Recent nominee for the United States Supreme Court."

"Of course."

"What was Thomas like as a child?"

"He was a good son. Paid mind to his mother and me. The stark opposite of his older brother."

"Was he a good student?"

"Always. He earned high marks throughout school. I think chemistry was the only class he ever took that tripped him up a little. But we got a tutor and he figured it out. Thomas had a remarkable memory. If he read it or heard it once, it was locked in a vault."

"When did he first show interest in law?"

"Early. Not sure exactly when, but Thomas was surrounded by the law from the time he could breathe. He probably understood a bit of it by the time he could walk."

"Did you ever think he would be where he is today? As a nominee for the Supreme Court?"

"Parents dream about what their children may do. But no one knows for sure what will happen. Things can change, sometimes in the blink of an eye." Cardin Senior motioned toward the cane leaning against his chair. "One minute I was able-bodied, the next I was put back together with enough metal to make money at a scrap yard."

"I heard that your wife passed away as a result of the same car accident that caused your injuries. I'm sorry for your loss."

"Thank you, Stacey."

"It's Pixie."

"Pixie. Right. I apologize."

"Did Thomas have a high school sweetheart?"

"No one regular. He had a lot of friends. Boys and girls. I remember some of the girls I wished he'd shown more interest in. Some of those girls probably wished the same thing."

"Did Thomas ever get into trouble?"

"What kind of trouble?"

"Any kind."

"Thomas played a lot of baseball from grade school right up until he graduated from high school. He probably put a baseball through half a dozen windows on our house and another half dozen up and down the street. They used to play in the streets and out behind the houses near the lake. But a few broken windows from baseball was better than basketball. His older brother played basketball, and he used to dribble the ball in the house. It drove my wife crazy."

"I was thinking something more serious than broken windows. Do you remember a man named Odin Rowe?"

"I do. Nasty character. Turned this city upside down for half a year."

"I met him yesterday."

"I don't think so. He's still incarcerated."

"He is. I met him at the prison."

"You went down to… What's the name of the prison?"

"Lee Correctional Institute."

"That's the one."

"Yes, I visited Odin Rowe at Lee Correctional Institute yesterday."

"Why?"

"I was curious."

"Why was Odin Rowe curious to you?"

"I met your old neighbor, Eleanor Watson. She told me about a girl named Mary Spears who went missing when your son was in high school."

"Yes. A girl named Mary disappeared. Odin Rowe confessed to killing her."

"And Mary was a friend of Thomas's?"

"They were friends. Mary went to the local public school and Thomas went to Hammond, but they were still friends. "

"Did Thomas ever talk about Mary or her disappearance?"

Cardin Senior looked in the direction of Arthur, who didn't move. "I can't say if he talked about her before her disappearance, but he never talked about her after that morning."

"Which morning is that? The day following Mary's disappearance?"

"Yes, that's right."

"What about that morning?"

Cardin Senior paused, seemingly unsure of how to respond. "I think that's all the time I have for questions today," he replied.

Arthur stood from his chair and helped Cardin Senior to his feet. Pixie stopped the recording on her phone, gathered her purse and legal pad, and stood. Arthur held the door open for Pixie as she exited the room, followed by Cardin Senior, cane in hand.

"It was a pleasure meeting you, Stacey," Cardin Senior said.

"It's Pixie," she replied. "Thank you for your time."

CHAPTER 19

DAN BALANCED THE brown bag on the box of documents under his right arm. With his left hand, he dragged his suitcase past the sea of chess players huddled around the concrete tables in DuPont Circle. A half-block away, he maneuvered his way through a set of revolving doors leading to the building's elevator. Moments later, Dan entered Dr. Joffee's office. He placed the box on the table in front of the sofa, reached into the lunch bag, and handed a sandwich to Dr. Joffee.

"Tuna on wheat," Dan said, confirming the doctor's order while sitting down.

"Perfect," Joffee replied.

Both men unwrapped their lunches and took hefty bites. Dan wiped his mouth with a napkin. Joffee pointed to the box.

"What's in there?"

"These are copies of the police files on our girl Mary."

"Any reason you're carrying them around?"

"Just landed. Haven't been to the office yet."

"What did you learn?"

"Her full name is Mary Spears. She was killed by a man named Odin Rowe."

"Never heard of him."

"Everyone in South Carolina over the age of fifty has. He confessed to murdering Mary Spears and two other students in 1986. I met him a few days ago. He's a piece of work."

"You met him?"

"I did. I had the distinct pleasure of visiting the most dangerous prison in the state of South Carolina."

"How was that?"

"Hot."

"And what was your impression of the man you met?"

"I have no doubt Odin Rowe is a killer. And he admitted to killing Mary Spears. His story hasn't changed in almost forty years."

"So you believe him?"

"He has all the hallmarks of a psychopath. But he's also been incarcerated since the late eighties. That much time in prison probably makes you crazy, even if you weren't before you went in."

"I can work with crazy."

"You *do* work with crazy," Dan said, taking another bite of his sandwich. "Anyhow, I got copies of the files from the murder cases to see if they can shed light onto Mary Spears's death."

"Is there anything in the files to indicate a certain Supreme Court nominee could have been involved in the murder? That's where the rubber meets the road."

"I haven't come across anything concrete to support your client's claim. But Thomas Cardin was one of the last people to see Mary Spears before she died."

"That sounds like something."

"I also asked Odin Rowe if he knew Thomas Cardin."

"And?"

"He said everyone in town knew at least one Cardin."

"Adding a Supreme Court justice to the family will make them even more prominent."

"Unless that Supreme Court nominee is a killer," Dan said. "Let me ask you a therapy question."

"Shoot."

"You have this patient who claimed, under hypnosis, that Thomas Cardin killed her."

"That's the short version of the story."

"So what happens to the patient after something like that? From a mental health perspective, how does remembering that incident—or any incident from one's past—help?"

"Let me start with the caveat that this is not my area of expertise. But I have been reading up on the topic."

"I acknowledge that you've successfully covered your ass with that disclaimer."

"Good. From what I understand, there's no definitive answer to that question. For some reason, it seems that just remembering a past life, or an incident from a past life, is enough to help most patients overcome their related mental health issues."

"They remember something, and that alone cures them?"

"Treatment is usually continued for a period of time but, yes, remembering a past life, or an event from a past life, is enough of an impetus for healing."

"And how is your patient doing? The one with the claim against Thomas Cardin. Has her condition improved?"

"We've only had two sessions since the past-life regression. As of now, the patient has not made a measurable improvement. We plan on continuing sessions for now and will reassess as we move forward."

"I have another question. How does truth play into this past-life regression equation?"

"What do you mean?"

"Does the patient have to believe what's discovered during a hypnotherapy session in order to see improvement in their mental health?"

"From what I understand, most patients believe the recollections to be true. But not all."

"And in this case?"

"Let's just say my patient is not ready to embrace their recollection at this time."

"That puts us in a tough spot. Your patient, albeit subconsciously, and a convicted murderer claim different people killed Mary Spears. One of them is the killer. One of them is the victim. And I don't know if we can prove that either of them is lying."

CHAPTER 20

THE BUZZER FROM the door at street level echoed through Dan's office one floor above. A second buzz pulled Dan's eyes off the open folder on his desk. He turned his attention to the bank of security monitors on the wall. The screen in the upper left showed a female visitor wearing sunglasses at the door. Dan stood from his desk, crossed his second-floor office, and pressed a button on the intercom near the top of the stairs.

"Can I help you?" Dan asked.

"You can if you're Dan Lord, private investigator and attorney," the woman said.

Dan glanced back towards security camera as the woman removed her sunglasses. Something about his visitor's face rang a bell, and Dan unlocked the ALON security door at the top of the staircase. At the bottom of the stairs, he slipped his laser-cut key into a second ALON security door. In the small foyer, he entered the code for the steel front door and pushed it open.

"Pixie on Politics," he said.

"That's right."

"I thought I recognized you."

"And I recognize you."

"Is that right?"

"Yep. You held the door open for me at The Happy Cock."

"Guilty as charged."

"Can I come in?"

"Not if you're writing a story about me."

"I think you might be interested in what I have to say."

"Why's that?"

"Because I also had a meeting Odin Rowe."

Dan paused.

"We should talk," Pixie said.

Dan motioned for Pixie to enter.

Dan reset the code for the front door and performed his multi-step security routine in reverse. At the top of the stairs, he noticed Pixie staring at the CCTV camera in the corner.

"You seem to be quite security conscious," Pixie stated.

"I am."

"I imagine the bomb attempt on your life last year didn't help."

Dan flashed Pixie a cautious look. He opened the office door on the second floor and flicked his head in the direction of the interior. "I see you've done some background on me."

"I have."

"Well, for the record, it wasn't a bomb *attempt*. The device successfully detonated."

Pixie looked around the office. "The place looks great for having been bombed."

"Most of the damage was to the art gallery downstairs."

"That couldn't have been good for business. Or for art. I hope they had insurance."

"It worked out, actually."

"Records indicate that you own the whole building. Which is most of the block."

"I do. But that's not why you're here, is it?"

"No."

Dan led Pixie to a small table near the front windows and they sat down. "So, what did you find in South Carolina that compelled you to hunt me down in Virginia?"

"It's what I didn't find, actually. I was hoping you could help me out."

"How's that?"

"I was at the courthouse in Columbia looking for the files related to our friend and serial killer, Odin Rowe. It's my understanding that you also went to Columbia to obtain these records."

"Not exactly. But for the sake of argument, it's close enough."

"And did you get a copy of these files?"

"They're public. Nothing would prevent you from obtaining a copy."

"Except one thing."

"What?"

"They're missing."

"The files?"

"Yes. When I spoke with Odin Rowe, he told me you had visited him. He said you had his files and that you'd been reading through them."

"You can't believe everything you hear."

"Especially from a convicted murderer?"

"You said it. But I didn't check out the files. The Columbia Police Department obtained the files and made copies of them on my behalf."

"I still think that makes you the last person to receive a copy of them."

Dan shrugged. "Maybe, but I had nothing to do with anything that may have gone missing."

"I didn't say you did."

"You implied it," Dan answered.

The two stared at each other.

"So, you spoke with Odin Rowe?" Dan asked.

"I did more than speak with him. I visited him in person. A true Southern gentleman, that one."

"What interest is Odin Rowe to you?"

"I could ask you the same question. Maybe we can help each other out."

"I doubt it. I'm not interested in being featured in a news article."

"Do you still have copies of the Odin Rowe legal files? I was hoping I could make copies of them."

Dan buried the urge to mention that the files Pixie was seeking were on the floor by his desk, fifteen feet away.

"I'm just talking about copies. As you said, they're public records."

Dan mulled over Pixie's predicament. "I'll tell you what, let me make a quick phone call. I have a contact in the Columbia Police Department who can probably help you out with what you need."

"That would be great."

✍

Dan returned and sat down.

"What did you find out?" Pixie asked.

"Nothing. I left a message. But, as an attorney, I'm confident the files will show up."

"And if you're wrong?"

"Someone in Columbia could be in a lot of trouble. Theft or destruction of court records is a punishable offense. Title 18 US Code 1506 clearly states that court records are treated as sacred because the content of court documents is presumed to be truthful. It is a federal crime to steal, alter, or falsify any official court records."

"That won't help me much," Pixie replied. She motioned toward the pictures on the office walls. "You've traveled a lot."

"I have."

"Any chance you'll tell me why you traveled to South Carolina? Any reason why you visited a man who has been incarcerated for nearly forty years?"

"A case."

"What kind of case?"

"I'm not at liberty to say," Dan replied.

"Fair enough, but you are aware that my job is digging up things people don't want discovered."

"We have similar professions in that regard."

"Is that why you went to South Carolina? To dig up information people don't want discovered?"

"I'm not at liberty to say."

"Who is your client?"

"I'm not at liberty to say."

"Okay. Maybe you can answer this question for me. Is it coincidence that you were investigating Odin Rowe, the killer of a girl who hung out with Thomas Cardin, the newly nominated Supreme Court justice?"

"I'm not at—"

"Liberty to say," Pixie said, finishing Dan's sentence. "I think Thomas Cardin is the reason you were investigating Odin Rowe. And assuming that, do you know what's particularly interesting about the timing of your visit to South Carolina?"

"I assume you're going to enlighten me."

"I cannot figure out why you paid a visit to Odin Rowe *before* Thomas Cardin's nomination was made public."

With that observation, any remaining question in Dan's mind on whether Pixie on Politics was going to be a pain in the ass was answered.

"Not at liberty to answer that one either?" Pixie asked.

"I think we're done here," Dan added, rising from his chair.

"Are you really not going to share the Odin Rowe files?"

"I'm going to think about it. Why don't you give me your number? I'll give you a ring."

"I don't think you will."

"You're entitled to your opinion."

"That's it?"

"No, that's not it. Next time you want to stop by, call first. I only see clients by appointment. And with a referral. Consider this meeting your free consultation. My standard rate will apply on your next visit."

"What's your standard rate?"

"Four hundred and fifty an hour."

"I hear those are Lee Correctional Institute rates for a legal consultation."

"Have a good day, Pixie," Dan said, leading her toward the stairs and the exit.

Dan stood in the doorway and watched as Pixie bounded down the brick sidewalk toward the Potomac.

CHAPTER 21

DAN SAT UNMOVING, reading until the rays of sunlight on the wall extinguished with the arrival of evening. If successful completion of law school proved anything, it was that you could read. Sometimes, that's all it proved.

Dan finished his second pass of the files, dropped a folder on the floor, and rubbed his eyes. Something about the Odin Rowe case gnawed at him. And it wasn't just that one of Rowe's victims was alive and well, living another life in another body.

His mobile phone vibrated. He answered, "Dan speaking."

"Dan, this is Roy Huff."

Dan could envision Huff's face on the other end, his white mustache dancing. "Hey, Roy, thanks for returning my call."

"Sorry I didn't get back to you earlier. Been busy. Something you might be interested in, actually. Some news."

"Good or bad?"

"Depends on how you look at it. Odin Rowe was stabbed today. He's alive, but it's touch and go. It was a bloody scene."

"Stabbed by another inmate?"

"Looks that way."

"How did you hear?"

"One of the guards gave me a courtesy call."

"Why you?"

"Odin Rowe doesn't get a lot of visitors. I guess when you bring a lawyer from DC to visit a man who's been in jail for four decades, people think you have some interest in him."

"Any suspects?"

"A whole prison full. Nothing definite beyond that. A fight broke out in the line to the exercise yard and Odin Rowe was attacked in the melee. It was pretty vicious. He had multiple puncture wounds to his liver and kidneys."

"That's professional efficiency."

"The Lee Correctional Institution is known for it. They transported him to a hospital in Sumter. I drove over as soon as I heard, hoping for a final conversation with him. I thought maybe I'd get him to tell me where Mary Spears's body is really buried."

"You wanted a deathbed confession?"

"A man can always hope."

"And…"

"Rowe was largely unresponsive. Made some sounds."

"I'm on my way down. I'll be there in the morning."

"You're coming back?"

"Yes. If Odin Rowe regains consciousness, I'm interested to see if he'll tell you where Mary Spears is buried."

"I'll share anything he says with you."

"No offense, but I'm ready to hear some firsthand information on this case."

"Offense taken."

"I have a request."

"Shoot."

"Any chance, you can get your hands on the visitor log for Odin Rowe?"

"Probably. It may take a few calls, but it shouldn't be much of a problem."

"Thanks."

"You really don't have to come all the way back down here."

"I want to check on a couple of other things in Columbia."

"Such as?"

"Local lore."

Detective Huff breathed heavily into the phone.

"How about a little fishing tomorrow evening?" Dan asked. "You can show me the ropes. We can discuss the case."

"I'll set up an extra tackle box for you."

"I'll call you tomorrow," Dan said.

Dan hung up and called Dr. Joffee.

"Hey, Doc. It's Dan Lord. Got a sec?"

"Just finishing off a glass of wine. How can I help you?"

"I wanted to give you a heads up. Odin Rowe, the convicted killer I mentioned earlier, was stabbed in prison today. His condition is serious. I'm planning on heading back down to Columbia tomorrow."

"That's an interesting development."

"One of two, actually. I also had a reporter come by my office today asking questions about Thomas Cardin and Odin Rowe. Her name is Pixie, and she writes the column Pixie on Politics. You may have heard of her."

"I know the name. What did she want with you?"

"She was looking for some files that allegedly have gone missing from the courthouse in Columbia. Evidently, I was the last person to receive copies of the files, which never made their way back to the records floor. She wanted copies of the copies I received."

"Did you give them to her?"

"No. I'm not convinced helping her will help us."

"Any idea why she's looking into Odin Rowe?"

"Probably going through Thomas Cardin's past with a fine-tooth comb. She won't be the last one."

"How did she make the connection between Thomas Cardin and

Odin Rowe? I thought you were the only one who had stumbled upon that."

"I'm not sure. But however she did it, you can bet someone else will figure it out."

Joffee didn't respond.

"I don't know exactly what angle she's working, but she seems to have a heavy dose of bulldog in her. She smells a story. And a Supreme Court nominee who knew a convicted serial killer will sell papers."

"That it will. And there's nothing to stop her. Freedom of the press." Joffee paused. "What are the chances that this serial killer survives his wounds?"

"I don't know. Part of me hopes he pulls through. As much as I don't want to admit it, he may be our best chance at finding out what really happened to Mary. Either that, or the best chance for getting to the bottom of our mystery may be having a face-to-face with Thomas Cardin and asking him point blank if he killed your patient."

"I don't think anyone wants to go that route."

CHAPTER 22

THE AUTOMATIC DOORS opened as Dan approached the front entrance of Sumter Regional Hospital. Three women in matching pink outfits smiled as he stepped up to the information desk. A security guard sat on a stool near the entrance. A woman with her head under a blanket was stretched over several chairs.

"Hi. I'm looking for Odin Rowe."

"Are you with the prison?"

"I'm not. I'm an attorney. I'm supposed to meet a retired detective here."

"You must mean Detective Huff."

"That's right."

"Odin Rowe is on the fourth floor. Just look for the men in uniform."

Dan exited the elevator and looked down the hall in each direction. He spotted Roy Huff standing amid a gathering of officers. The retired detective came forward and extended his hand.

"Any trouble finding the place?"

"Google Maps did all the work. What's the word on the patient?"

"He's in there. They have him hooked up to a few machines. The doctors estimate he lost between four and five pints of blood."

"Has he spoken?"

"He made a few sounds but that was it."

"Does anyone mind if I go in?"

"No, you're cleared. Holler if he starts talking."

"Thanks."

⌘

Dan stood at the side of the bed, looking down at Odin Rowe's body. A nasal cannula provided a steady stream of oxygen. An IV bag hung from a drip stand on the other side of the bed, pumping antibiotics straight into the killer's veins.

"Rowe, if you can hear me, this is Dan Lord. I visited you last week. I paid you $450 for a conversation. Not sure I got my money's worth. And now, here we are, together again. I'm going to be honest with you. I'm wondering if you're just biding time here in the hospital. Even in your current condition, this has to be better than a prison cell."

The steady faint beep from the heart monitor in the corner was the only reply.

Dan pulled the blanket off Rowe's feet and grabbed a toe. "Let me know if you feel this."

Dan cranked the toe back toward Rowe's head and twisted.

No response.

Dan took two steps toward the head of the bed and leaned his ear toward Rowe's mouth. He grabbed Rowe's tattooed hand and dug his knuckle into a pressure point between the patient's thumb and index finger.

Again, no response.

Dan stole a glance toward the door to the room and shoved a finger into the crevasse between Rowe's ear lobe and jaw. He waited for several seconds but Rowe remained motionless.

"Well, Rowe, maybe I was wrong. Maybe this isn't an act. No hard feelings. But if you're not going to help us find Mary's body, then I think it's time for you go to hell," Dan said. "Just head down the dark tunnel and follow the red guy with the pitchfork."

❧

Dan left Rowe's room and Huff approached.

"Anything?"

"Not even a grunt of pain."

Huff squinted, as if trying to determine whether Dan was lying. "He's not out of the woods. The doctor said he could still go either way. There's a lot of organ damage."

"Even if he makes it, I don't think he'll tell us anything."

Huff shrugged at the assumption. "What do you have planned for the rest of the day? Still interested in fishing?"

"I have some things to look into this afternoon, but I'm down for a fishing lesson later."

CHAPTER 23

HENRY'S PIZZA HAD ceased to exist seven years after Mary Spears had gone missing. By the time the sign was removed from the building, Odin Rowe, convicted murderer, had collected six years of penal dust. Ultimately, the owner of Henry's Pizza—Henry Dymond—was done in by his own product. With a diet that consisted of at least one meat-laden pizza a day, obesity and heart disease had joined forces to snatch Henry as he slept.

Dan stopped at the door of Za's Pizza on Devine Street and glanced back at his rental car in the parking lot. He tried to go back in time, to envision what Za's Pizza had looked like when it was still called Henry's. Dan peered into the interior of the restaurant. The booths, tables, chairs, and fixtures exuded modern industrial charm. Just inside the door, a sign reading "Seat Yourself" compelled Dan to a corner booth with a view of the parking lot.

A college-aged student with a tuft of hair on his chin and notepad in hand approached the table. "Can I get you something to drink?"

"How long have you worked here?" Dan asked, throwing the waiter off his usual routine.

"A couple of months," the waiter replied.

"Are you a local?"

"No, I'm from Georgia. I'm a sophomore at the university."

"Any chance the owner of the establishment is in?"

"The owner isn't, but the manager is. Her name's Bridget."

"Can you call her over for me?"

"Sure. I'm assuming I haven't done anything wrong. You haven't even ordered yet."

"You haven't done anything wrong," Dan replied. "I just have a few restaurant questions."

A minute later, Bridget pushed open the kitchen door, her black apron lightly dusted in flour. Her salt-and-pepper hair was pulled into a ponytail. As she approached, she wiped her hands on her apron. "Your server tells me you want to speak with the manager."

"That's right. My name is Dan Lord. I'm an attorney."

"If you have a legal issue, you'll probably need to speak with the owner."

"It's not a legal issue."

"Then what can I do for you?"

"Any chance you're a local?"

"Born and raised."

"This may seem like an odd question, but did you ever come here when it was still called Henry's Pizza?"

"Of course. Heck, everyone in town probably has at least one Henry's Pizza story. First date. Friday night football celebrations. Fist fights."

"The good ol' days."

"Some would say."

"I'm curious what the inside of this place looked like when it was still called Henry's."

Bridget tilted her head to the side. "Well, I could tell you or you could see for yourself."

"How's that?"

"Follow me," she said with a flick of her head before walking across the restaurant floor in the direction of the sign for the restrooms. Turning the corner, she stopped and faced the wall in the short hall. "That's what Henry's looked like back in the day. Not that different from a lot of pizza parlors from the seventies and eighties. Right down to the orange tabletops."

Dan's eyes danced over the old photographs plastered to the wall and whistled. Bridget nodded as if affirming Dan's reaction.

"Henry's was a real institution. I have no doubt it would still be here if old Henry was alive, or if he'd had any kids to take over the business. But he didn't. A few folks tried to keep it going for a while, but when Henry passed, he took a lot of the magic with him. A few years later, it closed. It was empty for a while before the new owner bought it. Obviously, the new owner was going for a different vibe."

"But he kept pictures of the old place on the wall?"

"I don't think he wanted to. But customers kept bringing in photos of the old place and telling stories about how important Henry's Pizza was to their lives. Eventually, the photos ended up on this wall. It's a monument of sorts."

Dan scanned the wall, examining the faces of customers, photographs of people smiling, mouths stuffed with pizza. Groups of kids in soccer uniforms and parties with birthday balloons tied to chairs. Several pictures of a jukebox caught Dan's attention, and he leaned in for a closer look. Standing motionless, staring at the photo, Dan saw the first crack in the storyline of a forty-year-old mystery.

"I heard a car once drove through the front window of the place when it was Henry's Pizza," Dan said, tapping the photograph with his finger.

"That it did."

"Do you remember that jukebox?"

"Remember it? We still have it. It's on the other side of the restaurant, near the bar. It still has records in it, but the coin slot is taped over. It's plugged in at night, but just for the ambiance. Most kids these days don't even know what it is. All they know is that it lights up."

"I don't doubt that," Dan replied. "Can you tell me where this jukebox was located back in the day?"

"Sure thing," Bridget replied, walking back in the direction of

Dan's corner booth. Bridget stopped along the back of the shop and stretched out her hands in opposite directions. "This is where the jukebox was. More or less."

"And this room is where the car crashed through the window?"

"Yep."

"Do you remember anything else about the shop after the accident?"

"I remember the windows were boarded up. It was the talk of the town for a while. Some kid on prom night. Needed to work on his parking skills."

Dan's mind churned as Bridget kept talking. "But, you know, that sort of thing happens every once in a while. Usually an old person or a drunk college student who misses the brake pedal or hits the gas by mistake. Columbia has a lot of both."

"Both of what?"

"Old people and drunk students."

Dan stared through the front window and faded out of the conversation. He was brought back to the present when Bridget said she had to finish making dough in the kitchen. "Are you staying for lunch?"

"It would be rude not to. What do you recommend?"

"Well, seeing that you're so interested in Henry's, I'd suggest Henry's Heartstopper. Unless you're a vegetarian."

"You're kidding."

"Nope. It's not officially on the menu, but customers in-the-know still order it. A little nod to the memory of the previous owner. We probably sell two or three Henry's Heartstoppers a day."

"What's in it?"

"Everything that's bad for you and nothing that's good. And it's delicious."

"I'll give it a try. Do you have Wi-Fi?"

"Half of our customers are college students. We wouldn't be in business if we didn't. The password is on the back of the menu."

❧

Dan ate half of his Henry's Heartstopper and called it quits before tempting fate. He wiped grease from his lips, dabbed his fingers on the same napkin, and picked up his phone. Googling, his eyes ran down the screen and focused on the fourth search result. He clicked on the link, perused the single-page website, and called the number.

"Bailey and Sons," a male voice with a thick Southern accent answered.

"Hi. I wanted to inquire about a jukebox that may or may not have been repaired by you."

"Not much to go on. When was it?"

"Would've been 1986."

"Did you say '86?"

"I did."

"I was only five years old at the time."

"Is there anyone there who was around that far back?"

"Sure. My father and his brothers. My aunt still helps out in the office. This place has been a family business for three generations."

"Any of the older generation available?"

"Let me get your information and someone can get back to you."

Dan provided his name and contact information.

"And what can you tell us about the jukebox?" the man asked.

"It was in a pizza restaurant in Columbia. Henry's Pizza."

"Okay. I got it. Jukebox from Henry's Pizza in 1986. Someone will call you back."

Before Dan could complete the ten-minute drive to his hotel, his phone rang.

He put the call on speaker and answered as he drove through the University of South Carolina campus.

"This is Dan Lord."

"Hi. This is Audry from Bailey and Sons. You called us about a jukebox repair."

"I did."

"I think I have the answer to your question. According to my husband, we did repair work on the jukebox that Henry Pizza's had in the late eighties. He remembered it pretty clearly. Says it was the only jukebox he ever worked on that was damaged by a car. He said it took some time to fix. He picked it up from the pizza shop and brought it back here for repairs. Kept it for a month or two."

"You wouldn't happen to keep records from that far back, would you?

"I'm sure we don't. We don't do contracts. We work on a handshake."

Dan pondered the answer. "Thank you for the call back."

"You have a good day."

CHAPTER 24

THE WOOD-PLANKED STAIRS connected Detective Huff's backyard to the shoreline of the Saluda River a hundred feet below. Dan followed Huff down the worn steps until they reached the edge of the water. A weathered shed with a fish cleaning station stood at the corner of an L-shaped pier.

Huff stopped at the shed, opened the door, and pulled out two folded camping chairs. With a nod, he motioned for Dan to grab them. Huff disappeared back into the shed and reemerged with several fishing poles and two tackle boxes. Dan followed Huff as he walked to the end of the dock and placed the tackle boxes on the squeaky planks. Assuming they had reached their final destination, Dan unfolded the chairs.

"Welcome to the Saluda River," Huff said. "Well, technically, this section is the Lower Saluda River."

"Is there an Upper Saluda River?"

"Sort of. A hundred years ago, the Saluda was dammed upstream to create Lake Murray. Before the dam, the whole thing was just called the Saluda River. After they built the dam, everything downstream of the lake became the Lower Saluda."

Still standing, Dan focused his gaze on the water. Rapids rippled over rocks in the distance. "How deep is it?"

"Deep enough to drown. It varies a bit. They open the dam

occasionally, and when they do, the water gets right up to the pier. The electric company announces it beforehand so as to not catch people off guard."

"And what do we fish for here?"

"The best bang for the buck is small mouth bass. But there's a little bit of everything."

A six-person flotilla on inner tubes floated by, waving to Dan and Detective Huff. A man in a hat was anchored in a canoe on the other side of the river, casting his lures toward the far shore. Another man was fishing from his kayak, just downstream of the rapids.

"It's busy out here."

"Most people will be off the water in an hour or so. Once the sun starts heading down. And that's when the real fishing starts. Let me get your rig set up and we can knock back a beer or two. I have a small fridge in the shed."

"I thought you were going to teach me how to fish."

"Drinking beer is the first lesson."

Dan sat and Detective Huff returned with two beers. He slipped one into the drink holder on the arm of Dan's chair. Sitting down, Huff pulled his tackle box closer.

"Before I set up your rig, I have something for you," Huff said. He reached into his shirt pocket and handed Dan a folded piece of paper.

"What's this?"

"That's the list of Odin Rowe's visitors for the last month. From one of the guys at Lee Correctional."

Dan unfolded the piece of paper and looked at the entries on the page.

Huff spoke. "Three visitors in the last month. Odin Rowe's mother, Felicia, you, and a woman named Patricia Flynn."

"She's a reporter. From DC. She covers politics. I was wondering if she was on the list."

"She's there."

"I was expecting more names."

"Like I said before, not a lot of interest in a convicted serial killer who's been in prison as long as Rowe has been." Detective Huff flipped open the lid on his tackle box and grabbed a rod. "You still haven't told me why you doubt that Mary was murdered by Odin Rowe."

"I can't tell you why, but I can tell you that I may have found a clue."

"You come into town for a couple of days and you found a clue for a thirty-some-year-old murder that was solved?"

"What do you remember about Henry's Pizza?"

"They made good pizza, but somehow I don't think that's what you mean."

"It's not."

"Is this something about Rowe having dinner at Henry's Pizza the night Mary Spears went missing?"

"It is."

"Rowe was a regular at Henry's. Nothing suspicious about that. A lot of people were regulars."

"Rowe's confession included details of his visit to Henry's Pizza that night."

"It did."

"Here's what bothers me. For a guy who couldn't remember where he supposedly buried a body, he sure remembered a lot about the night Mary Spears went missing and his time at Henry's. He remembered the type of pizza and beer he ordered. Remembered the price. Remembered where he sat. Remembered playing Aerosmith on the jukebox."

"He was a regular."

"No argument there. Do you recall anything about a high school kid driving through the front window of Henry's Pizza in 1986? On prom night. Probably in June, assuming that's when the schools around here get out. That would put it about a month before Mary Spears went missing."

"Now that you mention it. I wouldn't have necessarily remembered the timeframe off the top of my head, but yeah, I recall something along those lines."

"Last time I was here in Columbia, I met a former Henry Pizza's employee from the summer that Mary went missing. He was just a high school kid at the time. Both he and the guy who drove through the window went to the same school as Mary Spears. He seemed to remember that summer pretty clearly."

"I know who you're talking about. He is an accountant in town. He provided testimony as to the timeline for Rowe's movement the night Mary Spears disappeared."

"'Timeline' is an interesting choice of words."

"I'm not sure I follow."

"Here's what's bothering me. When I met Rowe at the prison, he verified everything in his confession."

"Because he killed Mary Spears."

"Maybe. But his confession was a little too neat for me. He recalled an amazing level of detail and then 'poof,' he can't remember the most memorable part of the evening? He can't remember where he buried a body. Seems unlikely."

Huff stared at Dan without replying.

"I stopped by Henry's today. As you probably know, it's now called Za's on Devine."

"Been there. Decent pizza, but it isn't the same place."

"But do you know what is the same? The jukebox. It's on the bar side of the restaurant now. They don't use it for music, but they do use it for the lights and ambiance. Still has vinyl records in it. Even has a couple by Aerosmith."

"That was in Rowe's confession."

"It was. Here's the problem. The night Mary Spears went missing, there was no jukebox in Henry's Pizza. It was damaged when the car came through the window. It had been sent off for repairs to a place called Bailey and Sons. I called them today. They are only one of two places left in the state that fixes jukeboxes and the only one that was in business in the eighties."

Huff took a hefty sip from his beer and stared out at the river. When he glanced back in Dan's direction, he asked, "Are you sure about that?"

"I'm sure. After the car crashed through the window, Henry's Pizza set up picnic tables outside. The former employee who provided details of Rowe's visit to Henry's on the night Mary went missing remembers putting posters on those same tables a few days later."

"So Odin Rowe claimed to have listened to music on a jukebox that had been sent out for repairs?"

"That's right."

"I'm not sure how that was missed."

"I'm not surprised. By the time autumn rolled around and Odin Rowe came onto your radar as a suspect, the temporary drive-through window at Henry's on prom night was probably a distant memory. It was a busy time. Mary Spears went missing and two girls were killed at the university. No one was going to remember that a jukebox had been shipped off to be repaired."

"That doesn't make me feel better. It was an oversight."

"I wouldn't beat yourself up over it. But it does bring into question the accuracy of Rowe's confession."

"Only the part about his music selection."

"It calls into question the validity of his entire testimony."

"I don't like where this is heading."

"Were you present when Rowe provided his confession?"

"Do you mean was I actually in the room?"

"Yes."

"No, I wasn't."

"Was Rowe's lawyer present?"

"Yes. He had legal representation."

"And who negotiated the plea bargain?"

"The plea was negotiated and agreed to by Nathanial Cardin Senior and Rowe's attorney, Clinton Stoll."

"Is Rowe's attorney still around?"

"Clinton Stoll? He was killed in a hunting accident a couple years after Mary Spears went missing."

"What did you think of him?"

"He was a court appointed defense attorney. Wasn't bad at his job, but you know how it goes. Detectives don't get along with defense attorneys very well."

"Where did the hunting accident happen?"

"Down in the Lowcountry."

"When you say 'Lowcountry,' how large of an area are we talking?"

"Thousands of square miles. Includes a half-dozen counties. If I remember correctly, Rowe's attorney was accidentally shot outside of Berkeley somewhere. He was duck hunting near the marshes. Killed by an errant bullet. Died before they could get him to a hospital. Never found who fired the shot. But that's not unusual. Particularly in the Lowcountry. All kinds of hunting down there... boar, deer, duck, quail, turkey. A handful of hunters are shot every year. Once in a while the shooter isn't found. Accidental discharge. Maybe someone had been drinking. People panic. You know how it goes." Huff swallowed a mouthful of beer. "I warned you before and I feel it's my duty to warn you again. Anyone who remembers 1986 is not going to look kindly at you stirring up buried feelings."

"Does that include you? Because the other day a homeless guy was waiting for me outside my hotel when I was in town. Someone had paid him a hundred bucks to warn me to go home. The homeless guy knew my name."

"Did you get a description of the guy who paid the homeless man?"

"A white guy."

"Not much to go on."

"Nope. When I went back to my room, I called the front desk from my cell phone. I asked them if someone named Dan Lord was staying at my hotel. They confirmed that I was. They wouldn't divulge my room number, but they confirmed I was a guest. They even offered to connect my call to my room without giving me the room number."

"I think that's the appropriate procedure. Legally speaking."

"I don't disagree. But it does bring me to an obvious conclusion. Someone either called every hotel in town looking for me or someone knew where I was staying. And if it's the latter, it's a short list of people in town who knew my name and that I was here. Captain Collins, Gerald Winters the accountant, the owner of The Happy Cock, Odin Rowe, the guards at the prison, and you."

"That may seem like a short list, but if all of them told a friend or a spouse, it could become a big number real fast."

"I remember what you said. 'A bad man went to jail, the killings stopped, and everyone moved on.'"

"That's right. Everyone moved on."

"I would feel a lot better with a body. And I think that Mary Spears's family would also feel better with a body. To have real closure."

"The Spears family has suffered enough. Nothing will make them feel better. If you go causing trouble with the Spears family, you and I will be done working together."

"I'll keep that under advisement."

"Good. You heading back to DC tomorrow?"

"Why would I do that? Things are just getting interesting down here."

CHAPTER 25

ELLEN STERN, EDITOR of *The Washington Gazette*, was staring out the window of her corner office when Pixie knocked on the open door.

"Good afternoon, Pixie. Grab a seat," Ellen Stern said without turning around.

Pixie sat and admired the framed front pages that lined the walls. Sealed moments of fame and infamy that her newspaper had covered in the past.

Ellen Stern finished staring out the window, turned, and sat behind her large desk. "The basic write-up on Thomas Cardin was fine."

"Thank you."

"I said it was fine. Fine is not great. Fine isn't even good. It was passable. But it was something that anyone else could have done. It lacked pep. Pizzazz. And you didn't visit the law school at Duke."

"I contacted them. They were unavailable. But I'm working other angles. There could be more to the basic Cardin story."

"Like what?"

"I'm not sure yet."

"Well, you better figure out a way to get sure."

"I will."

"You'd better." Ellen Stern reached for the pack of cigarettes on the corner of her desk. "You have an interview with Thomas Cardin's staff tomorrow morning. His office has set aside time for the press to meet with his clerks. You're on the list. I'll send you the information via email. I want you to stay out of the bars tonight. I need you bright-eyed and bushy-tailed for the meeting tomorrow. Do you understand?"

"Yes, ma'am."

"Good. I'm counting on you. Be the nosy bitch you were born to be and find me something that no one else can get."

❦

Pixie stood and extended her hand across the wood table to Grace Homan. "Thank you for your time this morning."

"You're welcome," Grace replied.

"I'll try not to take up too much of your day. I'm sure you have a busy schedule."

"We blocked off several hours for interviews today. Needless to say, Judge Cardin's nomination to the Supreme Court has made things hectic around here."

"Then let's get into it," Pixie said. "How did you feel about Judge Cardin's nomination when you heard the news?"

"Excited. Honored. I can say, unequivocally, the president nomi-nated the right man for the position."

"Even though Judge Cardin is just the second nominee in a hun-dred years to have not graduated from an Ivy League law school?"

"As I understand it, Judge Cardin was accepted into every law program he applied to, including most of the Ivy League schools. He chose Duke. He didn't settle for Duke."

"I wasn't aware of that. In your opinion, where does Judge Cardin fall on the political spectrum?"

"I think most people are cognizant of the fact that Judge Cardin was once a registered Republican. Then he switched teams and became a Democrat. Now, he officially supports neither party. He's a centrist."

"Which is very unusual."

"Unusual, but you might be surprised to know that political lean doesn't matter as much as people think when it comes to Supreme Court nominees."

"Why is that?"

"A lot is made of a judge's political views, but historically Supreme Court justices don't issue judgments along expected political lines. In fact, according to a study done two years ago, Supreme Court justices voted along expected political lines only 52 percent of the time. Meaning if a Republican president appoints a Republican-leaning judge, there is no guarantee the judge will make court decisions based on the political lean of the president that nominated him."

"That doesn't seem right to me."

"I agree it's counterintuitive. But the data speaks for itself. It was an interesting study."

"I may have to look it up."

"I can send you the link, if you want."

"That would be helpful."

For the next several minutes Pixie dragged Grace through Judge Cardin's behaviors, hobbies, interests, and family life. The end of the standard Q&A left Pixie agreeing with Grace's original assessment of Judge Cardin. By all accounts, he seems to be the right man for the job.

Both women looked down at their respective cell phones on the table and checked the time. "I had one final question for you," Pixie said. "Has Judge Cardin ever mentioned why he chose a career in law?"

"I think it's in his blood."

"I'm sure that's part of it," Pixie said. "But I'm curious if the judge has ever mentioned that when he was younger a classmate of his was murdered?"

A look of surprise washed over Grace's face. "No, the Judge never mentioned it."

"I asked because I was wondering if, perhaps, the murder of this classmate was an impetus to Judge Cardin pursuing a career in law."

"As I said, I think law is in his DNA. His father was a prominent lawyer. Ditto for his grandfather and great-grandfather."

"DNA only takes you so far."

❧

Grace could feel the waves of anxiety lapping against her mental beach. "I've never heard Judge Cardin mention the murder of a classmate or friend, or that such an incident was a driving force behind his desire to serve the law."

"Do you find that odd?"

Grace considered her answer. "No. There are things in every person's past they don't want to talk about."

The two women stared at each other for an extended moment. The weight of Pixie's stare pushed Grace deeper into the sea of anxiety.

"Do you have any other lines of inquiry regarding judge Cardin that I can help with?" Grace asked.

"As you know, Judge Cardin is from Columbia, South Carolina. Recently, I spent several days in Columbia, researching Judge Cardin. While I was in town, I interviewed a serial killer who has been on death row in South Carolina since the eighties. Thirty-some years ago, this criminal confessed to the murder of three young women. One of these women was named Mary Spears. Mary was Judge Cardin's classmate."

Grace Homan's head swooned, and she begin to perspire. She thought back on the audio recording of the hypnosis treatment she had undergone. "What was the girl's name that you mentioned?"

"Mary Spears."

"And what exactly happened to her?"

"She was allegedly strangled. Her body was never found."

Grace could feel her fingers begin to tremble. "I wasn't aware of this story, so it wouldn't be appropriate for me to respond." Grace dropped her eyes to her phone on the table. "Our time is up."

❧

Pixie watched Grace rise from her chair and steady herself with a palm on the table.

Pixie stood and extended her hand for the second time. "Thank you for your time." Pixie could feel the clamminess of Grace's hand and noticed the perspiration on her brow.

"If you wait here, I'll send in your next interviewee, a colleague. He's been a clerk for Judge Cardin for the last six months. He's a Yale graduate and a brilliant legal mind."

Pixie flipped through her legal folder as Grace Homan exited the room. She watched as Grace's shadow moved down the hall behind frosted, rippled glass.

Pixie waited for the next interview in silence for several minutes before standing and going to the door. Stepping out of the office, she asked a woman at the nearest desk for directions to the restroom.

"Down the hall, on the right."

"Thanks."

Moments later, Pixie opened the restroom door and came face-to-face with Grace, phone pressed to her ear. Tears ran down Grace's cheeks.

"I'll be there at eight tonight. Thanks for making the time," Grace said into the phone, smiling to Pixie as she grabbed a tissue from a box on the counter and exited the restroom.

CHAPTER 26

DAN WAS WALKING up the secure stairs to his second-floor office when his phone rang.

"This is Dan."

"It's Huff."

"My favorite retired detective."

"I'm calling to tell you that Odin Rowe succumbed to his injuries."

"He passed?"

"He did. In the same bed you saw him in. Organ failure. Not surprising."

"Did you get the confession you were hoping for?"

"No such luck. He died unceremoniously. Alone. In the early hours of the morning."

"I'm sad he didn't give you what you needed. But I imagine that's the end of anyone's sadness over his passing. Except for his mother. Maybe."

"Probably right on that. What's your next step? Does Odin Rowe's death put an end to your investigation?"

"I'm not sure. I'll keep you in the loop."

"Will you?"

Dan's phone vibrated in his hand. "Huff, I have to run. I have another call on the line," he said, hanging up before Huff responded.

Dan switched lines. "Hello, Dr. Joffee."

"Do you have dinner plans for this evening?"

"Not that I know of."

"Good. I want you to meet my patient."

"Do you mean *the* patient?"

"Yes. One and the same. She called me upset and wanted to meet. I think it's time I lay my cards on the table."

"Okay. I'm in. On a separate topic, I just received word that the serial killer who confessed to killing Mary Spears succumbed to his injuries early this morning."

"What does that mean for us?'

"It eliminates a line of inquiry. And there aren't a lot of lines left to investigate."

"What do you usually do in cases like this?"

"I've never had a case quite like this one, but typically when I find myself running out of leads, I start over from the beginning."

"How does that usually work out?"

"Something turns up. Send me the details on dinner for tonight and I'll see you then."

CHAPTER 27

PIXIE SPENT THE afternoon moving between the three coffee shops that offered a view of the building's front door. She was currently seated at the window counter of Baked and Wired. She pecked intermittently on her latest column, a halfhearted attempt to be productive while trying to appear normal.

At twenty minutes before eight in the evening, Pixie observed Grace Homan exit the front door and step onto the sidewalk. Pixie, fully caffeinated, quickly slipped her laptop into her bag. Moments later, she followed Grace from the opposite side of the street. Two blocks later, Pixie paused at the next intersection while Grace crossed the street. Pixie continued to follow Grace down the sidewalk as the sign for Old Ebbitt Grill came into view. Pixie slowed her pace and watched as Grace entered the establishment and approached the maître d'.

Perfect, Pixie thought. *I could use a little alcohol to balance out the caffeine.*

For 150 years, Old Ebbitt Grill had beckoned the city's elite with after-work drinks and dinner. A large wood bar stretched the length of the establishment. A multi-sectioned tray ceiling perched over the dining area.

Pixie kept her eyes on her mark as Grace was led to a table in the middle of the dining room. A man at the table stood and then waited for Grace to settle into her chair. Pixie approached the bar and slipped onto a stool.

The bartender quickly appeared and smiled. "Hey Pixie. What are we having tonight?"

"Martini. Dry. Triple on the olives. Two sticks."

"Coming right up."

From her vantage point, Pixie could see the back of Grace's head, blond hair tied into a bun. The face of the unfamiliar man sitting across from Grace was clearly visible. For the next few minutes, Pixie slugged and nibbled her way through her martini and six olives, all the while keeping her attention on Grace. When the bartender swooped in for her empty glass, Pixie grabbed his wrist and leaned in. "Do you see the man sitting over there, facing this way. The guy in the blue tie. He's sitting across from the blond."

"Let me take a look," the bartender replied. "I'll get you a refill on that martini and be right back."

The bartender returned with another martini and a dose of dining floor intelligence.

"The table's server says the man's name is Joffee. She said he's a medical doctor. He comes in every few weeks for dinner, usually with another doctor. A female."

"Thanks for the info."

"And he has a thing for raw oysters."

"I'm glad someone does."

"Anything else you want to know?"

"That'll do," Pixie replied.

Nursing her second drink, Pixie Googled Dr. Joffees in Washington, DC. One click later, she found a matching photograph. She perused several pages of the doctor's website, his biography, and a handful of research papers he'd penned for the AMA. As the alcohol from the martinis throttled the caffeine into submission, Pixie considered her next move. Her search for a plausible reason to interrupt a dinner between a doctor and law clerk came to a screeching halt when the private investigator from Alexandria, Virginia, stepped into the dining room.

Pixie shielded her face from the dining room with one hand and turned her gaze towards the mirror that ran behind the bar. In the reflection of the mirror, she watched Dan arrive at the table, pull out a chair, and sit between Grace and Dr. Joffee.

"What the hell?" Pixie said aloud.

The bartender diverted his attention away from muddling bitters. "Everything all right, Pixie?"

"Fine. Would you mind keeping an eye on my drink and seat for a second? I'll be back."

⚬

Before anyone at the table could protest, Pixie sat down in the table's fourth chair. "Pardon the interruption. I hope no one minds," Pixie said.

"What the hell are you doing here?" Grace asked, her face turning crimson.

Dan's gaze bounced from Pixie to Grace and then back to Grace. "How do the two of you know each other?" he asked.

"We met today," Pixie replied. "Members of the press interviewed Judge Cardin's clerks this morning. Background and legal stuff."

"I could use a little help here," Dr. Joffee said, unaware of the dynamics he was squarely in the middle of.

Dan spoke. "Doc, this is Pixie. As in Pixie on Politics. The reporter I mentioned in our previous conversation."

"You can call me Patricia if you'd like," Pixie said.

Dr. Joffee nodded. "And what exactly can we do for you? I didn't realize this was a dinner for four when I made the reservation."

"I want in on the story."

"What story is that?" Dan asked.

"The story that has brought together a doctor, a lawyer-investigator, and a clerk for a Supreme Court nominee. Oh, and a serial killer from South Carolina."

The server stopped at the table. "Shall I place another setting?"

"She won't be staying," Dan replied quickly. "I'm curious as to what you think you've uncovered here?" Dan asked, eyes on Pixie.

"I'm not sure. Not exactly. I think our most recent Supreme Court nominee has a darker side. Historically, problems with Supreme Court nominees and their approval by the Senate tend to deal with behavioral issues. Drinking. Sexual harassment. But I don't think that's the case with Thomas Cardin."

"What makes you say that?" Dan asked.

"I think the judge's clerk here is privy to information regarding nominee Thomas Cardin. Something juicy. And Dan was hired to investigate it."

Grace gestured in the direction of Dan. "I've never met this man before."

Pixie continued. "His name is Dan Lord. The serial killer I met in South Carolina told me that Dan had paid him a visit and that Dan mentioned he'd been hired by a doctor in DC."

The silence at the table provided the only answer Pixie needed.

"I'll take that as confirmation. But there's one small detail I just can't ignore. Why would anyone hire a private investigator to investigate a Supreme Court nominee *before* the nomination was announced?"

Dr. Joffee seemed on the verge of replying, but Dan shook his head and stood.

"Why don't you join me for a drink at the bar?" Dan asked Pixie, flicking his head away from the table.

"I'd love to."

✦

Dan sat in the stool next to Pixie and watched as she picked up her martini and, without spilling a drop, downed half in one swallow. The bartender looked over at the state of Pixie's drink and approached.

"Pixie, do you need another?"

Pixie nodded.

"Anything for you?" the bartender asked Dan.

"No. I'm seated at one of the tables."

The bartender turned to make another martini and Dan faced Pixie.

"We need to come to an agreement," Dan said.

"About what?"

"About the difference between what you know and what you think you know."

"Tell me what I know and what I don't."

"My investigation is not about Thomas Cardin. It's related to a missing girl."

"Mary Spears."

"That's right."

"One of the girls that Odin Rowe killed."

"That's correct."

"And Thomas Cardin was friends with Mary Spears."

"They were."

"Which means that a Supreme Court nominee had a friend who was killed by a serial killer. That's a story the people could be interested in."

"But it has nothing to do with whether or not Thomas Cardin is qualified to be a Supreme Court justice."

"It's an interesting story. And I'm up against a deadline. I need to produce."

"I'll make you an offer. I'll share the Mary Spears and Odin Rowe case files with you and bring you in on my investigation. In exchange you will not write about Odin Rowe or Mary Spears. Not yet. Not until we get more information."

"Why would I agree to that? You're offering to share information with me, but I can't use it for a story."

"You'll agree to it because there is a bigger story behind the story. For now, write about Thomas Cardin. His background. Education. Family. His legal career. Just leave Odin Rowe and Mary Spears out of the conversation."

"And if I don't agree?"

"Then you won't get copies of the file," Dan said. Pausing, he thought about the little black book that a deceased madam, and his close friend, had kept on her clients. In the wake of his friend's death, the book had eventually found its way into Dan's possession. "And if you can agree to hold off on certain aspects of the story, I'll agree to share information I have access to regarding improprieties by prominent individuals in this city."

"What does that mean?"

"That means I'm privy to the kind of information that can end careers. Names. Financial transactions. Sexual kinks. Drug usage."

"I'm intrigued."

"If you hold off on writing about Odin Rowe and Mary Spears until next week, I'll give you an exclusive glimpse into some of the information I have. It should be enough political fodder to keep you occupied for a year."

"I'm interested."

"Good. Know that if you write about Odin Rowe or Mary Spears before I give the okay, the deal is off."

"That's blackmail."

"That's not blackmail. You may not like it, but it's not blackmail."

"I'm starting to understand why someone tried to blow up your office in Alexandria last year."

"Maybe it's because I'm good at what I do."

"I don't trust you. No offense."

"The feeling is mutual. Do we have a deal?" Dan asked.

"Nothing holds an agreement together like distrust."

CHAPTER 28

DAN LEFT PIXIE at the bar as she received her third martini. He returned to the table and sat down.

"Where's your patient?" Dan asked.

"She is using the facilities."

"How upset is she?"

"She didn't want to speak with Pixie again. She's had press interviews all day today. I think she's burned out."

"I can't blame her. By the way, our reporter friend has agreed to a truce with regard to writing about Mary Spears."

"How did you pull that off?"

Dan shrugged. "Don't get too excited. I think she'll honor the agreement for less than forty-eight hours."

"That's not much of an agreement."

"Nope. But the silver lining is that when she writes her article, it may jar loose a piece of our puzzle."

⊰

When Grace returned from the restroom and reached the table, both Dan and Joffee stood.

"Is she gone?" Grace asked.

"She's gone," Joffee responded, motioning toward Dan. "Grace,

I would like to formally introduce you to an acquaintance of mine, Dan."

Dan extended his hand and Grace shook it. "It's a pleasure to meet you. For transparency's sake, my name's Dan Lord and I'm both an attorney and a private investigator."

"So the reporter was telling the truth?"

"Let's sit down," Dan said.

Grace seemed to consider the offer before nodding. Dan pulled out her chair and the three of them sat.

"Shall I order wine?" Joffee asked.

"Yes," Dan and Grace answered simultaneously without hesitation.

"Which one of you is going to tell me what is really going on?" Grace asked.

"I'll start," Joffee said. "I hired Dan to look into the possibility that Thomas Cardin may have been involved in the disappearance and murder of a high school classmate in 1986. The classmate's name was Mary Spears."

"That's the name the reporter mentioned in our interview this morning," Grace said before facing Joffee. "That interview was the reason I called you."

"After your session with Dr. Fabrizio, I researched Thomas Cardin's background and discovered he had a classmate named Mary who had gone missing. I hired Dan here to dig a little deeper into Thomas Cardin and this missing classmate. In doing so, Dan discovered that a known killer in South Carolina confessed to Mary's murder. Pixie, the reporter, also made this connection."

"You should have asked me before you hired someone to dig around in my boss's past."

"You're right. I should have. And you would have said no."

"Correct. I would have said no."

"Dan's specialty is working with high-risk clients and prominent individuals. Discretion is of paramount importance."

"That would be great. If I had agreed to hire him."

Dan cleared his throat. "If I may interject for a moment. While I certainly understand your feelings, there's an additional aspect I'd like to make very clear. At no point did Dr. Joffee tell me your name, your employer, or any other personal information."

Joffee nodded in agreement.

Dan continued, "In fact, as of this moment, I still don't know your full name. And I don't need to. I'm not looking into your background. I'm squarely focused on finding out what happened to a girl named Mary Spears who disappeared in 1986."

Grace again turned toward Dr. Joffee. "You still should have told me."

"I should have."

Dan spoke, "As I said, Dr. Joffee didn't divulge any information about you. The reporter put some pieces together and she got lucky."

"Her luck could end my legal career."

"It won't. I won't let it."

A bottle of wine arrived at the table, and Dr. Joffee tasted it after the requisite swirl and sniff. As the waiter filled their glasses, Grace faced Dr. Joffee.

"I'm still upset," Grace said.

"I understand. I apologize. But I did what I thought was best for my client without violating any HIPAA regulations."

"You honestly believe you did what was best for your client?"

"I did. Always."

"For what it's worth, I'm also charging him $450 an hour," Dan added. "So it's costing him to look into Mary Spears's disappearance. That's an extraordinary level of commitment to a patient."

Grace frowned. "As extraordinary as it may be, is this behavior acceptable for a psychiatrist? I can't image it is."

"No. It's a first for me," Joffee admitted.

"Why? Why did you go the extra mile for me? Judging by how full your schedule seems to be, I'm sure you have other worthy patients."

Joffee replied, "You remind me of my younger sister. She was much like you. Smart, driven. Always the best in her class. Always the best at whatever she decided to do. Then, one day, she began having panic attacks. Severe anxiety. Debilitating mental hiccups. She sought help. She tried dozens of medications and nearly as many doctors. Nothing worked. Nothing could silence the sloshing whirlpool of thoughts in her mind. So she silenced them herself. The authorities estimated she was going ninety when she crashed into large tree not far from where we grew up."

The silence at the table was deafening.

"I'm sorry for your loss," Grace managed to say.

"And I'm sorry for not including you in my decision to hire Dan."

"I'll try to move past it."

"Hopefully we can."

Dan suddenly felt like an intruder. "I think I'll leave the two of you to enjoy dinner without me," he said.

"Not so fast," Grace replied. "I want to know what kind of information $450 an hour can buy."

With a belly full of steak and his share of two bottles of wine, Dan returned to his office. He opened the court files regarding Mary Spears's disappearance and murder and flipped through the evidence until he found the section of witness statements. He removed Thomas Cardin's sworn testimony from the stack and put the document into his desk drawer. He placed the top back on the box of files, carried it toward the stairs, and turned out the lights.

CHAPTER 29

DAN DROVE HIS white SUV through Middleburg, Virginia, then headed south. A mile down the country road, he turned onto a long gravel driveway between a red mailbox and an old oak tree. Further up the driveway, he approached a house on a hill surrounded by a substantial security fence. Dan pulled up to a gate and pressed the intercom button on the stone column. As he waited, he admired the view of Virginia's horse country. On the neighboring estate, an equestrian rode a horse through a series of steeplechase jumps. The Blue Ridge Mountains waved from the west through the summer haze.

"Hey, Dan," a voice bellowed over the intercom speaker. "Come on in."

Dan looked up and waved at the small CCTV camera. The gate slid open, rolling silently on tracks that ran across the driveway. Dan pressed forward, dust from the driveway trailing behind him. At the parking circle in front of the house, Dan brought the vehicle to a stop, stepped out, and approached the front porch.

The door opened and a hundred pounds of canine charged out. The dog jumped on Dan with its front legs, tail wagging. Dan rubbed the dog's head and scratched its ears.

Tobias, owner of both the residence and the dog, appeared at the doorway of the house. "I'm glad you could make it. I've been wanting to show you a few things." Tobias motioned toward the interior of the house. "Please, come inside."

"I cannot wait to see what you've been working on," Dan said as he followed Tobias across the living room before descending a staircase to the basement. Downstairs, Dan noted the new rack of computer servers running down one of the walls. The temperature in the subterranean lair was noticeably chilled.

"Looks like you have some new equipment."

"Good eye. I have a dozen NVIDIA GPUs. They cost about thirty grand each. I've been working on some AI stuff."

"How are the sports gambling models you developed?"

"They're awesome. On top of that, the models are updating constantly. Getting more accurate every day. Last month, I received a request for a pickleball predictor."

"Pickleball?"

"The fastest growing sport in America."

"I've seen it. Kind of like playing ping pong while standing on the table."

"People are starting to bet on it. I'm working on the variables. Unfortunately, I'm a little short on historical data at the professional level."

Tobias sat down at the long desk in front of a bank of computers. Several bottles of medication and a glass of green-colored juice were on his left. He jiggled the mouse and a multitude of computer monitors came to life. Tobias patted his hand on the chair next to him. "Have a seat. What can I do for you? Tell Uncle Toby how he can help."

"Uncle Toby?"

"You can stick with Tobias if that's better for you."

"I'd like to gain access to a prison's visitor log."

"Virginia, Maryland, or DC?"

"None of the above. South Carolina."

"That seems out of your jurisdiction."

"In more ways than you can count."

"What's the name of the facility?"

"Lee Correctional Institution in Bishopville."

"Have you asked them for access to their visitor log? You're an attorney. They may extend you some professional courtesy."

"At this juncture, I'm trying to remain professionally anonymous. Besides, I already received a copy of their visitor log entries."

"So what I am doing?"

"I want to know if they were lying."

"Gaining access to most systems has never been a problem. Not a real problem, anyway. It's just a matter of time and computing power."

"Which means money."

"Yeah. Money. Now, let's see what we can find. Thinking aloud, the first step is to identify employees who work at the Lee Correctional Institution. The South Carolina Department of Corrections has to maintain some sort of list. It's a public entity. It may not include all employees, but it should be enough to crack the system open for us to slip in."

Dan watched as Tobias's first query produced a list of names, work numbers, and work email addresses. The data populated the middle screen in neat rows.

"Boom, there's our list of potential access points," Tobias said.

Dan perused the names and titles. "It looks like a company directory. We have multiple employees from the prison's medical department, from operations, even finance."

"A prison is very much like a subsidiary of a large company, in this case the South Carolina Department of Corrections."

"So what do you do with the names, titles, numbers, and email addresses?"

"As that cook on TV likes to say, 'were going to kick it up a notch.' It'll take the name of each employee, and it will interface the name with a series of public databases. The query should provide each employee's birth date, spouse's name, anniversary, past and present addresses, their children's names, the names of any registered pets, their Facebook friends, their favorite teams, etc."

"How long will this take?"

Tobias worked the keyboard and hit enter. "One, two, three… boom, it's finished."

The screen listed the names of all the contacts from the Lee Correctional Facility and their subsequent personal information.

"Impressive."

"Based on what we see here, the work email addresses for employees are created using the employee's last name and the first initial of their first name. We'll try to access the system using that as potential User IDs. The password will be a separate query."

"Understood."

"You know, on the dark web there are thousands of compromised organization user names and passwords, with hundreds of millions of credentials. On top of that, there's a list of the most common password elements compiled from that stolen data."

"Sounds promising."

"Within that data, nearly 20 percent of people use their birthday, their kids' birthdays, or their anniversary as part of their password."

"Any other common ones?"

"Date and name combinations, addresses, curse words. 'ABCD1234' is in the top ten. 'Password!123' is another contender."

"Why am I not surprised by any of those?"

"You can't fix stupid by making a password more difficult. Most people will still use some variation of numbers and letters that is meaningful to them."

Tobias took a sip of the green liquid in the glass on the desk and then continued. "Let's take a peek into Lee Correctional Institution's internal system."

Dan watched as Tobias accessed the system and perused the back-end directory until he located the visitor log files. A different screen view appeared on the monitor to the right.

"As I thought, the User ID is the employee email, which, as I just mentioned, is based on an employee's last name and first initial. Now here comes the first dash of magic sauce. I'm going to run User ID and password combinations using AI."

"I thought AI wasn't needed."

"Technically it is not. But AI makes things so much faster."

"I'm listening."

"Historically, the search for a data point or information required a query or multiple queries. Think about your average Google search. You know what you're looking for, and you query to find it. With AI, the query becomes much more powerful. You provide as much data as you can, run your AI algorithms, and AI will produce results that you didn't even know you were looking for."

"Interesting."

"And dangerous."

"Why's that?"

"Hallucinations. Fabrications by AI. On occasion, AI has a tendency to make things up. So an AI algorithm may provide you with ten data points, connected in ways that you hadn't imagined. But with those ten data points, you may have one hallucination."

"Sounds like having a genius friend who occasionally lies to you."

"That's exactly what it's like. And humans need to figure out how to identify the lie from the truth."

"What could possibly go wrong?"

"You're reading my mind," Tobias replied. "But that's a longer conversation. For years, people have claimed AI was going to be the future of computing. Some say the future of mankind. And now the future is here. At least in my basement it is."

Tobias cracked his knuckles for show, tickled the keyboard, and pressed enter.

"One, two, three, four, five... boom."

"You're in?" Dan asked.

"Affirmative. Thanks to Operations Manager Adam Korf. Adam

used a combination of his anniversary, his dog's name, and the year he graduated from college."

"How many User ID and password combinations did your AI program just try?"

"Let's see… Two hundred and twenty-two thousand combinations. It sounds like a lot, but compared to the billions of combinations that the brute force method would have had to work through, two hundred thousand is nothing."

"Watching you do that makes me think it's time for everyone to get off the internet."

"Way too late. The cat is out of the bag. Or rather, personal data is out of the bag. What exactly are you looking for in the visitor log? It looks like we have fields for dates, inmate names, visitor names, and visitor contact information."

"Can you provide a list of all visitors for a prisoner named Odin Rowe."

"What timeframe?"

"The last two weeks."

Tobias typed on the keys and the printer behind them came to life. Tobias flicked his head in the direction of the printer. Dan took the hint, reached over, and grabbed the printout. He put it on the desk and both men read it.

"Not a popular guy," Tobias said. "There are only four names on the list, and you're one of them. The other three are Felicia Rowe, Patricia Flynn, and Nathaniel Cardin."

"Son of a bitch."

"Not the list you expected?"

"The last name wasn't on the original list of visitors I received."

Tobias read the last name aloud. "Nathaniel Cardin. Who is he?"

"I'll give you a hint. The last name is a giveaway."

"Is Nathaniel Cardin related to the Supreme Court nominee, Thomas Cardin?"

"It's his father."

"I feel like I'm going to regret this next question, but who is Odin Rowe?"

"He's a serial killer."

"I've never heard of him."

"It was a long time ago."

"And why are you and Thomas Cardin's father visiting this serial killer the same week the Supreme Court nomination was announced."

"Would you believe me if I said coincidence?"

"No."

"How about I let you know when I know?" Dan stood and began pacing the floor behind Tobias's chair.

"Anything else I can help you with?"

"Not today. But I'll be back. It's time for me to see who else has been lying to me."

CHAPTER 30

BACK IN COLUMBIA, South Carolina, Dan pulled his rental car up to the curb. From the driver's seat, he read the No Trespassing sign in the grass next to the driveway. For those who ignored the first warning, a No Soliciting sign stood by the sidewalk. Dan stepped from the car and the humidity of Columbia hit him like an anvil. He raised his gaze and focused on the front of the home. The brick residence was under siege. The left side of the structure had been swallowed by ivy. Paint flaked off the window trim. Dan tried to picture the house before its decline, before tragedy struck and rendered upkeep an unnecessary distraction from grief. He envisioned kids playing on the front porch and the second-floor windows illuminated with light and life.

Dan ignored the lawn signs and headed for the front door. On the porch, he rang the bell and listened to a muffled two-tone chime fade into the interior of the house. A moment later, a voice on the other side of the door cut through the silence.

"Can't you read?"

"Yes, ma'am, I can."

"Then you must be stupid."

I might be, Dan thought. "My name is Dan Lord. I'm an attorney. I'm sorry to disturb you. I was hoping to have a conversation with Angela Spears."

"You're an attorney? Whose? What do you want?"

"If you're Angela Spears, I would like to talk to you about your daughter, Mary."

The long pause that followed was interrupted by the rattling of locks. The door pulled open several inches and a wrinkled face peeked out.

"Do you have ID?" she asked.

"I do," Dan replied. He reached into his wallet and pulled out his driver's license and bar identification card.

The woman took the identification and compared it to the face of the man on her porch.

"I guess that's you," she responded, shutting the door and releasing the chain lock. She pulled the door open halfway and the cool breeze of the air conditioning wafted over Dan's face. "Your ID says you're from Virginia. What do you have to do with my Mary?"

"Can you confirm that you're Angela Spears?"

"I am." Beyond her wrinkled skin, her bright blue eyes were framed by long gray hair that hung past her shoulders.

"Well, Mrs. Spears, frankly, I'm looking into the possibility that your daughter wasn't killed by the man who was convicted of the crime."

Angela turned her head. "And just where in the hell would you get that idea?"

"It's a bit of a long story. I was hired by a doctor who has a patient who claims to have information regarding your daughter's death. This patient believes that your daughter was murdered by someone other than Odin Rowe."

"What are we talking about here? Some kind of eyewitness?"

"Something like that."

"Who is it?"

"I don't have a name. And I couldn't tell you, even if I knew. Attorney-client privilege."

"Hogwash. You don't drop a load like that on someone without an explanation. Maybe I should call the police. Get Roy on the phone."

"Detective Huff?"

"That's right. Roy Huff. Detective on the case. Retired."

"I've met with Detective Huff. I assure you there's nothing untoward about my visit. I'm not looking for money. I don't want to cause trouble. I'm searching for the truth."

"You ever seen a unicorn, Mr. Lord?"

"Not sober."

"Well, they're about as rare as the truth."

Dan could feel the opportunity for information slipping away. "I just want to talk to you about your daughter for a few minutes. You don't have to invite me in. We can grab a seat here on the porch."

"I don't know."

"Just give me a couple minutes of your time. If you don't like what I say, you can tell me to leave."

Angela's head bobbed slowly. "Grab a seat."

Angela stepped out of the house and sat down on a metal chair with a rusty creak. Dan sat in an identical chair to her left.

Without prodding, Angela spoke, "You know, people are funny. I'll have conversations with folks I've known forever and they won't utter Mary's name. As if it would have some ill effect on me. But the truth is, I like hearing her name. It reminds me of her. That she was alive and lovely. Maybe people think I don't want to be reminded, but I do."

"Some people are uncomfortable talking about death or the dead."

"How about you?"

"I lost my father, brother, sister-in-law, and their son—my nephew—not long ago."

"And your mother?"

"She's still alive. But we're estranged."

"She's your mother, so you better figure out how to fix it before it's too late."

It's already too late, Dan thought, recalling the last time he had seen his mother and the firearm that had been between them. "Yes, ma'am."

"What do you want to know about Mary?"

"I'm not really looking for anything in particular. I think I'll know it when I see it."

Angela stared out across her yard.

"Was there anything about Mary's disappearance that didn't ring true to you? I've read the police reports and legal documents, and they all indicate Odin Rowe met Mary on her way home from Lake Katherine. After they crossed paths, Odin Rowe offered her some grass and she accepted. One thing led to another, and she was killed."

Angela wiped a tear from her face. "That sums it up."

"Anything about that story bother you?"

"Everything about that story bothers me. No one wants to picture their daughter's last moments of life. I'd prefer to remember her from other occasions. Happier times."

"I understand that."

"Mary was a free spirit. She had a strong individual streak. Had it ever since she was little. She always did her own thing. But she was a good kid. Was never in any trouble."

"Did she smoke pot?"

"I never heard that she did, and we wouldn't have condoned it. But let's face it, kids know how to get drugs. If a kid wants them bad enough, no parent in the world is going to prevent their child from dabbling."

"What about talking to strangers?"

"This is the South. Kids are raised to speak when spoken to. And Columbia was a much smaller city way back then. I imagine Mary would have stopped and talked to someone on her way home. And Mary knew who Odin Rowe was. He didn't live a half-mile away. Kids know kids. At least they used to when kids played outside. Back in the day."

"Had you ever heard your daughter speak about Odin Rowe before?"

"Not that I recall."

"What about Thomas Cardin?" Dan asked. "Did Mary ever talk about Thomas Cardin?"

"That's an interesting question given the recent news."

"I'm aware he was nominated as a Supreme Court justice."

Angela pushed back into her squeaky chair and sighed. "Mary and Thomas knew each other."

Dan pressed, "Did they date?"

"Not exactly. Mary liked Thomas and Thomas liked her. I got the impression that Thomas's parents didn't think Mary was up to Cardin standards. Thomas's parents were busy setting him up with debutants. Young ladies from wealthy families with memberships at the country club."

"Did Mary ever refer to Thomas Cardin as her boyfriend?"

"Not even in her diary."

"Mary kept a diary?"

"She did."

"Did the police ever look through it?"

"Of course. When Mary was missing that summer, the police were digging through everything. Her clothes, her books, her photographs. They also took some items for the dogs to pick up her scent."

"Did they find anything surprising?"

"Nothing that helped them."

"Do you still have her diary?"

"Of course. I'll have it until the day I die. It's one of my most cherished possessions."

"I'm sure it is."

"You know, years ago we had a fire in the kitchen, and my first reaction was to run upstairs to get the diary and Mary's photo albums. I was still married at the time, and I ran past my husband in the living room. I was running to go up the stairs, and he was running toward the kitchen with a fire extinguisher. Later, we had a good laugh about it. A rare laugh after Mary was gone. Now, I keep her diary in a fireproof safe box in the bedroom. Just in case."

"Would you mind if I took a look at her diary?"

"You think you're going to find something the police didn't?"

"You never know. Would you mind?"

"You can read it if you want."

"Can I copy it?"

Angela paused, seeming to consider the request.

"Give me a few minutes to put on some makeup. There's a copy center in Five Points, down the street. We can make copies there."

"That will work."

⁓

Dan sat in a wobbly chair next to a bank of photocopiers. He watched as Angela Spears copied each page of her deceased daughter's diary. She handled the book with a gentleness reserved for rare manuscripts and fine works of art. It took nearly two hours for the diary to be copied in its entirety. When Angela Spears was finished, she handed Dan a thick stack of paper.

Angela caressed the outside of the diary and clutched it to her chest.

"Thank you," Dan said. "I know you had some trepidation."

"I still do," Angela replied, walking toward the door and the car parked outside.

Five minutes later, back in front of the Spears house, Dan walked around the front of the car. He opened the passenger door and offered a hand to Angela, who kept both arms wrapped around her daughter's diary as she got out of the vehicle.

"I can make it back to the front door by myself," she said.

"Very well," Dan said. "Thank you again for your help. And I know it was a long time ago, but I am sorry for your loss."

"Don't be sorry, Mr. Lord. Instead, do me a favor."

"What did you have in mind?"

"If you find something in that diary that leads you to my daughter, bring her home. Give me a body to bury. I always wanted to have a proper burial. Find her body so she can finally rest in peace."

Dan felt as if he had been punched in the stomach. "I'll do everything I can. I promise."

CHAPTER 31

WITH THE EVENING temperature and humidity running neck-and-neck near ninety, Dan shortened his standard jog from seven miles to five. At the intersection of Lady and Lincoln, Dan turned the corner and slowed his pace to a walk. With his hotel's sign in the distance, thunder rumbled overhead. Dan glanced westward at the dark clouds as the streetlight overhead exploded with a pop, sending a shower of glass shards down around him.

Dan froze and looked up at the light pole. His eyes scanned the street. Car traffic was light, a smattering of vehicles driving the speed limit between the lines. Down the street, a public bus pulled to the curb, unloading passengers.

Curious, Dan thought as he stole a second glance at the broken light and continued walking back to his hotel. Seconds later, as he passed under the next streetlight, another pop was followed by another shower of glass.

Again, Dan stopped, his eyes moving from ground level to the multistoried buildings around him. After a momentary pause and scan of the street, Dan headed down the sidewalk. As he approached the next streetlight, he slowed his gait. Concentrating on the sounds of his environment, he heard a distinct *pffft* as the third streetlight exploded. A small piece of brick tumbled from the wall of the nearest building onto the sidewalk.

Again, Dan froze, his eyes settling on the parking garage on the opposite side of the street. As the public bus he had previously spotted approached, Dan dashed across four lanes of asphalt. Seconds later, he pulled open the exit door to the parking garage and stepped into a stairwell. As the thick door shut, Dan closed his eyes and listened. Ascending stairs two at a time, Dan reached the top floor of the garage. From the stairwell, he looked through the small window in the door, and then he entered the empty floor.

Dan approached the edge of the short wall that ran around the perimeter of the garage. From his new vantage point, he stared down at his previous location on the sidewalk. As the public bus pulled away, he could clearly see the dark stretches of sidewalk caused by the broken lights on the far side of the street. Dan turned his attention to the ground, scanning the concrete floor for evidence of a shooter. As he scoured the area for clues, a door on the far end of the garage slammed shut.

Adrenaline pumping, Dan sprinted across the empty floor, past the exit ramp down, and into another staircase. Descending four steps at a time, Dan arrived on the first floor and exited the stairwell leading into the garage. Again, he scanned his surroundings.

The sound of a car door slamming and an engine revving on the street outside the garage spurred him to move. He threw his legs over the short wall of the garage and landed on a strip of grass between the building and sidewalk. Staring down the street, Dan saw the outline of a white pickup truck turn the corner a hundred yards away.

Son of a bitch.

As Dan stood on the sidewalk, the first drops of rain began to fall. He contemplated calling 911, reconsidered, and headed back to his hotel.

∾

Dan dried his hair with a hotel towel and picked up his phone to make a call.

Roy Huff answered in a groggy voice.

"Hey, Roy. It's Dan. I'm back in town and someone just took a shot at me. Three shots, actually."

"Are you okay?"

"I'm fine."

"Did you call the police."

"I didn't."

"Why not?"

"They weren't trying to hit me."

"How did you come to that conclusion?"

"Whoever it was shot three consecutive streetlights as I walked underneath them. Anyone who's that good of a shot didn't miss me by accident."

"Where did this happen?"

"On Lady Street. Five minutes ago. Not far from my hotel. The shooter was in the parking garage."

"The parking garage on Lady is closed for resurfacing. The city uses the summer lull in students to do a lot of repairs and general maintenance."

"The garage was empty. Except for me and the shooter."

"Did you get a good look at them?"

"No, but they may have been driving a white pickup. And they were definitely using a suppressor."

"That's unusual."

"Unless you're a sniper."

"That may be true. Do you want me to make a few calls?"

"Can you ask around and see if there are any security cameras that may have caught the license plate on a white pickup truck?"

"I'll put in the request."

"Thanks."

"Keep your head down."

CHAPTER 32

THE MORNING SUN shone over Dan's shoulder as he read pages from Mary Spears's diary. His suitcase was packed, its wheels on the carpet near the door. Check-in was complete and his boarding pass ready. A pulsing vibration on his leg sent Dan digging for his phone in the cushions of the chair.

"Dan here."

Roy Huff's gravelly voice boomed, "Where are you?"

"Still in Columbia."

"Did you hear the news?"

"No. Good or bad?"

"Nathaniel Cardin Senior was found dead."

"What happened?"

"Sounds like a heart attack. They found him outside in his back yard, sitting in a chair near his firepit. From what I heard, there's nothing to indicate foul play."

"Was this at the house on Lake Katherine?"

"No. He was down in the Lowcountry. The Cardin family has a hunting retreat named Pine Hall near a town called Smoaks."

"Who has jurisdiction in Smoaks?"

"Colleton County Sheriff's office."

"Who found the body?"

"A housekeeper."

"Do you know any of the local law enforcement down that way?"

"Not anymore. Everyone I knew is long gone, one way or another. Captain Collins has connections."

"Think we can get a look?"

"At what?"

"The house."

"Probably. But I'm not sure why."

"Call it curiosity."

"You know how that worked out for the cat."

"I'll take my chances."

"Let me get back to you. Sit tight."

Dan stared out the window of his hotel room, eyeing the pool deck below. His phone vibrated again and he answered it.

"We're on," Detective Huff said. "You want to ride together?"

"Sure. I'm going to run to the ATM around the corner. I should be ready in fifteen minutes."

※

Dan sat on the bench in the smoking area where days earlier the homeless man had warned him to get out of town. Cigarette butts littered the gravel between the bench and the parking lot. Dan stood as Huff's car came to a halt in front of the hotel.

"Thanks for picking me up and for getting approval," Dan said, climbing in the passenger seat.

"Thank Captain Collins the next time you see him. He cleared the way for us. We can visit Pine Hall, the Lowcountry estate, and meet with the coroner's office. From here, it's about ninety minutes down the road."

As the car merged onto Route 20 heading south, Huff's tone seemed to change.

"I have a bone to pick with you."

"What's that?" Dan asked.

"I heard you went and visited Mary Spears's mother."

"Where did you hear that?"

"Don't you mind where I heard. The question on the table is whether or not it's true."

"It is."

"I told you not to bother Mary Spears's mother. She's been through enough."

"I treated her with kid gloves. I actually think she may have enjoyed the company."

"Did you find out anything?"

"I don't know yet. When you were investigating Mary's disappearance, did you ever read through her diary?"

"I did."

"Why wasn't it mentioned in the case files?"

"It was determined nothing in the diary was pertinent to her disappearance or useful to the subsequent murder investigation."

"Nothing?"

"That's right. And the police chief at the time didn't want a missing girl's diary to become some sensationalized piece in *The Enquirer*."

Dan mulled over the explanation and let it slide. "While we are on the subject of complaining, I have a bone to pick with you as well."

"What's that?"

"Where did you get the list of Odin Rowe's visitors while he was in prison?"

"From Lee Correctional."

"Well, it wasn't a complete list."

"What do you mean?"

"The list was incomplete. Edited. The question I have is whether it was manipulated before it reached you or after it reached you."

"That's quite an accusation."

"It's fact. I gained access to the Lee Correctional visitor log via other means."

"How did you do that?"

"Don't you mind how I did it."

"That's illegal."

"Only if it can be proven. Want to take a guess who also visited Odin Rowe last week?"

"Who?"

"I'll give you a hint. He was found dead this morning in his backyard."

"You're kidding."

"I'm not."

"I don't know what to tell you."

"Tell me you had nothing to do with it."

"I had nothing to do with it."

"I'm not sure I can believe you."

"Here's a thought. Don't burn bridges while you're still on them," Huff said.

"What can you tell me about Nathaniel Cardin Senior?"

"He's been a prominent figure in these parts for over half a century. His family name has been a pillar of the legal community for twice as long."

"What do you know about the man, not the family?"

"Cardin Senior was circuit solicitor for twenty years. Then he opened a private law practice with one of his brothers, and named the firm Cardin & Cardin."

"Creative."

"Wealthy. Powerful. Well-connected."

"How old was he?"

"Early eighties would be my guess. Rumor has it he'd started slipping, mentally. No one is going to confirm it, but that's the rumor. Last I heard, he still had an office at the law firm, but I think the days of actively practicing law were behind him."

"After this morning's discovery, his days of practicing anything are behind him."

❧

The state road rounded a curve and Huff applied the brakes. A Colleton Sheriff's cruiser was parked on the shoulder. A news van was on the opposite side of the road. Huff turned onto the driveway, and the vehicle passed under a wooden archway with the name Pine Hall engraved on it. As evidence of an appropriately named estate, the shade from thick southern pines cast the car into shade. A quarter mile down the driveway, the Cardin's Lowcountry house came into view. A second police car was parked near the steps to a sweeping front porch replete with a row of rocking chairs.

Dan and Huff climbed from their vehicle and a deputy sheriff stepped forward. Introductions and handshakes ensued.

"What do we have?" Detective Huff asked.

"One deceased. Nathaniel Cardin Senior. Housekeeper found him in a chair out back. Time of death was estimated to be between 10:30 and midnight. Cause of death is undetermined, but no foul play is suspected. Probably a heart attack."

Dan measured the deputy sheriff's appearance and estimated the young man could start shaving soon. "Any security system?" Dan asked.

"Alarms on the front door, back door, and garage door. A passcode is needed."

"Any cameras?"

"The front door has a camera. It provides a view of the driveway coming to the house. We examined the video. It shows Mr. Cardin Sr. arriving yesterday evening."

"Was he alone?"

"He was. Apparently that is unusual."

"Why is that unusual?"

"Mr. Cardin didn't drive much these days."

"What kind of car is it?"

"A late model Mercedes-Benz."

"Newer Mercedez-Benzes have Drive Pilot. Hands-free and eyes-free driving assistance," Dan explained.

"Either way, from what we've learned, it was unusual for him to head down here alone," the officer said. "After he arrived, he never left. It all seems pretty straightforward. Evidence shows that he cooked some food on the grill out back, had some drinks, and smoked a cigar."

"What time did the housekeeper arrive?" Huff asked.

"Around 8:30 this morning. This was also verified on the front porch camera. The housekeeper entered through the garage, which she claimed was the norm."

"Did the housekeeper always come on the same day of the week?"

"Yes."

"Do you mind if we look around?" Huff asked.

"No, sir. You're cleared. The only stipulation is that you have to wear gloves. I have some in the trunk."

Dan dropped his voice to a whisper as the deputy walked to the back of his car. "Is it normal for a prominent, wealthy family to have minimal security? A camera and door alarms aren't much."

"Nathaniel Cardin doesn't need a security system. Everyone in these parts knows him or his family. They know where he lives. People look out for the neighbors down here. Not to mention everyone within twenty miles owns at least one gun. Including most school kids."

The deputy returned with gloves. Moments later, Huff and Dan walked through the front door of the house. A large foyer led to an even larger living room. Several sofas faced toward the back of the house, a scenic view of the Lowcountry framed by a stone fireplace on one side and a bar on the other. The kitchen was off to the right, separated from the living room by an oversized island with a line of stools.

Dan stopped and admired the room and the view. "Nice place."

"It is."

"And recently cleaned," Dan said, pointing at the vacuum tracks in the carpet at their feet. Dan took out his phone and took photographs of the carpet.

"The housekeeper did come."

Dan and Huff explored the first floor. Dan paused every few seconds to take more photos. A wine cellar off the kitchen held an impressive supply of European reds. Next to the wine cellar was a humidor the size of a broom closet. Dan perused the cigar options and determined the selection to be that of an aficionado. Moving to the kitchen, the two men rifled through the cabinets, opening doors, and examining their contents. Dan opened the cabinet beneath the sink and pulled out the trashcan.

"New bag. Nothing in it."

"The housekeeper was doing her job."

Dan opened a door that led to a mud room. He traversed the room, passed the washer and dryer, and opened the door to the garage. A Mercedes was parked in the spot on the right, next to an empty bay. Dan spotted a large trash can on the opposite side of the car. He stepped around the vehicle, flipped open the trash can lid, and removed the lone bag from the can.

"Want to take a peek?" Dan asked.

"By all means."

Dan untied the top of the trash bag and spread the contents across the garage floor of the empty bay. "Not much in here. We have corn husks, green beans, and some butcher paper with blood on it." Dan held the butcher's paper up and examined the small sticker. "Filet mignon. Good choice. From a place called The Purple Cow."

"It's a boutique butcher in Columbia," Huff said as he leaned over and flicked through a wad of napkins.

"Not much else here," Dan admitted.

"Makes sense," Huff replied. "If he came down yesterday. He didn't have time to produce much trash."

Dan stood silently in the garage, the gears in his mind racing through possibilities.

"Let's make our way outside to where the body was found," Huff said.

Dan followed Huff, stopping at the bar on their way to the back door. Dan measured the alcohol offerings and took more photos. "He has quite the lineup of booze."

"The Cardin family enjoyed the finer things in life. Particularly Nathan Cardin Senior."

Dan admired several photographs on the wall next to the bar. He pointed to a framed photo on the right, four men standing over the carcass of a lion and a Cape buffalo. "Do you recognize any of the men in that photo?"

Huff squinted. "The man on the right is Nathaniel Cardin Senior. Before the car accident, obviously. That photo is probably from the 1990s."

Dan snapped a picture of the framed photo. He then took a final photograph of the Cardin liquor collection and followed Huff toward the large glass doors leading to the rear deck. From the deck railing, Dan scanned the yard in front of him. A large firepit was surrounded by multicolored Adirondak chairs, intermingled with matching side tables. Yellow police tape encircled the firepit and one of the chairs.

"I guess that's where he was found," Dan said.

"Let's have a look-see," Huff replied. The two men descended the stairs from the deck and arrived at the yellow police tape. They walked the perimeter of the tape, eyeing the final location of Nathaniel Cardin Senior. One of the side tables stood next to the chair where the deceased had presumably been found.

"What do you see there?" Dan Lord asked, pointing at the table.

"A couple of rings from a couple of glasses. One circular. One square."

"Just making sure we're seeing the same thing," Dan replied. Huff stood by as Dan finished taking pictures of the table. He followed Dan as he circled the firepit twice, eyes locked on the extinguished ash.

"Anything else you want to point out?" Huff asked.

"Not at this time."

"You'll forgive me if it's my turn to say I don't believe you."

"Call it even for the visitor log."

"I gave you the names I received from the prison."

Dan shrugged his shoulders and took close-up photographs of the extinguished ash in the firepit. "Let's go see the coroner."

❦

The Colleton County Coroner's office was in a flat brick building that could easily be mistaken for military housing. Similar buildings dotted the county property. Sandy soil meandered around the buildings and the surrounding pines. Heat shimmered off the metal roofs.

A man behind a desk stood and Huff introduced himself. "My name is Roy Huff, retired detective. We're here to see the coroner."

"Dr. Gibson is expecting you. I'll buzz him and let him know you're on your way back. Through the doors, head right."

Dan and Huff pushed through two double doors and followed the signs in the direction of the autopsy room. Entering, they were met by a fit black man in medical scrubs.

"Dr. Gibson, I presume," Huff said.

"Yes, sir."

"I'm Detective Roy Huff, retired."

"And I'm Dan Lord, attorney at law," Dan added.

"I was told you would be stopping by. What can I do for you gentlemen?" Dr. Gibson asked.

"We wanted to discuss Nathaniel Cardin Senior."

"I figured as much."

"What can you tell us about the circumstances surrounding his death?" Huff asked.

"Nathaniel Cardin died of natural causes. His body was found by his housekeeper in the backyard of his property. Body temp and rigor mortis put the time of death at roughly eleven o'clock last evening. No signs of trauma were reported."

"Are you planning to perform an autopsy?" Dan asked.

"Not at this time and not unless something changes."

"May I ask why not?"

"There's nothing suspicious about the death. Nathaniel Cardin was eighty years old. He had health issues and was on medication."

"Such as?" Huff asked.

"High blood pressure. Type 2 diabetes. High cholesterol. Arrhythmia. Ongoing pain management from a car accident that broke a dozen bones. He was on a long list of prescription meds."

"Is that enough to forgo an autopsy?" Dan asked.

"I confirmed his health issues and prescribed medications with his personal physician. Law enforcement had no indication of foul play. An autopsy will not be required. And the family didn't request one."

"But the decision whether to perform an autopsy is ultimately yours, correct?" Dan asked.

"It is. And in my professional opinion, an autopsy is not required on a senior citizen with multiple health issues confirmed by their physician. Nothing at the scene of death was suspicious."

"Do you have a list of the inventory taken from the scene?" Dan asked.

"I do."

"Can I get a look at it? I'm curious what Mr. Cardin was drinking before he died. We just toured the backyard and noticed some marks on the table next to the deceased's chair."

Dr. Gibson opened a folder on the counter and motioned for Dan to have a look. "This is the inventory list and photographs. Based on the evidence found on site, Nathaniel Cardin had consumed half a bottle of wine and a couple glasses of scotch. The names of the wine and scotch are written down under the photograph of each. We also have a cigar that was almost completely smoked. The second page is a write-up of his prescription medication, when they were last filled, and the remaining dose count."

Dan pulled out his phone and took pictures of the inventory and the list of medications. After taking a photo, Dan perused the list of medications.

"It says here that Mr. Cardin had a prescription for fentanyl. I assume that's unusual."

"Contrary to popular belief, fentanyl has been prescribed by doctors for pain long before the fentanyl epidemic. Mr. Cardin had long-term, ongoing pain management issues as the result of a serious car accident."

"Did you check the pill count on the fentanyl?"

"I did. He had a prescription for twenty tablets. Three hundred micrograms in each. The prescription indicated he was to use them as needed. Based on his prescription history, he didn't take fentanyl very often. The last time the prescription was filled was over a year ago."

"So he could have ingested fentanyl with alcohol."

"It's possible. But Mr. Cardin has had a fentanyl prescription for over a decade. I assume he understood the appropriate dose and not to mix it with alcohol."

"Did you check Mr. Cardin's BAC?"

"Blood was drawn. His BAC was a little over one. He'd qualify for being under the influence, but he wasn't driving."

"And that's the end of the story?" Dan confirmed.

"Unless something else comes up," Dr. Gibson replied.

"Thank you for your time," Huff said.

The sun beat down as Dan and Huff walked toward the car. Dan froze, patted his pockets, and swore. "I left my phone inside."

"I'll get the car," Huff replied with a wave of his hand.

Dan headed inside and passed the man at the reception desk. "I left my phone."

"You know the way," the man replied.

Dan knocked on the double door and pushed his way into the

room. Dr. Gibson was sliding a body into one of the refrigerated morgue drawers.

"You're back," Dr. Gibson said.

Dan reached into his pocket and removed a folded stack of hundred-dollar bills. Then he placed his business card on top of the cash. Dr. Gibson stared at Dan as he approached and extended his hand.

"What's that for?" Dr. Gibson asked.

"Payment to run a comprehensive toxicology on Nathaniel Cardin Senior."

"I can't do that."

"Sure you can. We both know you're the sole decision maker when it comes to autopsies and toxicology. You wouldn't be breaking any laws. You can order an autopsy and toxicology for any reason you see fit."

"Not for a bribe." Dr. Gibson stared at Dan for a long moment.

"I'll tell you what. I'm going to place my offering and business card on your desk. You can decide what to do. If you don't like the idea of a cash infusion, give it away to charity. If you choose to run the toxicology, give me a call with the results."

"You can take your money with you when you leave," Dr. Gibson said. "And the time for you to leave is now."

Dan put the cash back in his pocket but left his business card on the desk. "I would be remiss if I didn't mention potential extenuating circumstances involving the deceased."

"Such as?"

"I can't say for certain yet."

"Then speculate."

"The reason I'm here in South Carolina is to investigate a teenage girl who went missing in the eighties. She is believed to have been killed. Her body was never found."

"And what does the deceased have to do with it."

"I hope nothing. But he was involved in the case. And his son was a friend of the missing girl."

Dr. Gibson pursed his lips.

"It's just a toxicology report," Dan said, turning away. As he headed toward the exit, he glanced back just long enough to see Dr. Gibson pick up the business card he'd left. A minute later, Dan was outside, climbing into Detective Huff's car.

"Did you find your phone?"

"I did."

"Are you satisfied with our trip to the Lowcountry?" Huff asked.

"The death of a prominent individual—particularly one with an estate the size of the Cardin family's—and the fact that Thomas Cardin is a nominee for the Supreme Court should require that an autopsy is performed."

"You're ignoring an important piece of the equation. The coroner said the family is not requesting an autopsy. If the Cardin family doesn't want an autopsy, then one isn't going to happen. This is South Carolina. The Cardins will get what they want. That's just how it is."

"Tell me, could Nathaniel Cardin Senior have gotten his hands on the police and court files for Odin Rowe without anyone knowing?"

"You mean the missing case files?"

"Yes. Would Nathaniel Cardin Senior have had that ability?"

"Nathaniel Cardin wouldn't have needed to sign for files. Everyone knew him. On top of that, Nathaniel Cardin was the circuit solicitor on the case. It was *his* case. No one would have questioned his authority."

"Do you think it's a coincidence that as soon as Thomas Cardin was nominated for the Supreme Court, the police and court records for Mary Spears and Odin Rowe, including witness statements, disappeared?"

"It's irrelevant what I think. But if you're asking what's possible, my answer is that Nathaniel Cardin could have made just about anything in this state disappear. And no one would have questioned him."

"Is it possible that Nathaniel Cardin Senior took the legal files, paid to have Odin Rowe killed, hired someone to scare me off my investigation, and took his secrets with him to the afterlife?"

"Possible? Yes. The question is a little short on motive, but a man of Nathaniel Cardin's standing could do pretty much anything without being questioned."

"That's a powerful statement."

"Welcome to the South," Huff said.

Dan swiped through the photos he had taken with his phone. "Any luck on identifying the white pickup truck?"

"No dice. Not yet."

"Keep me posted."

The two drove in silence until Huff spoke again, "Dan, what do you think killed Nathan Cardin?" Huff asked.

"Most likely, he died from a heart attack."

"Then you agree with coroner. Case closed."

CHAPTER 33

KELLY'S IRISH TIMES on F Street in Washington, DC, was as much a bar as it was an institution. It's faded yellow facade and red tile roof stood out among the shiny office building that peered down on it. Inside, Kelly's prided itself as a drinking hole for law enforcement and first responders. Donated police shoulder patches plastered the walls. Baseball caps with a variety of three- and four-letter acronyms filled a shelf in the corner. Newspaper clippings and photographs hung over the bar. A pair of doors off an actual police car were used as barriers near the dart board.

Dan walked through the bar and found Detectives Wallace and Fields at a corner table near the back wall.

"Right on time," Wallace said, tapping his watch.

"Sorry I'm late. I just landed at Reagan National."

"We ordered already," Fields said apologetically.

"I'm not hungry."

"They have good Reubens," Wallace said.

"It's an Irish bar. The only thing good is the beer," Dan retorted.

"Suit yourself," Wallace said.

Dan placed a manila folder on the table. "Thanks for coming. I need a sanity check on something. There's really no one else I could ask who would give me a straight answer."

"You need a sanity check from the same people you just insulted for eating food at an Irish bar?" Wallace asked.

"Yep. Those same people."

"What do you need?" Fields said.

"Opinions regarding evidence that's important to a case I'm working. I figured my resident wine drinker and cigar smoker might prove helpful."

Wallace and Fields stole glances of each other's reactions.

Dan continued, "Let's start with wine." Dan unzipped a folder and placed a series of photographs on the table. Each photograph showed a single bottle of wine with its label in clear focus. Motioning toward Fields, Dan posed his first question. "You're the resident wine expert here. Check out these wine bottles. Does anything about this collection strike you?"

Detective Fields picked up each photograph in turn and examined the label on each bottle. After several moments of contemplation, Fields offered her assessment. "It's a nice collection of reds. Amarone, some Bordeaux blends, Barolo, a Faust Cabernet. All good stuff."

Fields picked up one of the photos for a second look. "But this one right here is in another league all together. That is a 2018 Domaine Faiveley Pinot Noir. A single bottle costs in the neighborhood of five grand. It's by far and away the best of the bunch."

"How would you know about a bottle of wine that cost five grand?" Wallace asked.

"Because my stepfather is a wine connoisseur."

"Thank you for your expertise," Dan replied. He placed the photograph of the expensive wine on the top of the stack of reds.

Next, Dan turned to Detective Wallace. "Now, we are going to run through the same exercise, this time with cigars."

"Oh, man, this is going to make me want to smoke one," Wallace said. "I have haven't had a puff in a month."

"You're a grown man; you can smoke if you want."

"Cigar smoke is hard to hide. My wife threatened to kill me the last time she caught a whiff of it on my clothes."

"Something is going to kill you, one way or another. Might as well be something you enjoy." Dan laid the photographs of cigars on the table.

Detective Wallace followed the same assessment process that Detective Fields performed on the red wines.

"It's a solid collection of cigars. We have Arturo Fuente Opus. Padron 1964 Anniversary edition. Montecristo number 2. Partages. Ashton. A couple of Olivas."

"Any of those available at a gas station mini-mart?"

Detective Wallace raised an eyebrow. "You can't find some of those in a cigar shop." Wallace handed the photo of the pick of the litter to Dan. "But that one right there is a Cohiba Behike 52. Cost several hundred dollars per cigar."

"Have you ever smoked one?"

"Not on a detective's salary."

Dan reached into his pocket and removed a Behike 52. "A gift."

Wallace examined the cigar suspiciously. "Where did you get this?"

"I got it and it's yours."

"Why didn't I get a bottle of wine?" Detective Fields asked.

"Because it cost five thousand dollars."

"Wait a second. That means you knew how much it was before you asked for my opinion of the wines?" Fields asked.

"I did. Like I said, I'm here for a sanity check."

"Fields, never forget that Dan here is a lawyer, and lawyers don't ask questions they don't already know the answer to," Detective Wallace said.

Fields frowned. "What are the remaining photos?"

Dan flipped the third stack over. "This is a picture of all the liquor behind an in-home bar. The good stuff." Dan ran through the photographs one by one. "Balvenie 21 Year. Johnnie Walker Blue. Macallan

25. Whistle Pig. Yamazaki 18. Weller 12. Blanton's Gold Edition. All top shelf."

"And then we have this one," Dan said, placing the photograph face up on the table. That is a twenty-three-year-old Pappy Van Winkle. It runs about twice as much as the expensive wine you just saw. A couple of bottles went up for auction last year and sold for twenty grand."

"Jesus," Detective Fields said.

"And I hope now is when you to tell us what this is all about," Wallace said.

Dan put the photograph of the most expensive wine, cigar, and whiskey on the table. "What if I told you someone consumed these three before their death?"

"I'd say I wish we could all be that lucky."

"And what if this someone also had a filet mignon with his dinner?"

"God bless them and this great country. That's what I call going out in style," Wallace said.

Dan glanced around the bar surreptitiously. "Well, the last meal we just identified was that of Nathaniel Cardin Senior."

"The Supreme Court nominee's father? The one in the news?" Fields asked.

"Yes."

"How in the hell did you get involved in that?"

"I can't explain. Not now. But I took those photographs this morning in South Carolina. I think it paints a clear picture."

"It does. Someone had expensive taste."

"More than that. I believe that Nathaniel Cardin Senior took his own life. He was found in his backyard, near a firepit. I think he drank expensive wine and bourbon and smoked his Cuban cigar as he watched a box of legal files burn in the firepit. Then I think he took some fentanyl and said goodnight. Permanently."

"What legal files was he burning?"

"Ones that could prove his son, the recent nominee for the

Supreme Court, may have committed a serious crime when he was in high school."

"You gotta be kidding," Wallace said.

"That's my theory."

"You might want to keep that theory to yourself unless you have proof."

"I've been warned several times already. Someone fired a warning shot at me the other night. Three shots, if you want to know the truth."

"Jesus, Dan," Fields replied in surprise. "I hope you were wearing one of your special shirts," she added in reference to a high-tech garment made from a thin ballistic-resistant material that had once saved Dan's life as Fields had stood nearby.

"They weren't trying to hit me."

"So you say. I'd offer some help, but South Carolina is a little out of our jurisdiction," Wallace added.

"Actually, there may be something you can do for me. If I can work out how to pull it off."

"I don't like the sound of that. All things being equal, leave me out of it," Wallace said.

CHAPTER 34

DAN STOPPED AT the gate, pressed the button, and waited for Tobias to answer. The rolling gate chugged open and Dan drove up to the house. Per usual, Tobias met Dan at the front door. On cue, Peso appeared from behind Tobias and pushed his way outside to greet Dan.

"You promised to come back and, if nothing else, you always keep your promises."

"I'm short on time."

"The bat cave awaits."

Dan began asking questions as the two men traversed the first floor and headed down the stairs.

"I need to go back to the prison's visitor log."

"Easy peasy."

"This time I need you to search the logs for any other instances of Nathaniel Cardin Senior?"

"Thomas Cardin's father again?"

"That's right."

"What timeframe?"

"Let's try for the entire year."

Tobias sat down and, with a flick of his head, pointed to the chair next to him.

"I need to close out a few of the things I'm working on," Tobias said as he typed. After a long minute, Tobias performed his count-down. "One, two, three... boom."

Dan leaned toward the screen as Tobias read the results. "Nathaniel Cardin Senior made three visits to the prison in the last year. All of them last week. The first visit was to Odin Rowe. We already knew this from the first time we accessed the visitor log. The day after Nathanial Cardin paid Odin Rowe a visit, he met with two other prisoners. The first one is Earl Brown. The second is Jose Consuelo."

"What are they in for?"

"Let me see," Tobias replied. "Prisoner one is serving life for rape and first-degree murder. Prisoner two is an arsonist. Serving a three-hundred-year sentence for burning down a daycare center."

"Sounds like Nathaniel Cardin was making the rounds with some of the finer tenants of Lee Correctional."

"A murdering rapist and an arsonist walk into a bar..."

"I don't have a punchline for that. What do you know about prison bank accounts?"

"A lot of states use something called JPay for inmate accounts."

"When I visited Odin Rowe in prison, I deposited $450 dollars into his prison account. Any chance you can access the prison accounts of Earl Brown and Jose Consuelo?"

"Give me a minute to poke around."

"Can I use the restroom?"

"Sure," Tobias answered without taking his eyes off the screen. "Down the hall."

When Dan returned, Tobias smiled like the Cheshire cat. He pointed to the screen on the right. That is Earl Brown. The day after Nathaniel Cardin visited him, Earl Brown received a five-thousand-dollar deposit into his JPay prison account. The deposit was from a prepaid debit card."

"Five thousand dollars on a prepaid card?"

"I've seen ten thousand before."

"What about Jose Consuelo?"

"Identical deposit. Same day. Also five thousand dollars."

"I'll be damned."

"What are you thinking, Dan?"

"I'm thinking that Nathaniel Cardin put five thousand dollars into the accounts of two convicted lifers in exchange for them killing Odin Rowe."

"That might be hard to prove."

"I'm not interested in proving it."

"Then why did you ask?"

"Because it may help me with another case I'm working on. A case that I'm very interested in solving."

"Which is?"

"Finding out what happened to a girl who disappeared nearly forty years ago."

Dan reached into his pocket and removed a new mobile phone. He placed it on the computer bench next to Tobias's mouse. "That's an untraceable burner. I'll only call that number from another burner. If it rings, I'd appreciate it if you'd answer."

Tobias touched the screen on the phone and it illuminated. He reached for a yellow Post-it note, scribbled Dan's initials on it, and stuck the Post-it note to the phone.

"I don't know, Dan. I don't like the sound of this. You're talking about murder for hire and a Supreme Court nominee. That could ruffle the feathers of some powerful people."

"I'm aware."

"Time to be careful. In case you didn't know, things in the South operate a little differently. Everyone knows everyone else. Kevin Bacon made six degrees of separation popular, but in the South, it's probably closer to two degrees."

"You're right about that. I have another query for you. I need you to figure out who's in a photograph that I took of an older photograph. Give me a second and I'll send it to you."

Dan swiped at the screen of his phone, and a moment later the photograph of the four men standing over a lion and Cape buffalo filled one of the monitors.

"Who do we have?" Tobias asked.

"The man on the far right is Nathaniel Cardin Senior. I don't know who the other three are, but I'm betting one of them has a white pickup truck."

"A white pickup truck in South Carolina? That really narrows it down."

"Just let me know when you can identify them."

CHAPTER 35

ELMWOOD WAS THE oldest funeral home in Columbia. Founded in the mid-1800s, a section of the adjacent, eponymously named cemetery was the final resting spot of two hundred Confederate soldiers. The stone building that housed the main hall boasted a sense of Southern regal air.

Shiny black four-doors filled the parking lot, sprinkled with the occasional Tesla.

Dan parked his rental car on the edge of the lot. The sign posted at the entrance to the main hall clearly indicated that the day's viewing was a private event for family and friends only. Dan strolled past the sign in his dark suit and black tie, nodding to other guests and pausing to hold the door open for an elderly couple with a slow shuffle.

Inside, the queue of men with gray hair and dark suits wrapped around the large room. Chairs lined the middle of the floor in rows. On the opposite side of the large room, the line disappeared into an open doorway. Dan moved to the end of the queue and listened to Southern gossip make its way around the room, wafted words spoken too loudly to remain secret.

After several minutes in line, the man to Dan's rear cleared his throat and spoke. "How do you know Nathaniel?"

"I always called him Mr. Cardin. It was a habit I couldn't break, as hard as I tried."

"Work associates?"

"In the past. My name is Dan Lord, attorney."

"Most of this crowd are attorneys, or the wives of one. Some have been the wives of more than one."

Dan smiled. "It happens."

Dan shifted the small talk to the weather and the man ran with the topic until Dan was near the doorway of the viewing vestibule. Peering ahead, Dan caught a glimpse of the open casket. A large photograph of the deceased rested on an easel with the dates of his life printed beneath it. Dan scanned the room and recognized Thomas Cardin to the left of the casket. The Supreme Court nominee shook hands with each visitor who stopped at the casket for a final viewing.

Dan followed the line into the room. Arriving at the casket, he stopped and bowed his head. Seconds later, he was extending his hand to the latest Supreme Court nominee.

"I'm very sorry for your loss."

"Thank you for coming," Thomas Cardin replied.

Dan sunk his fingers into his suit pocket and removed a business card. He quickly reached up and slipped the card into Thomas Cardin's breast pocket. "I apologize for the timing, but you and I need to talk. When the dust settles, give me a call."

Thomas Cardin seemed as if he wanted to pursue Dan out of the room, but the line of well-wishers continued unabated. Dan looked over his shoulder as he exited, and Thomas Cardin seemed to give him a single nod of his head.

In the main hall, Dan swooped by the hors d'oeuvres table and popped a deviled egg into his mouth. As he moved to a tray of pimento cheese sandwiches, a woman in a red dress stumbled into the main hall. A strong stench of booze followed in her wake.

A younger man in a suit attempted to corral the woman, who began slinging and slurring obscenities. The first man to intercept the inebriated guest was quickly joined by a second, each grabbing the woman by an elbow. Escorting the woman toward the exit, Dan heard one of the men call the woman trailer trash. The passing insult sent the woman into a full-fledged fit that was mercifully silenced by the closing of the front doors.

The old man who had been behind Dan in the viewing queue chimed in from the hors d'oeuvres table, "I'm always fascinated by funerals. You never know who's going to show up to say whatever has been on their mind."

✺

Dan loosened his tie as he headed for his rental car on the far end of the lot. He opened the driver's door to let the hot air escape before climbing in, starting the engine, and turning on the A/C.

As his car cooled, he scanned the parking lot until his gaze came to rest on a white pickup truck parked at the end of a row. The front wheels of the vehicle were off the pavement, the cab of the truck successfully position under the shade of a tree.

Dan remained in the car, A/C blasting. From behind the wheel, he observed the guests as they exited the funeral home, assessing each one as a potential shooter. When a bald man with a patch of gray hair on his chin began walking in the direction of the white pickup, Dan exited his vehicle.

Dan approached quietly as the bald man reached the back of the pickup. By the time the man clicked on the truck's fob and reached for the door, Dan was standing next to the bed of the truck.

"Thank you for your service," Dan said, offering a nonconfrontational segue into a conversation.

The bald man with the gray chin patch turned around. Thick wrinkles covered his forehead.

"The sticker on the back window of your cab indicates you were in MACVSOG."

"What do you know about it? You're a little young to be a Vietnam War buff."

"You're right. I'm not. But I knew another member of MACV-SOG. He was a diplomatic security officer when I was a teenager. We were living in South Africa at the time. My mother was working at the US Embassy there. We trained together in a dojo. Once he even showed me his MACVSOG get-out-of-jail-free card."

"Not many people have seen those."

"It was the first and last time for me. But it left an impression." Dan extended his hand. "My name is Dan."

The bald man seemed flustered by Dan's offer of an introduction and a handshake.

Undeterred, Dan continued, "But I'm guessing you already knew my name was Dan. And you knew where I was staying in town. You probably watched my routine."

"Are you finished?"

"No. I believe you paid a homeless guy a hundred bucks to warn me to get out of town. When I didn't heed that warning, you decided to it was time for something more persuasive than words. Only I don't think you decided. I think the dearly departed Nathaniel Cardin Senior was making the calls."

The bald man's eyes seemed to darken as a stern look washed over his face.

Dan forged ahead, "A few nights ago, you were in an empty parking garage and you took three shots at me from the fourth floor. With a suppressor. You missed. But I think you intentionally missed."

The bald man glanced around surreptitiously. "When I shoot, I don't miss."

"Exactly my point. Three shots, three streetlights are proof of that."

"You'll have to excuse me. I have somewhere I need to be."

"Before you go, we have one more thing to discuss. Now that Nathaniel Cardin is deceased and he's taken all of his secrets with him, I assume your interest in me has waned. Unless he paid you ahead of time to finish the job."

"Nathaniel Cardin and I knew each other for sixty years. You don't take money from a friend you've had that long."

"I can respect that. So, unless you say something to the contrary, I'm going to assume we've concluded our business."

"Have a good day, Mr. Lord," the man said, intentionally using Dan's last name. "We have nothing further to discuss."

◈

Thomas Cardin finished his day in the home he had grown up in. Standing in the kitchen, he looked out a back window to the still water of Lake Katherine. In silence, Thomas Cardin removed his suit jacket and tie. He checked the pockets of his suit and emptied the contents onto the kitchen counter. He spread several business cards on the counter and then plucked Dan's card off the cold granite. *Dan Lord. Attorney at Law.* Cardin flipped the card over and read the handwritten note scribbled across the back. *I believe your father paid to have Odin Rowe killed. We should talk.*

Cardin's attention fell to a stack of mail on the counter teetering near a bowl of brown bananas. Without thought, Cardin began flipping through the mail, parsing the pile into junk mail, bills, and correspondence. At the bottom of the pile, he stared down at a plain white envelope with his name written across it in his father's unmistakable penmanship.

Cardin moved the three piles of mail, pulled open two kitchen drawers, and came away with a letter opener. He carefully opened the envelope and slowly unfolded the single-page letter. Cardin grabbed a pair of reading glasses from the counter and began reading.

By the time he finished the letter, his eyes were wet and his hands trembled.

CHAPTER 36

TOBIAS LOOKED OVER at the burner phone on his desk as it began to vibrate. The yellow Post-it note attached to the screen of the phone fluttered, giving the impression that the device had come to life. Tobias pulled off the Post-it note and answered.

"If you called this number, then you know who you're talking to."

"I like that," Dan replied.

"My man, Dan. How did the trip South go?"

"Nothing like a Southern funeral."

"Let me guess. Sweet tea and pimento sandwiches all around."

"Both were served."

"I found a potential name for one of the men in the hunting photograph. The guy on the left is named Franklin Bosh. I found him by running the photo through some facial recognition software. According to a high school reunion Facebook page, Franklin Bosh has been friends with Nathaniel Cardin Senior for sixty years. And he owns a white pickup truck, one of 1,718 such vehicles in that color registered in the greater Columbia area."

"Let me guess the rest of his background. He was in the military and served in a group called the Military Assistance Command, Vietnam. Studies and Observation Group. Colloquially known as MACVSOG," Dan said.

"You met him," Tobias stated.

"I did. I didn't get a name, but I met him."

"Okay. Moving on. Do you need anything else on this Franklin Bosh?"

"Not at this time. But I need your help with something else. A list of names. I need you to run a query on the names I provide and tell me if, or where, those people intersect."

"Nothing we haven't done before. As long as there's an intersection between those people in some form of online records or social media. How wide of a net do you want to cast?"

"As wide as I can."

Tobias hummed. "Fair warning, I won't be able to get to this until later. I'm putting out a fire, dealing with an entourage of Chinese card counters who have descended on Las Vegas. They're working as a group and employing next-level statistics and mathematical models. Some of the casinos on the strip have taken major losses. I'm tracking their movements in real time."

"Squeeze it in when you can."

"Give me what you got." Tobias grabbed a notepad and pen. "Depending on the output, you may need to streamline your query results. But we'll see. Let's run some names through and see if it helps. What names do you want to start with?"

Dan ran through his mental list. "Let's do this in two parts. The first part is the Cardin family. I think this will be the largest dataset. Afterall, the Cardin family is well-known in South Carolina, so I'm assuming there are a lot of potential relationships to discover."

"Probably," Tobias replied, scribbling.

"Thomas Cardin and his father are at the top of the list. Thomas Cardin's mother died years ago. Ditto for his brother. I'm not sure what you'll find on them seeing that they both passed before a lot of data was online."

"Okay, that's group one."

"For group two, I want to look into Mary Spears's family. I've met the mother. The father supposedly disappeared the year after Mary went missing. May or may not be divorced. May or may not be alive. I'm not sure about the rest of the family. That query is pretty open."

"And this is the dead girl from the eighties, correct?"

"Yes."

"Okay. Mary Spears and family. That's group two."

"Give me a holler when you find something."

CHAPTER 37

DAN SAT AT his desk with a bourbon on ice. His phone rang and he checked the incoming number. Against his better judgment and current disposition, he answered the call from the unknown contact.

"Hello."

"Good evening. This is Thomas Cardin. I would like to speak with Dan Lord."

"Speaking," Dan answered, straining to mask his surprise.

"You left your business card with me at my father's viewing. Your handwritten note on the back of your card suggested that we need to have a conversation."

"I did. Thank you for your call. And before we get started, I would like to offer my sincerest condolences for your loss."

"Thank you.

"And I apologize for my method."

"It was unorthodox."

"I realize that. I'm sorry for any perturbation it may have caused."

"Depending on how this phone call goes, I may be willing to put it in the past," Cardin said.

Dan paused. "With all due respect, it may be better to have this conversation face-to-face. Would it be possible to get on your calendar? I realize you are exceptionally busy."

Cardin audibly sighed. "Are you available now?"

"Right now?"

"Yes. I'm back in DC. I'm at work. We can use my office."

"What's the address?"

Dan wrote the address on a piece of paper.

"I can be there in twenty minutes, depending on traffic."

"I'll let security in the lobby know you're coming. They will escort you up."

"Thank you."

⁂

Thomas Cardin was standing at the bank of elevators when the door opened. A uniformed security guard motioned for Dan to step out. Cardin thanked the security guard, who nodded. As the elevator doors closed, Dan Lord and Thomas Cardin shook hands.

"This way, please," Cardin said, walking into a sea of cubes and glass-walled offices. Dan measured Judge Thomas Cardin as he walked ahead. A couple of inches over six foot, thin with broad shoulders and long arms. Salt-and-pepper hair, the majority still pepper. In Cardin's private corner office, Dan sat in a chair across from the judge, who sat at his desk. Shelves of books and stacks of files filled the room.

"I poked around in your background," Thomas Cardin said, beginning to loosen his necktie.

"And?"

"There's not a lot there."

"I prefer it that way."

"In this day and age, avoiding a digital presence takes effort."

"It does."

"Shall we get started?" Cardin asked, placing his untied tie on his desk.

"As you know, Odin Rowe was stabbed in prison last week. He was in the hospital for several days before he succumbed to his injuries."

"That's my understanding."

"This may come as a shock, but I believe there's a chance your father paid to have Odin Rowe murdered."

"That's an accusation I'd be very careful about repeating outside the walls of this office."

Dan noted that the Supreme Court nominee projected a calmness that was palpable despite the seriousness of his accusation. "I can appreciate your position. But what I'm suggesting is not without merit. I have a copy of the visitor log from Lee Correctional Institute. The visitor log indicates that within forty-eight hours of your nomination, your father paid a visit to Odin Rowe."

"I was not aware of that."

"I don't know that anyone else is."

"It doesn't prove your accusation."

"In and of itself, it does not. But the day after your father visited Odin Rowe, he returned to the prison to visit two other inmates. Earl Brown and Jose Consuelo. They were both serving life sentences. One for rape and murder, the other for arson."

"And...?"

"Those two inmates received five thousand dollars each, deposited into their prison accounts. The deposits were made via prepaid debit cards. Virtually untraceable. I believe this was done intentionally."

"By my father?"

"That is my belief."

Thomas Cardin considered Dan's alleged evidence.

"What angle are you working, Mr. Lord?"

"No angle. And to be clear, I'm not interested in pursuing what your father may or may not have done."

"Then what are you after?"

"The truth about Mary Spears."

"Mary Spears? Why?"

"I don't think Odin Rowe killed Mary Spears. I think your father knew this. I think Rowe was offered a deal to avoid the death penalty if he confessed to Mary Spears's murder and disappearance."

Thomas Cardin's face turned stoic. "Odin Rowe was a murderer."

"Of that, I have no doubt. But it's possible he didn't kill Mary."

Thomas Cardin seemed to stew in silence, his eyes drifting toward the window and the city lights outside.

"So what are we discussing? As you're aware, given your presence at the viewing, my father is dead. Odin Rowe, a serial killer, is dead. Mary has been deceased for nearly forty years. Those are all truths. What resolution are you looking for?"

"I want to find Mary Spears. I would like to return her body to her mother for a proper burial."

"And you're threatening a judge to achieve this?"

"I'm not threatening you. For the record, I think you're as qualified as any judge to serve on the highest court. Provided that you didn't kill Mary Spears."

"I didn't kill Mary."

"You were the last one to see her alive."

"How do you know this?"

"I read Odin Rowe's files and the police records related to Mary's disappearance. Your name is in the files, and you are identified as the last one to see Mary alive. The detective in charge of the investigation also indicated that you had been drinking the day she went missing."

"We had all been drinking."

"Underage."

"That's right. We were teenagers. It was summer. Someone got their hands on some beer and a couple bottles of Mad Dog 20/20."

Dan grimaced. "You want to walk me through that day?"

"If you read the court files and police records, then you have the story."

"I'm not sure I have the whole story. What happened when Mary left? Let's start there."

"Okay, Mr. Lord, I'll play. Around sunset on the day in question, Mary said she had to go home. I walked her to the end of the neighborhood and watched her cross Kilbourne Road. From there, it was a straight shot back to her house. I watched her pedal off. By the time I went to bed, I was a staggering fool. I felt sick for two days."

"Mad Dog will do that to you."

Cardin made a face as if he could still taste the cheap alcohol.

"Were your parents home?"

"No, they we're at a silent auction at the country club."

"As a judge, you're aware that, statistically speaking, when someone is the last person to see another person before they disappear, they move to the top of the suspect list."

"I was never treated as a suspect. I was never labeled a person of interest."

"The question is whether you should have been."

Cardin's face turned crimson.

"Your father was a circuit solicitor. You were friends with a missing girl. He shouldn't have been involved in the case. One could easily see the conflict of interest."

"I was never a suspect."

Dan strained to see through Cardin's veneer. "I'm wondering, if under the right circumstances, you would be willing to take a polygraph?"

"Regarding?"

"Mary's death."

"That would be very unusual."

"It may help to prove your story."

"I'm not aware anyone is doubting my story."

"They could. In fact, I know a particularly nosy political reporter who is hot on the case."

Thomas seemed to reconsider Dan's inquiry. "Why would I subject myself to a polygraph?"

"For Mary Spears. A childhood friend of yours. That's the only reason I can give you."

Cardin rubbed his chin and leaned back in his chair. "I'm going to pass. There's not much upside in your proposal, but a whole lot of downside."

CHAPTER 38

DAN STOPPED FOR coffee and croissants from a bakery in Middleburg. Ten minutes later, he headed down Tobias's long driveway and pressed the intercom button at the gate. In front of the house, Peso appeared as regular as clockwork and welcomed him with slobbery licks.

"You're up early," Tobias said, standing in the doorway.

Dan tried to pet the dog without spilling the small tray of coffee and croissants. "I'm usually up early. Something tells me that you're the night owl."

"I'm a night owl and a day owl. I survive on naps. Come on in."

"Can I assume you found something regarding one of the queries?" Dan asked as he followed Tobias across the main floor.

"I found something, but I'm not sure how useful it will be. We can figure it out."

Dan sat in his customary chair next to Tobias, in front of the wall of monitors.

"I ran the two queries you requested. At the top of the list was Thomas Cardin and his father, Nathaniel Cardin Senior. As you are probably aware, they are members of a very successful family. Several circuit solicitors, one state attorney general, members of state legislature, university professors, a dean of the law school. Not to mention the business side of the family."

"I knew they were a big deal."

"They own more companies than Crayons have colors. The most profitable is the law firm of Cardin & Cardin. Nathaniel Cardin Senior began the firm after he retired as a circuit solicitor. Judging by cases with his name on them, he was mostly retired before he died. The second most prominent firm in the Cardin business realm is a construction company. That company was instrumental in developing some of the larger projects in South Carolina over the last fifty years. Two shopping malls. A hospital. A residential planned community near Myrtle Beach. They donated money for the new law school library at the university. Nathaniel Cardin has a younger brother named Jonathan. He seems to be involved in most of the family businesses. He has an MBA on top of a law degree."

"Anything out of the usual?"

"Not for the Cardin family and their businesses. Everything appears to be legitimate. If you want me to dig into any specific aspects of any of the companies, then let me know. I wasn't sure if you had any more parameters to include. A query about everything related to every business dealing of the Cardin family may be too large to be useful."

"Let me mull it over."

"On to the second query: Mary Spears and her family."

"I hope these results are more insightful."

"First and foremost, the Spears family is quite large."

"I didn't get that impression. I only met the mother. She seems like a recluse."

"Nothing wrong with being a recluse."

"I get the feeling she never recovered from the loss of her daughter."

"A recluse with loss issues. Right up my alley."

"Point taken. What did you find?"

"Mary Spears's father is alive and well in Coeur d'Alene, Idaho. Mary Spears's parents divorced three years after her disappearance. Records indicate he never remarried. He makes a living carving woodwork using a chainsaw. The mother only had one sister. She went to

Florida State University. She got married and has been in Tallahassee ever since."

"Where's the large family you referred to?"

"Mary Spears's mother had thirteen uncles and aunts on her mom's side. Another nine on her dad's side. On average, those thirteen uncles and aunts had three kids. Between them, there are over fifty first cousins in state. If you count first cousins once removed, we're over a hundred relatives. If you add second cousins, the number is twice that amount."

"What was Mary Spears's mother's maiden name?"

"Huff. And there are a lot of them."

"Did you say Huff?" Dan asked.

Tobias pointed at the screen.

"Is there a Roy Huff in that family?"

"Give me a sec," Tobias replied. He hit several keys, and a family tree appeared on the screen. "There isn't a Roy Huff. But we do have a LeRoy Huff."

"I've been reading the diary of the missing girl and I'm pretty sure she mentioned an Uncle LeRoy. It has to be the same person."

"I can confirm it." Tobias's fingers danced across the keyboard and two photographs appeared on side-by-side monitors "Indeed, they are one and the same."

"Son of a bitch," Dan cursed.

"You want copies?"

"Yes. Digital and printouts."

"Coming right up," Tobias answered. "You can grab them off the printer and I'll send them to your email."

Dan fetched the photographs and stared at them.

"What are you thinking, Dan?"

"Can you ask your AI model to develop its own queries?"

"That's not exactly how it works. I can expose it to certain datasets and develop algorithms. In the AI world, that step is referred to as training. Once it has data, or access to data such as vital records, census records, property records, court records, state corporation records, education records, tax records, what have you, then AI can get to work."

"Meaning…?"

"AI has the ability to see trends and anomalies that would take humans months, if not years, of work."

"Okay. Train your AI and run a deep dive on Nathan Cardin Senior. See if your AI model can identify anything out of the ordinary."

"What exactly is your definition of out of the ordinary?"

"I'll know it when I see it."

CHAPTER 39

FOR REASONS KNOWN only to the Department of Transportation, the opening stretch of Route 50 from the rolling horse farms of Middleburg toward Washington, DC, was a series of newly constructed traffic circles, which the natives had yet to figure out. As Dan practiced his arc-by-arc driving dexterity, he placed a call.

"This is Huff," the familiar voice answered.

"Retired Detective Roy Huff or Uncle LeRoy Huff?" Dan asked. After a pause, Dan could almost hear Huff stewing on the other end of the line.

"It's Roy to you."

"Now, why do you sound angry? I'm the one who has been lied to."

"I never lied to you."

"You lied by omission. Mary Spears was your cousin's daughter."

"I have more cousins than you can shake a stick at. And if you include all of their kids, there are probably enough to start a school."

"You should have told me."

"For what? For your investigation into an already-solved murder?"

"It's called professionalism."

"My relationship with Mary Spears is irrelevant to the Odin Rowe case."

"The lead investigator was the victim's cousin, and the circuit

223

solicitor was the father of the last person to see the victim alive. That case would be thrown out of any legitimate court by any legitimate judge."

"And yet it wasn't."

"Not in the great state of South Carolina," Dan retorted sarcastically.

"You said it. The simple fact is we had a confession from a man who murdered three young women. No jury in this state was going to overlook those facts. Your investigation into this case was never going to get you the results you wanted."

"What about Mary Spears's mother? Your cousin. Don't you want her to know what happened to her daughter?"

"She knows. Her daughter was killed. It wasn't an unsolved crime. She hasn't been sitting around for thirty-some years waiting for her daughter to walk back through the front door."

"She told me she would like a body to bury."

"We all did. But at some point, everyone has to realize that isn't going to happen."

"Not everyone," Dan said, hanging up as he approached two 18-wheelers converging from opposite directions in the next traffic circle.

Dan came back to his office and changed into running shoes and shorts. Over the next hour, he pounded out seven miles along the Potomac River while contemplating his current case. Near the old Torpedo Factory, Dan's phone buzzed. Covered in sweat, he stopped and answered.

"Hey, Dr. Joffee."

"Good morning. Any chance you've seen the paper?"

"I haven't ingested my daily news yet."

"Your girl Pixie wrote an article on Thomas Cardin."

"My girl?"

"Pixie on Politics."

"She's not my girl. And I'm not surprised she wrote an article. I told you I had a feeling she was going to ignore my request."

"I'm sending the link to the article."

Dan checked his text messages and opened the link that Joffee had just sent. "Give me a second to read through it."

"Supreme Court Nominee Thomas Cardin Confronts Past Tragedy After Convicted Killer's Death"

By Patricia Flynn

Thomas Cardin, the President's nominee for the US Supreme Court, is grappling with the resurfacing of a painful chapter from his past after the recent death of Odin Rowe, a convicted killer responsible for the 1986 disappearance of Cardin's childhood friend, Mary Spears. Rowe, who was convicted in 1986 for the murders of Mary and two other university students in Columbia, South Carolina, died last week after being stabbed in prison.

Mary Spears was just sixteen years old when she vanished without a trace while biking home from the Lake Katherine neighborhood in Columbia. Her disappearance shocked the community and left many—including Cardin, who had been a close friend of Mary—searching for answers. Rowe's arrest and confession brought some measure of closure to the families; however, Mary's body was never recovered.

Rowe's death in prison, after serving nearly four decades for his crimes, has reopened old wounds. His passing, resulting from a stabbing in the state penitentiary, marks the final chapter for the families of his victims, who have long struggled with the weight of unanswered questions.

Police records indicate that Rowe cooperated in revealing the location of Mary Spears's remains. Despite this claim, her body was never found.

Cardin has not spoken publicly about the impact Mary's disappearance had on his worldview or his approach to the law. One can assume that the tragedy of losing a close friend at a young age impacted his belief in the importance of justice—not just in terms of punishment, but in the pursuit of truth, transparency, and victim's rights. It is expected that Thomas Cardin will address the passing of his high school classmate as the Senate nomination hearings proceed.

As a judge on the US Circuit Court of Appeals, Cardin has consistently advocated for stronger victims' rights. His confirmation would give him an opportunity to further his commitment to ensuring that justice systems across the country address victim needs and those of victims' families.

"Well," Dan said, "there's nothing in that article that's incorrect."

"How does it impact your investigation?" Joffee asked.

"It puts me under the gun. It's likely to pique the curiosity of others in the press."

"So no real damage?"

"No. But Pixie doesn't know that," Dan replied, wheels turning.

CHAPTER 40

THE EIGHTEENTH STREET Lounge had moved to Ninth Street after the COVID epidemic. A converted townhouse, the plain gray exterior hid one of the city's gems when it came to music and atmosphere. Located in the Shaw neighborhood, the townhouse boasted four floors of small stages, lounge furniture, narrow bars, and nooks and crannies where people could hide in plain sight. A rooftop patio with city views was the cherry on the sundae.

Dan climbed the narrow stairs between the second and third floors. Turning the corner, Dan stared down a long bar that stretched the length of the room. A quartet of wingback chairs surrounded a low table littered with colorful cocktails. In the next room, Dan spotted Pixie snuggling with a musclebound younger man on a sofa in the corner. Without a word, Dan approached and sat in the vacant seat on Pixie's other side.

"Good evening, Pixie. I've been trying to reach you. You've been avoiding my calls."

"Oh, really?"

"Yes. You've obviously been ignoring me."

"I don't owe you a thing."

"Is this guy bothering you?" asked Pixie's muscle-laden man for the night.

"No, I'm not bothering her. And you don't want to go down that street," Dan answered.

"Which street is that?"

"The one where you end up on your backside."

"By you?" the man asked, glancing down at his formidable biceps that stretched the fabric of his shirt sleeves.

"Yes," Dan replied without blinking. "Why don't you go buy us all a round on me. I need a couple of minutes with Pixie."

Dan pulled out a hundred dollars and placed it on the table. The man took the money and headed toward the bar. "Take your time," Dan added.

"How did you find me?" Pixie asked.

"I asked the bartender from Old Ebbitt Grill where else you liked to drink."

"How many places did you try before this one?"

"Two. Turns out, he had pretty good intel on your drinking habits."

"I guess so."

"Pixie, I thought we had a deal."

"We did. And the deal had ifs. If I did this, you would do that. If I did that, you would do this. I told you I was under pressure to produce at work. So, I took stock of the options and made my decision."

"It may hinder my ability to solve the Mary Spears mystery."

"Your mystery is not my investigation. I'm a political reporter. I'm doing my job, which is protected by the First Amendment."

"True. The constitution affords you the right to freedom of the press and to speak your mind."

"So what's the issue?"

"I'm having negotiation remorse. I knew you couldn't be trusted."

"The feeling is mutual."

"Then you won't be surprised to learn that I didn't give you all of the contents from the Odin Rowe and Mary Spears files."

Pixie remained silent for several seconds, visibly sulking.

"Part of me knew you wouldn't be able to resist writing something once Odin Rowe passed away," Dan added.

"If you're looking for an apology, you're going to be waiting a long time."

"I have one more thing to share with you. I believe the original police and court files that went missing have now been destroyed."

"You said there would be legal ramifications for destroying court records."

"Indeed. But I never said I destroyed them."

"Then who did?"

"Someone named Cardin," Dan answered. "And if you had waited, I would've cut you in on the full story."

CHAPTER 41

THE MEETING ROOM on the top floor boasted large windows and a polished table that nearly ran the length of the room with enough chairs for fourteen. Thomas Cardin sat at the head of the table, waiting for his staff to fill in the seats. As the audience settled in, Cardin poured himself a glass of water, stood, and closed the door to the room. Facing his staff, Cardin cleared his throat.

"As many of you are aware, there was an article written about me in *The Washington Gazette* this morning. For those who haven't seen the article, I would like to provide a minute for you to peruse the article. It's a short read."

Half of those around the table clicked and swiped their way to *The Washington Gazette's* website and began reading. One by one, each looked up as they finished. In turn, Judge Cardin made eye contact with each individual at the table.

"If everyone is caught up, I would like to request that all laptops be closed and all mobile phones are turned off."

With a surprising level of unplanned synchronization, computers were shut and pushed to the middle of the table. Seconds later, mobile phones joined the laptops.

"I wanted to make sure you all understand the article that was written. I'm aware it may have come as a shock. And before you ask, the gist of the article is accurate. When I was a junior in high school, a good friend of mine disappeared. Her name was Mary Spears. Several months after Mary went missing, two college students were murdered on the campus of the University of South Carolina. The man who murdered those two college students confessed to killing my friend Mary. That man's name was Odin Rowe. He spent over thirty years incarcerated in South Carolina. Late last week, he was stabbed and subsequently passed away. All of that was included in the article.

"What wasn't written in the article is that the day Mary went missing, we had been hanging out. I grew up on a small lake in Columbia, South Carolina, called Lake Katherine. I had a view of the water from my bedroom window. The day that Mary went missing, a bunch of kids from the neighborhood hung out at the lake. I was there. Obviously, we were all shaken by Mary's disappearance and the subsequent legal proceedings. For many of us, it was life-altering.

"Given that, some of you may be wondering why I never mentioned Mary's disappearance as an impetus to my legal career. The simple answer is because it wasn't. I come from a long line of attorneys. The law was in my blood before it ever entered my mind. On top of that, I refused to use Mary's disappearance as a tool to help further my career. I wanted to prove my worth based on the quality of my work, not from sympathy. That is the reason no one has heard me speak of Mary."

Numerous heads around the table nodded in silence.

"Some of you may be wondering about the impact of this news on my recent nomination. My response to that is nothing has changed. I plan to continue onward. Each of you who wishes to continue to work on my team going forward will have a position."

A collective sigh of relief was audible.

""If anyone has additional questions or concerns, my door is open. That is all. Meeting adjourned."

Computers and mobile phones vanished from the top of the table as Cardin's staff members stood from their seats and began filing out.

Cardin held open the door and thanked each person as they exited.

Grace Homan was the last in the staff procession, and Cardin watched as his prized clerk seemed to move in slow motion.

"Grace, is everything okay?"

❧

No more than three feet separated Grace from her boss. She tried to respond to him, but no words came out. She could feel tears welling in her eyes and struggled to keep them contained.

Cardin repeated his question and a tear broke free, trickling down Grace's cheek. She swiped at her face with her free hand. "I'm fine," she managed to mumble. "I haven't been sleeping well."

A look of concern washed over Judge Cardin's face. Grace watched her boss's mouth move but heard only silence. Barely hanging on, her mental faculties faltered as an emotional dam burst. There were no more fingers to put in the dike. A torrent of intrusive thoughts gripped her. As full panic set in, Grace quickly put distance between herself and her boss. In a full-fledged crisis, she dropped her computer off at her desk without breaking stride and headed for the stairs. Outside on the street, Grace hailed a cab.

"Take me to GWU Hospital," she said as she climbed into the rear of the vehicle and began to sob.

Blocks of downtown Washington, DC, turned into a blur of nondescript buildings. Streets she knew well turned into foreign stretches of asphalt. The interior of the car seemed to shrink. She closed her eyes and tried to breathe. When the cab pulled to the curb and announced the amount of the fair, Grace pushed a handful of cash through the security window.

Out of the cab, she cut across a throng of college students on the sidewalk and headed for the emergency room entrance. Inside, she approached a woman at the reception desk. "I need a doctor. I'm having a breakdown," Grace said.

As the receptionist reached for a clipboard and asked for insurance information, Grace Homan threw up and lost consciousness.

∽

The GWU Hospital had a twenty-bed inpatient psychiatric unit on the second floor.

Dressed in a shirt and tie, with a visitor's badge around his neck, Dr. Joffee entered Grace's room and smiled. "Hi, Grace."

"I'm sorry, Dr. Joffee. I didn't know who else to call. Thank you for coming."

"How are we feeling?"

"Embarrassed."

"I was more interested in the state of your anxiety."

"My anxiety has been replaced by humiliation. I threw up in the lobby. In front of a bunch of people."

"Yes, you did. But I'll tell you what. Throwing up at the reception desk in the emergency room won't be remembered tomorrow."

"I'll remember it."

Joffee shrugged, lifting his palms upward. "You want to tell me what's going on?"

"Everything I feared came to fruition in a matter of seconds. Judge Cardin called a staff meeting to discuss the article that was written about him in *The Washington Gazette.* He explained to the staff how he knew a girl named Mary who disappeared while he was in high school. And that triggered an avalanche of anxiety. Worse than anything I've experienced before."

"Maybe there's some therapeutic value in there somewhere. That's a very specific incident that triggered one of your attacks."

"I stared my boss in the face, started to cry, and then ran out of the office without saying a word."

"You'd be surprised how often this happens. Every day in this city. In all types of employment. Trust me, I know."

"This doesn't happen to me."

"Today, it did. And we can put it behind you."

"I need to get out of here."

"The doctor is waiting for the CT scan results. I spoke with the doctor on duty. I can take you home when you're cleared to leave."

"Great. That's what I need. My own personal shrink picking me up from the ER and driving me home."

"It's either that or find someone else who would be willing to sign you out."

"Everyone I know is a lawyer. They cannot know about this."

"Then it's me or nothing," Joffee said. "Let me see where you stand and how much longer you need to be here."

Joffee pulled out of the GWU Hospital parking garage and headed north.

"Thank you again for the ride, Dr. Joffee."

"You're welcome."

"I probably ruined your afternoon."

"I wouldn't say it was ruined. But I'm going to need to do some rescheduling."

"Now you're probably wishing I would've just come to your office unannounced. And we both know how much you love that."

"Are you feeling better?"

"Anxiety-wise, yes. My humiliation continues unabated."

"Some things take time."

"I don't have time, Dr. Joffee." Grace peered out the window. The buildings that had melted into a blur on her way to the hospital were back in focus. The streets were once again familiar.

"I want to try another session of hypnotherapy," Grace said.

"You do?" Joffee asked incredulously.

"Yes. I can't continue to deal with this. I'll take whatever slim possibility another hypnosis session may offer for relief."

"I can contact Dr. Fabrizio and arrange another session. But before I do, I want to be sure it's something you really want."

"It is. And do you know why?"

"I don't."

"Because I'm at the end of my rope. And because I believe in you."

"A vote of confidence born out of desperation?"

"I checked out your sister's story. I found several articles on her. Everything you said was true. She did pass away in a one-car accident at a high rate of speed. Her obituary suggested donations to a mental health nonprofit in lieu of flowers."

"I don't know how to respond."

"You don't have to. All it means is that I believe you had only good intentions when you hired that private investigator."

"I did. Even if the execution was less than stellar."

"How is the investigation going?"

"It has hit a wall."

"How's that?"

"Attrition."

"Meaning?"

"Almost everyone involved in the disappearance of Mary Spears is dead."

"What about Judge Cardin?"

"Dan offered the judge a chance to clear the air with a polygraph. Specifically to address his knowledge of Mary Spears's disappearance."

"And?"

"Judge Cardin declined."

"I've always considered Judge Cardin to be a good person. With the exception of what I said under hypnosis during my initial session with Dr. Fabrizio, I've never wavered in that belief."

CHAPTER 42

DAN'S HEAD WAS nestled tightly between Detective Emily Fields's legs. As Dan struggled to breathe, Detective Earl Wallace cheered on his partner from a chair just off the mat of the police department's main gym.

"She's got you where she wants you," Wallace said.

Trying to breathe, Dan fought to escape. In a last-ditch effort to release the jujitsu hold, Dan grabbed Emily's thighs and stood up. Holding Detective Fields's full weight with his neck and shoulders, Dan began to spin until Fields resembled a kid about to fly off a merry-go-round. Emily tapped one of Dan's arms and the impromptu amusement ride came to a halt.

"That's quite a core you have," Emily said, her back on the mat.

"Nice head scissor."

"I was promised a submission. I want my money back," Wallace added.

"Take off your shoes and get over here," Fields taunted.

"I wouldn't get on the mat with either of you for all the cigars in Cuba."

"He's smarter than he looks," Dan said to Fields.

"Not always."

Dan stepped off the mat, grabbed a towel off his gym bag, and wiped his face. He checked his phone, saw he'd missed a call, and dialed the number.

"This is Dan Lord. Someone called my phone from this number."

"Yes, Mr. Lord," a male responded in a voice Dan vaguely recognized. "This is Dr. Gibson. We met several days ago pertaining to an autopsy of an elderly gentleman who passed away in the backyard of his estate. I hope you can understand the reason for the cryptic explanation."

"Yes. I understand."

"Good. What I'm about to relay to you is not a conversation for public consumption."

"Understood. I assume the fact that you're calling means you had a change of heart?"

"No, I did not. However, after I met with you, a family member of the deceased requested that I run a toxicology report."

"Interesting."

"It made me wonder."

"Did you comply with the request?"

"I did. I expedited the request. Given the circumstances and the public status of the family member in question, I wanted you to be aware that your assumption was correct."

"The deceased had fentanyl in his system?"

"Affirmative."

"Enough to kill him?"

"Enough to kill a few people."

"Did you inform the family of the results?"

"I did."

Dan contemplated the news for a second. "I appreciate the call. I'm surprised you reached out, but I appreciate it."

"I mulled it over for a while. But I couldn't shake what you said about a possible connection to a girl who went missing in the eighties."

"You did the right thing."

"That's up to you to prove."

"May I ask how the family member reacted when you told them the toxicology results?"

"Something between disbelief and relief."

"I may need a shrink to help identify what that feeling is. Thanks for the call."

"No need to thank me. This call never happened."

&

Dan wiped sweat off his arms while considering the implications of the call that just ended. A young man torturing a heavy bag ten feet away snapped Dan out of his momentary stupor.

"Was that good news or bad?" Wallace asked. "You seem concerned. And you mentioned you may need a shrink. Not that I was eavesdropping."

"I'm fine. Just taking a minute for the blood to return to my head after the thigh clamp."

"I call bullshit," Wallace replied.

"Do the two of you remember the wine and cigar challenge from the other day?" Dan asked.

"Yes. I'm still waiting for my five-thousand-dollar bottle of red," Fields said.

"I smoked my Cohiba. It was better than I imagined it would be," Wallace added.

"Well, the person who I speculated may have killed himself in an effort to protect his son did consume a lethal amount of a dangerous pharmaceutical. That was on top of the wine, cigar, and Pappy Van Winkle."

"Don't forget the filet mignon," Wallace added.

"By the way, you never told us what crime his son allegedly committed," Fields said.

"Murder."

CHAPTER 43

GRACE WAS ON her back on the sofa in her own living room. A thin pillow rested under her neck. Dr. Fabrizio sat in a chair next to the sofa. Dr. Joffee took the middle of a small loveseat on the other side of the room.

Dr. Fabrizio glanced down at the yellow notepad in her lap. Three glasses of water stood on the coffee table. Grace's iPhone leaned against one of the glasses, the camera focused on her upper body and face.

"Okay, Grace, any questions before we try this one more time?" Dr. Fabrizio asked.

"Nope. Let's get it over with. And we agreed there will be no video or audio other than my own."

"Understood and agreed to," Dr. Joffee said.

Dr. Fabrizio nodded in agreement. "If you're comfortable, take a deep breath, and we'll get started."

⊰

"Your eyes are becoming heavy. It takes effort to keep them open. Soon they are going to slowly close as you relax the muscles around your eyes. You can allow yourself to relax with your eyes shut and let yourself fall into deep relaxation. You feel comfortable warmth all around you. Take deep comfortable breaths as you let yourself relax.

You can feel yourself falling deeper into relaxation as you listen to the sound of my voice. Your eyes are shut, and your breathing is deep and relaxed. You are at ease."

Dr. Joffee watched as Grace was slowly guided into complete hypnosis.

"Keep listening to the sound of my voice as you continue to relax every muscle. All is well. Now, see yourself at the top of a long staircase. You have no fear. Slowly, you take your first step and begin descending the stairs, each step bringing you down into a state of deeper relaxation. You have no anxiety. Each step is welcomed…"

Dr. Fabrizio repeated herself for several minutes. "Allow your mind to gently float back in time. You can still hear my voice and you, too, can speak. Your mind is moving effortlessly through your memories."

"Hmmmm," Grace mumbled ambivalently.

"You feel good. You are at peace. All is well."

Dr. Fabrizio continued to bring Grace into a deeper trance. "Feel free to go back in time. To a time that is important to you. All is well. You are at ease."

A moment later, Grace spoke. "I see people."

"Where you are?"

"I'm in a crowd. Everyone is in a chair," Grace replied. "We are all wearing black. It's hot."

Dr. Fabrizio recognized the description of Grace's graduation from the first hypnosis session. "Is it graduation from law school?"

"Yes."

"And the year is 2016?"

"Yes. The banner over the stage says, 'congratulations to the law class of 2016.'"

"Okay, that's good. All is well. Allow your mind to move on to your next memory. Allow yourself to drift back to other memories that may be important to you."

Grace remained silent as Dr. Fabrizio repeated her guidance.

"Grace, can you tell me what you see. How do you feel?"

"My name is not Grace. My name is Mary."

"Mary?"

"Yes."

Dr. Fabrizio raised her eyebrows in Dr. Joffee's direction.

"Do you know your last name, Mary?"

"My name is Mary Martin."

Dr. Fabrizio scribbled on her notepad.

"Do you know where you are, Mary?"

"I'm outside. I'm near a river. It's hot and humid. There's music playing."

"What kind of music is it?"

"It's a new band. People are singing along. 'Come on, baby, light my fire.'"

"Okay, Grace. Good. Can you tell me who is with you?"

"Grace is not here. My name is Mary." Dr. Fabrizio tapped the side of her head, signaling that she realized her mental flub.

"Yes. I meant Mary. Mary Martin. How old are you, Mary?"

"I'm in high school."

"Do you remember the name of your high school?"

"Cedar Falls High School."

"Who are you with? Are you with classmates?"

"There are many people. I'm with friends and classmates. I am with a boy I like. His name is Pierce. I've known him for a long time."

"Pierce?"

"Yes, Pierce."

Dr. Fabrizio pursed her lips.

"Okay, Mary. What else do you remember from that day?"

"Pierce says he wants to show me something."

"What is it?"

"He says he wants to show me when we are alone. But I am happy where I am. It's a nice day."

"Okay, Mary. All is well. Do you go somewhere with Peirce?"

"No. Pierce has a gun, and I am afraid."

"Is he threatening you?"

"No. He says the gun is not loaded. He is showing off. Spinning the gun around his finger like a cowboy. I ask him to stop. He laughs. I'm getting upset."

Suddenly Grace's voice breaks into a guttural explosion, the same gargled, wounded animal howl exhibited in the first hypnosis session.

Dr. Fabrizio quickly began to bring her out of the hypnotic trance. "I'm going to count backward from five, and when I do, you will wake, refreshed…"

⁊

Grace sat up slowly and put her feet on the floor. She reached for her phone and then for the glass of water her phone had been leaning against. She took several sips of water and returned the glass to the table. "Judging by your expressions, it must have been another interesting session."

"We're going to let you decide for yourself."

"How long was I under?"

Dr. Fabrizio checked her notes. "Twenty-six minutes from the time we started."

"Dr. Fabrizio and I are going to go for a stroll. Take your time and watch the video. Text me when you finish, and we'll come back up to discuss it," Joffee said.

"Sounds like a plan," Grace replied, staring at the screen of her phone.

⁊

Grace answered the door and motioned for Dr. Fabrizio and Dr. Joffee to reenter her apartment.

"How was your walk?" she asked.

"It was a nice night for it," Joffee answered. "How did you manage with the video?"

"I watched it."

"How do you feel about it?"

"It was less strange than watching the video of the first session."

"Supports the argument that humans can grow accustomed to almost anything."

"I wouldn't go that far," Grace said, returning to her sofa. "What did the two of you think of the session?"

Dr. Fabrizio answered first. "You achieved what I consider full hypnosis. In that state, you described what I can only define as past-life regression. This was a similar result to the first hypnotic session."

"Except the boy who I was with was named Pierce."

"True," Dr. Fabrizio said. "We're not sure what to make of that. In the first session you identified the boy you were with as Thomas. In this session, he was named Pierce."

"My legal mind considers that a red flag with regard to credibility."

Dr. Joffee nodded. "I can understand that."

"So where do we go from here?"

"I would like to share the information from this session with the private investigator and attorney who has been looking into the disappearance of Mary Spears," Joffee said.

"That video is not leaving my possession. No one is copying it. No one is sending it. No one is editing it."

"Understood," Dr. Joffee said. "Maybe there's another alternative."

Dan opened the steel security door at the bottom of the staircase that rose to the second floor. He led his two guests through the series of keypads, locks, and bulletproof doors into the main room of his office. His two guests sat in chairs around a small table with a view of the Old Town Alexandria skyline and the Masonic Temple.

"Anyone interested in joining me in a glass of wine?" Dan asked. "It's after hours."

Dr. Joffee waited for his patient to respond.

"Sure, what the hell?" Grace replied.

"Three glasses," Joffee confirmed.

Dan disappeared and returned with a bottle of red and three glasses. He filled each one and placed the bottle in the middle of the table.

Grace spoke. "Before we discuss anything, I would like to formally introduce myself. My name is Grace Homan. Dr. Joffee is my psychiatrist. He has my permission to use my name and discuss any of my medical issues or treatments with you."

"Nice to officially meet you. I introduced myself at the restaurant the other day when the reporter intruded on us. But one more time, for the record, my name is Dan Lord. I'm an attorney. I'm also a private investigator. Dr. Joffee hired me to look into the death of a young woman named Mary Spears who disappeared in 1986."

In lieu of a needless introduction, Dr. Joffee offered a more traditional "L'chaim."

Dan and Grace repeated the phrase and all three touched glasses.

"Thank you for agreeing to see us on such short notice and after hours," Dr. Joffee began. "We have information that may prove useful to your investigation into Mary's disappearance. Grace agreed to a second treatment of hypnosis and that treatment provided surprising information."

"I'll add it to the long list of surprises."

"If you're interested, Grace has a recording of today's session. Video and audio," Joffee said.

Grace nodded. "You're free to listen to it, but one of us will have to leave. I can't bear to watch someone watching a video of me under hypnosis. It's just too bizarre."

"I can take it into the back room," Dan replied.

Grace punched her passcode into her phone, swiped at the screen, and handed the device to Dan. "All you have to do is hit play. The first portion of the video is Dr. Fabrizio putting me under. It gets interesting when the Q&A starts."

"I'll take a gander and be back." Dan pointed at the wine bottle on the table. "There's more where that came from, so help yourself."

❧

When Dan returned, he sat down across from Dr. Joffee and Grace. He handed the phone back to Grace and reached for his wine glass.

"What did you think?" Grace asked.

"It's interesting. Not the least of which is the fact that your name in the latest session is Mary Martin. It throws a wrench into the mystery of Mary Spears."

"I agree. We also have to consider the name Pierce. That's distinct from Thomas."

"You mentioned a couple of other pertinent facts such as Cedar Falls and a song that was being played. In the recording you referred to the song as a new one."

Dan retrieved his laptop from his desk, returned to his seat, and began typing.

"According to Google, The Doors' first hit was 'Light My Fire.' It was released in 1967," Dan said. "And if we focus on 1967, we can look through death records for a Mary Martin who may have died in Cedar Falls. I'm going to assume we're talking about Cedar Falls, Iowa, unless either of you know of another Cedar Falls."

Dan typed, searched, and continued his play-by-play. "Okay, here we go. In the state of Iowa, vital records are maintained by the Iowa Department of Health and Human Services. And it looks like they have a website that can be searched for a small fee."

Dan entered his credit card information from memory. "Let's see what ten dollars buys us in Iowa."

Dan clicked his way through vital records as his guests drank wine and listened. "All right. I'm in. Death records for Cedar Falls, Iowa, for 1967. Usually I would ask for a drumroll at this juncture, but not for a death record. Too morbid."

"Agreed," Grace said.

A one-line entry appeared as the search result. Dan read the file record. "We have name, birthplace, birth date, death date, and the deceased's mother's maiden name. Mary Martin, born in Cedar Falls in 1949, died in Cedar Falls in 1967. Mother's maiden name is Franklin. That's all it has."

"No cause of death?" Dr. Joffee asked.

Dan's eyes dropped to the bottom of the screen. "It says additional vital records may be available at the local city or county office."

Dan clicked two more times. "And for Cedar Falls, complete death certificates are kept by the Cedar Falls Historical Society."

The three sat in silence for a moment.

"It's your move, Doc," Dan said. "What do you want to do with this information? The choice is pretty straightforward. Close up shop or see it through."

Before Joffee could respond, Grace interjected. "Oh, we're going to see it through. There's no way in hell I'm going to just let this slide."

Dr. Joffee shrugged his shoulders and raised his palms toward the ceiling.

"I'm down. I've never been to Iowa," Dan said.

"I have," Dr. Joffee replied. "You haven't missed much."

CHAPTER 44

LEAVING WATERLOO REGIONAL Airport, Dan drove past the Cedar Falls Utility smokestack, the tallest structure for a hundred miles in any direction. On the other side of the river, he stopped for a coffee at Maid-Rite, a red-and-white checkered diner and mainstay of downtown Cedar Falls. One block up and three blocks over, Dan pulled into a parking spot on the street.

Stepping into the hundred-and-fifty-year-old Italianate house felt like going back in time. He strolled through the entrance hall, eyeing a multitude of display cases holding the historical wares of Cedar Falls, Iowa. At the information desk, an elderly woman turned to greet him and removed her reading glasses.

"Welcome to Cedar Falls Historical Society. How can I help you today?"

Dan introduced himself with his inquiry of the day. "I'm looking for someone with historic knowledge of this town."

"Well, you've come to the right place."

"I hope so."

"What part of Cedar Falls history are you interested in? I can provide a good overview, but we have a lot of volunteers. Many of us have our own areas of expertise."

"I'm looking for information on a woman who died here in 1967."

"Oh my. That's not the typical question."

"I found a database entry for her death in the Iowa Department of Health's vital records. But I was looking for a copy of the actual death certificate. They told me they don't keep records at the state level for deaths that old. So here I am. It's my understanding that you keep these older records."

"We do, but boy, oh boy."

"That doesn't sound promising."

"Have you ever used microfilm?"

How young does this woman think I am? Dan wondered. "Many times."

"That's good. You'll have a fighting chance. A lot of young folks these days have never even heard of microfilm, much less microfiche."

"I'll work it out. Just point me in the right direction."

"Follow me."

The woman exited the confines of the information desk, crossed the room, and pushed open an old wooden door. As she descended the narrow set of stairs, she began to provide Dan with a rundown of the procedure.

"Everything is pretty well organized down here. We have three film machines. Most of them work most of the time. We have marriage, birth, divorce, and death records going back to 1880 for Cedar Falls. All of the records are organized by year. Once you have the year, they are listed in alphabetical order by last name."

Dan followed as the woman waddled down a row of filing cabinets. She turned right at a break in the aisles and took a left. She put her reading glasses back on her nose and tapped the top of the filing cabinet. These are the death records from 1967. Or the beginning of them."

"Thank you for your help."

"The film machines are along the wall. Come upstairs if you need me for anything. I'm running the info desk by myself today, so I better get back to it."

"Thank you again."

❧

Dan's eyes darted over the tabs of the filing cabinets, shuffling his feet side to side as he worked his way down the aisle. Near the middle of the row, Dan pulled a drawer handle. He ran his finger across the top of small boxes until he found one identifying last names from M to P for 1967. He removed the box, took it to the microfilm machine, turned on the screen, and threaded the film.

Minutes later, Dan was looking at the death certificate for Mary Martin. Dan scanned to the bottom of the death certificate and stopped when he saw the cause of death. *Accidental Death. Loss of blood. Gunshot.*

Dan's mind began to churn, and his gaze dropped to the illegible signature of the coroner on the bottom line of the death certificate. Dan followed the instructions on a poster on the wall to print out a copy of the certificate and then returned the box of film to its location to gather dust for another decade.

Back at the information desk on the main floor, Dan proudly showed off the death certificate.

"Wow, that was fast. I assume you found what you were looking for," she said.

"I did," Dan replied. "But I could still use your help. I can't read the coroner's signature." Dan placed the certificate on the desk.

The volunteer bent over and peered at the certificate. "I don't think I'm going to be able to help you out with that one."

The woman then placed her finger on a line halfway down the page. "But I do recognize the patient's physician's name. Raymond G. Kelleher. Most people around here call him Dr. Ray."

"Does that mean he's still alive?"

"Dr. Ray? Sure, he's alive. He delivered half of the population of Cedar Falls back in the day. He did a bit of everything. Set broken bones, delivered babies. Rumor has it, he floated a few horse teeth from time to time."

"Where is Dr. Ray these days?"

"Over at Greenwood."

"What's Greenwood?"

"A cemetery."

"But you said he's not dead."

"He's not. Dr. Ray's son is the sexton over at Greenwood. Dr. Ray helps out."

"Is Greenwood far?"

"Couple of minutes by car. Right on Franklin, left on First, right on College. You can't miss it."

"Famous last words whispered to the permanently lost."

The woman cocked her head seemingly unsure of whether to smile.

"Thank you for your time and the information. I put the microfilm back where I found it."

⁓

Greenwood Cemetery was, indeed, impossible to miss. Dan parked his car outside a small stone building and removed his sunglasses. Entering the front door, an old man stepped out from behind a frosted glass wall.

"Good afternoon. Don't suppose you're the guy who was just at the historical society?"

"News travels fast. Are you Dr. Ray?"

"Guilty as charged. Raymond G. Kelleher. But everyone calls me Dr. Ray. Not sure when that started, but it's been a long, long while."

Dan introduced himself and offered a handshake.

"What can I do for you, Mr. Lord," Dr. Ray asked.

"I'm looking for information on Mary Martin. She died in the summer of 1967. An accidental gunshot."

"That's a while back. I reckon before you were even born."

"It was."

"Well, it's not really my business, but what interest do you have in Mary? Some kind of lost inheritance?"

"It's a long story. It may be hard for me to explain in a meaningful way."

"Try me."

"I'm interested in the specifics of her death. I know a few things, but I was interested in knowing who shot her. Assuming she didn't shoot herself."

Dan unfolded the printout of the death certificate and handed it to Dr. Ray.

"It was an accident," Dr. Ray stated bluntly.

"That's what it says. Do you remember her or what happened? Anything may be helpful."

Dr. Ray seemed flustered by the request. "Let's take a walk."

Dan followed Dr. Ray as he headed down an asphalt path that meandered through the cemetery. A pair of freshly dug graves stood out against the green landscape.

"I take it that you remember Mary Martin," Dan said.

"What gave me away?"

"You invited me on a walk."

"Maybe I don't like walking alone."

"I doubt it."

"As a doctor in a small town, you pretty much know everyone. Everything. And in the 1960s, Cedar Falls was a small town. A lot smaller than it is these days. Back then, if someone came into my office with a case of gonorrhea, within a couple of months, I would know exactly who was sleeping with who."

"I'm not here about STDs. I'm wondering if you treated Mary Martin after she was shot."

"I didn't. And it wouldn't have mattered. No one could have saved her."

"Why's that?"

"The day Mary died, there was a group of a few dozen kids up at Ulrich Park. Most of the kids were from Cedar Falls High School. Back in the late sixties, Ulrich Park was new. I think it opened in 1965 or so, but there wasn't much there. There's not much there today, either, really. It's a nature preserve on the river. A hundred acres or so. Back then, it was just far enough from town that no one was worried about the cops, making noise, having bonfires. In the sixties, teenagers took to the park like ducks to water."

"And?"

"A group of kids was hanging out. At some point, Mary's boyfriend shot her in the neck. He was playing with a gun and it went off. The bullet tore through part of her clavicle and severed the carotid. She bled out in minutes. Probably lost consciousness in twenty seconds. Even with today's medicine, Mary would not have been saved."

"What was Mary's boyfriend's name?"

"Pierce Lamont."

"Where did Pierce Lamont get the gun? Did anyone ever ask?"

"In 1967, anyone with money could buy a gun, no questions asked. No age restrictions. No background checks. Put your bubblegum money on the counter and you could be a gun owner. If I recall correctly, it wasn't until '68 that the government passed the Gun Control Act."

"Did you know Mary Martin's family?"

"I knew almost every family."

"What about the boyfriend?"

"I knew him too."

"Is he still around?"

"Pierce Lamont drowned the year after Mary's passing. In the spring. He and his brother were fishing out on the river. The current was strong, and the boat tipped over. Pierce's body was found downstream the next day."

"I'm sorry to hear that. What was his brother's name?"

"Alvin."

"How old was he?"

"Ten months younger than Pierce."

"Irish twins," Dan muttered. "I'm curious about something. There was no mention in public records of Mary Martin's death or of an accidental shooting. I searched through old newspapers. Nothing."

"No mystery there."

"There is for me."

"Pierce Lamont's father was the editor of *The Waterloo-Cedar Falls Courier.*"

"The local paper?" Dan asked.

"Yes. It was actually an afternoon paper, delivered every day of the week except Saturdays. And Pierce Lamont's father made damn sure the paper didn't cover the story of his son shooting his girlfriend. Of course, at the time, everyone in town knew what had happened. The rumor mill is strong in Cedar Falls. The internet, social media, and all that jazz has nothing on the speed of rumors in a small town."

"So, Pierce Lamont and Mary Martin went to Cedar Falls High School. Mary died in 1967, and Pierce died in 1968."

"That's right."

Dan realized that Dr. Ray had walked him on a circular path and the two were heading back toward the stone building.

"I'm still curious why you're interested in the specific cause of death and the surrounding circumstances of someone who died sixty years ago."

"You wouldn't believe me if I told you."

"Try me. I'm at the age where I can confidently say I've heard it all."

Dan laughed. "You think so?"

"Yes, sir."

"Okay. I believe that Mary Martin was reincarnated, and in her next life became someone important to the recently nominated United States Supreme Court justice."

"Thomas Cardin?"

"That's correct."

Dr. Ray stopped walking and turned to face Dan. Dan could feel the doctor's penetrating glare, pupil to pupil. "You don't look like you're on drugs."

"I'm not."

"Then I stand corrected. I hadn't heard everything."

CHAPTER 45

DAN SAT ON an uncomfortable plastic chair at gate four, the highest numbered gate in Waterloo Regional Airport. A full-size John Deere tractor encased in the world's largest glass display box was the terminal's only attraction. Refreshments were limited to a row of vending machines near the bathrooms.

Dan's laptop teetered on his thighs as he scrolled through Google search results. He entered the URL for a website offering scanned images of old high school yearbooks and, for the price of a beer, he purchased a digital copy of the 1967 Cedar Falls High School yearbook.

Dan clicked through the pages of teachers and accolades before the student photo section began. He continued to scroll until the last names began with the letter M. He proceeded slowly until he found himself looking at Mary Martin's photo. He zoomed into the black-and-white photo and a vaguely familiar face filled the screen. "Holy shit," he said aloud.

Dan continued to click his way through the yearbook and stopped again when the last names began with the letter L. Again, he slowly scrolled until he found the photo of Pierce Lamont and zoomed into the picture. Staring hard at the face of the young man, he whispered under his breath. Dan placed his laptop on the empty chair next to him, stood, and began pacing back and forth. As he considered the case of Mary Martin, the terminal's PA system came to life and announced his flight to Washington, DC, was delayed. Dan checked the time on his phone and placed a call.

"This is Dr. Pando," the voice on the other end of the phone answered.

"Hi, Dr. Pando. This is Dan Lord. We met last week in Charlottesville. You graciously allowed me to observe a conversation in Western Neo-Aramaic."

"Dan, yes, of course. I was wondering if you got everything you needed."

"Do you have a minute? I have some follow-up questions."

"I have about fifteen minutes before my next meeting."

"I apologize in advance if the questions seem random. I'm thinking on the fly."

"Understood."

"Is there an average amount of time between lives for those who claim to have experienced reincarnation? What I mean is that if person A dies and is reincarnated, is there an average amount of time between death in one life and rebirth in another?"

"There's no average that I'm aware of. I've read cases where individuals seem to have been in what I call 'the in between' for many decades. But there are instances where the end of the last life and the beginning of a new life is a year or less. Of course, that cannot be determined until the individual is old enough to speak and reflect."

"So John Smith dies. Then John Smith is reborn. And when John Smith is able to speak, he references his past life and when it was?"

"Something along those lines. Often, we have to piece together the exact timing based on what is said."

"What about the cases where there's been decades between lives?"

"Longer periods of time between lives may be the norm. But it also becomes harder to verify."

"And what about people who have been reincarnated with other people who have been reincarnated? Friends from a past life are reincarnated as friends again in a new life."

"I sent you an email on the topic. It was the follow-up on the fire chief who found photos of himself in the Civil War."

"I never saw that email. What was the subject line?"

"Soul groups."

"Sounds like a band from the 1960s. Let me check."

Dan grabbed his laptop off the chair next to him and checked his inbox to no avail. A cursory search of his spam folder pinpointed an email with the subject line Dr. Pando had mentioned.

"Sorry. It was in my junk folder. I missed it," Dan said.

"Not a problem. Did the attachments go through?"

"I'm staring at the photographs. I recognize the Civil War soldier turned fire chief with the damaged ear." Dan clicked through additional photos of different Civil War soldiers. "Who are these other soldiers?"

"They're soldiers from the same unit as the fire chief. Continue with the next couple of attachments."

Dan opened the remaining photographs. "What am I looking at here? A group of guys in front of a firehouse?"

"You're looking at the photograph of the members of Firehouse 58 in Monroe Township, New Jersey."

Dan zoomed in on the faces of the other firemen. He then revisited the previous photos of the Civil War soldiers. "What the hell?"

"I know. It's remarkable."

"Are you telling me that a group of men from the same unit in the Civil War were reborn and served in the same firehouse in New Jersey a hundred and thirty years later?"

"That's exactly right. Only I'm not saying it. The images are."

"Are these verified? Did these guys go under hypnosis?"

"Several of the fire fighters subjected themselves to hypnosis after seeing the same photographs you are looking at. Three of the men were able to recall some elements of their past lives, including the fire chief with the damaged ear."

"Is this common? People going from life to life with a sustained connection between them?"

"I can't classify it as common, but it happens. As the subject line of the email indicates, unofficially, we call them soul groups. It's rather unusual to discover an instance where so many individuals are reincarnated together. It more often occurs with couples, siblings, and family members."

Dan remained silent long enough for Dr. Pando to wonder if they were still connected. "Are you still there?" Pando asked.

"I am."

"May I ask why you're asking?"

"I think I may have found another case for you to investigate."

CHAPTER 46

DAN WAS STILL digesting the concept of soul groups, the images of Civil War soldiers turned first responders, and the hundred and thirty years the men must have spent in "the in between." Adding fuel to the fire of disbelief was the Cedar Falls High School yearbook for the class of 1967. In the midst of Dan's struggle through the fog of improbability, the airport's PA system again came to life and announced, for a second time, that his flight was delayed. Taking a break, Dan made his way to the vending machine and purchased a bag of stale corn nuts and a bottle of water. As he sat down, the burner phone in his bag began to ring.

"Dan speaking."

"This is who you think it is," Tobias said.

"You're the only person with this number."

"I may have found something on your query request. Particularly about Nathaniel Cardin Senior."

"Let's hear it."

"I ran Cardin Senior through the wringer, so to speak. I wrote some new algorithms for my AI programs to identify anomalies across a long list of databases. Most of them are public. Perfectly legal. Others are more restricted. My AI query identified something unusual that I wouldn't have looked for. Actually, it identified something that no person would know to look for."

"Do tell."

"Cardin Senior owns, or partially owns, a multitude of businesses and real estate. When I ran my AI algorithms against real estate records for all forty-six counties in South Carolina, the query identified several dozen properties. Of those, one property was identified by the AI system as anomalous when compared to the rest."

"Anomalous how?"

"It was a double-wide trailer purchased by Nathanial Cardin Senior for thirty-one thousand dollars. That price was substantially lower than all the other properties owned by anyone in the Cardin family."

"A trailer could be a hunting cabin."

"It could be. But this isn't. When I dug around on that particular property, records indicated it was transferred to someone named Stacey McSween less than a month after Nathaniel Cardin Senior purchased it."

"He gave it away?"

"He did. To Stacey McSween."

"Who is she?"

"She was married to Thomas Cardin's brother, Nate Cardin Junior. And the same month that Nathanial Cardin Senior gave away this double-wide trailer, Stacey changed her name from Stacey Cardin back to her birth name of Stacey McSween."

"Interesting. I'm not sure what to make of it, but it's curious."

As Dan contemplated the new information from Tobias, the PA system announced that his flight from Cedar Falls to Washington, DC, was now canceled.

Dan stroked his chin. "Do you have an address on that trailer?"

CHAPTER 47

SOUTH CAROLINA'S CRESTVIEW Trailer Park was the state's largest. Stretching between Interstate 26 and Route 61, the sprawling acreage featured two hundred homes. Near the entrance, a customized trailer served as the community center and rental office. Beyond the entrance, an outdated playground, an algae-ridden pool, and a netless tennis court completed the list of amenities.

Dan slowed to a stop in front of a weathered mobile home. A blue racing stripe wrapped around the trailer, giving the residence a sense of motion that would never be realized. The tires on the mobile home were flat. Remnants of a bonfire stood surrounded by lawn chairs in the dirt yard.

Dan exited the car and followed the uneven walkway in the direction of the double-wide trailer. He stepped up three creaky stairs and knocked on the rusty screen door. Standing in the heat, Dan could feel approaching footsteps, the structure of the home bouncing.

"Be right there," a gravelly voice rang out from inside the trailer. Seconds later, the knob turned and the door opened. A woman's silhouette appeared from the dark interior of the trailer. Dan eyed the woman's jeans, worn T-shirt, and bare feet. Long greasy hair framed her face.

"Are you Stacey McSween?" Dan asked through the screen door.

"Who wants to know?"

"My name is Dan Lord. I'm an attorney from Virginia. Just outside of DC."

"No one here called a lawyer."

"I'm not here because someone called."

"Then what do ya want?"

"Can I assume this means you're Stacey McSween?"

"Guilty as charged."

"Formerly Stacey Cardin?"

Stacey cocked her head to the side.

"I was hoping to talk to you about your late husband, Nathan," Dan added.

"Well, that's a surprise. Nate's been dead a mighty long time. No one's come round to talk about him in years."

"I realize it was a long time ago, and I'm sorry for your loss."

"Thanks, I guess," Stacey replied. "Life goes on."

"It does. For all of us."

"I can't wait to hear why a lawyer from Washington has come to beautiful Crestview. Must be something to do with Nate's brother, Thomas."

"Yes and no."

"Figured as much."

"I think I saw you at Nathaniel Cardin's funeral. You were wearing a red dress."

"I was there for a hot minute. Wasn't one of my better moments."

"Funerals typically aren't a good moment for anyone."

"Truth to that."

"Do you have a few minutes to talk? I'll pay you for your time."

"How much?"

"Well, my going rate is $450 an hour. Seems fair to offer you the same."

"What if it only takes ten minutes?"

"You still get $450."

Stacey seemed to consider the proposition in front of her. She sighed and pointed at the chairs around the bonfire pit. "Why don't you grab a seat and we can have a sit down. Do you want a beer?"

"Sure," Dan replied.

"I'll be right out."

Dan crossed the dirt yard and sat down on a rickety lawn chair. The growl of an 18-wheeler downshifting in the distance echoed across trailer park. As the noise faded, Stacey Cardin stepped from the trailer with two beers. She handed one to Dan and kept one for herself. She pulled out a pack of cigarettes, fished around in her jeans for a lighter, and sat down.

Cracking open her beer and raising it in the air as a toast, she took a sip. "So, what do you want to know about Nate?"

"Anything you can tell me. What happened to him?"

"What happed to him is that he died from liver failure. Hepatitis. Eventually he just wasted away. A lifetime of drugs will do that to you. If an overdose doesn't get you first."

"What was he into?" Dan asked.

"Heroin. Meth. Coke. Ketamine. You name it, he did it. Hell, *we* did it. I've been in and out of recovery too many times to count. Been drug free for nearly a year this time around."

"Good for you."

"I take it day by day."

Dan looked at the woman's arms. Scars dotted her skin in the patches of flesh between her tattoos.

"I still drink," Stacey offered unapologetically.

"You're not going to hear a lecture from me," Dan said. "How long had Nate been involved in drugs?"

"We both started young. By the time we could legally buy booze, drugs already had their claws deep into both of us. And as fate would have it, that's about the time we met. Two disasters running into each other and turning into a bigger disaster."

"Did Nate ever try to quit?" Dan asked.

"Try? Sure. We all try. Sometimes for a few hours. Sometimes longer. But I'll tell you something. When you keep trying to quit, it's like the boy who cried wolf. Eventually, you're the only one listening."

"Everyone is fighting a battle."

"Amen to that. Demons, voices, the government, addiction."

"Did Nate ever get into any details about his family and the friction between them?"

"Tell me? No. He didn't have to tell me. I witnessed it. His parents disowned him."

"Because of drugs?"

"Mostly. I think they could have overlooked the drugs, or at least some of them, but the behavior that came with the drugs was hard for them to swallow."

"Such as?"

"Nate was first arrested when he was sixteen. Pulled over for speeding. The cops found a quarter pound of weed on the passenger seat."

"Under the passenger seat?"

"No, on the passenger seat."

"A quarter pound? I guess it wasn't for personal consumption," Dan said.

"Back in the eighties, a QP was a lot. Nowadays, pot is legal in so many places, I don't think anyone cares. If pot had been legal in the eighties, maybe Nate's life would have taken a different route. He could have gone another way."

"Pot ruined his life?"

"No, but it started there. When your father is a circuit solicitor, and a Cardin to boot, there are certain expectations to uphold. Even though his father saw to it that charges didn't stick, once Nate was arrested, the relationship with his father soured. With that first arrest, I think Nate's life veered into another lane. One he could never find his way back from. Without drugs, Nate could have been anything he wanted. Anything. But he barely squeaked out of high school."

"So the two of you met in your early twenties and got married?"

"That's right. Two stupid kids without a clue, who liked getting fucked up."

"And then?"

"And then nothing. Twenty years of lost days. A trip or two to Myrtle."

"Never had kids?" Dan asked.

"Nope. Not sure who had the bad bits, but we never used birth control and never got pregnant. A blessing in disguise, I guess."

"Why did you change your name after Nate died?" Dan asked.

Stacey took a drag off her cigarette. "That's an odd question. What are you after, exactly?"

"The truth," Dan said.

Stacey blew a cloud of smoke into the air. "The truth is that I was paid to change my name."

"You mean you were paid to relinquish the Cardin family name?"

"Yep. Like I said, when you're a Cardin, there are expectations to uphold. One of those expectations is not sullying the family name. Nate didn't live up to those expectations. Of course in Nate's case, it was particularly sensitive. Nate's father never came to grips with the fact that his son, who bore the same name, was running around high on drugs, getting arrested, what have you."

"And when Nate passed away, the Cardins decided you weren't qualified to keep the Cardin name?"

"Something like that. But for me, at the end of the day, who cares about a fucking name?"

"The Cardins do," Dan stated.

"Yeah, that's right. The Cardins and people like them. People with more money than sense," Stacey said. "So, when they offered to pay me to change my last name, I accepted."

"You don't regret it?"

"Regret it? No. My name was Stacey McSween most of my life. The deal was if I changed my name, they would buy me a house and give me some money."

"How much?"

"I got paid fifty grand to change my name. And you're looking at the house they purchased for me."

"Who arranged the payment for you?"

"The house was gifted to me by ex-father-in-law."

"Nathaniel Cardin Senior?"

"That's right. The payment to change my name came through one of their lawyers. It was pretty straightforward. He handed me an envelope full of cash and told me it was enough to pay the courts to change my name. Once that was done, I would receive $50,000 and the keys to a house. And they did what they said. Deposited directly into my bank account."

Dan paused as if considering his next question. "Have you ever heard the name Odin Rowe?"

Stacey seemed to wince. She sucked on the end of her cigarette and blew another thick cloud toward the sky. "Sure. Odin Rowe was a killer from Columbia. Back in the day. Died recently. Stabbed in prison."

"You heard the news?"

"The entire state heard the news."

"What else do you know about Odin Rowe?"

Stacey gulped her beer. "I know that when Nate was young, he bought drugs from Odin Rowe. A lot of people did. Right up until Rowe was arrested for murder."

Dan stared at Stacey.

Stacey grimaced. "I know how it sounds. It's fucked up. To look back and think you bought drugs from a killer. To think that you sat around and did drugs with a killer. That kind of thing could keep you up at night."

"Does it keep you up?"

"I never did drugs with Odin Rowe. I never met him. But I have other things that keep me up at night. Most nights I can drown out the thoughts, twelve ounces at a time. It was easier when I was using the hard stuff."

"Did Nate know Odin Rowe had a violent streak?"

"Nate knew Odin Rowe was dangerous. I don't think anyone knew just how dangerous."

"Did you know Mary Spears?"

The question seemed to hit a nerve, and Stacey downed more beer with audible swallows. "I know the name."

"Did Nate ever say what he thought happened to her?"

Stacey averted her eyes and looked toward the highway in the distance. "That's a dangerous question."

"And an important question."

"I don't think I'm the person to answer that one."

"You might be the only one left who can," Dan said.

Stacey tipped her head back and poured her beer into her open mouth as fast as gravity would allow. When she finished, she crushed the can with one hand and threw it in the yard.

"Nate knew what happened to her," Stacey said, her gaze still averted.

"Did you know that Mary's mother is still alive. She's still waiting to bury her daughter's body."

Stacey stared stoically ahead, almost catatonic.

"What did Nate know about Mary Spears?" Dan pressed.

"He knew everything."

"Like?"

"He knew everything about the night she went missing."

"How's that?"

"Dumb fucking luck. Bad timing. Call it whatever."

"Meaning?"

Stacey's face contorted. "I shouldn't be talking about this."

"There's no one left to tell the truth." Dan replied. "Nate is dead. Odin Rowe is dead. Nathaniel Cardin Senior is dead. You're not protecting anyone except for Thomas Cardin. And if he was involved, we all need to know. Everyone needs to know."

"No one will believe what I say."

"Unless you were there at the time, whatever you tell me is hearsay. Whatever you say could never be used in court, even if I wanted to, which I don't. All I want is the truth."

Stacey craned her neck, seeming to look around for neighbors. "I don't think anyone has asked me for the truth since I was a kid."

"You can trust me," Dan said.

"If you share anything about what I say, I'll deny it. I'm a recovering junkie who drinks beer for breakfast. Look at me. I'm what they call an unreliable witness. And I'll make sure everyone knows it."

"No one will know we ever spoke," Dan said.

Stacey slowly nodded. "I'm going to need another drink first."

CHAPTER 48

STACEY DISAPPEARED INTO the house and came out with two additional beers, one in each hand. "I'll tell you what Nate told me. And like I said, if anyone asks, I'll deny I said it."

"Agreed," Dan said.

"Go put your phone on the hood of your car where I can see it. And when you get back, I'll take the $450 you promised me."

Dan walked to the car and placed his phone on the hood as asked. On the return leg to his chair, he removed $450 in cash from his wallet. Sitting down, Dan handed the money to Stacey.

Stacey counted the cash, chugged her new beer, crushed the can, and threw it in the yard near the one she had finished minutes before.

"The only person I ever told this story to was a girl I was in rehab with. We were confessing things as we detoxed together. Poor girl was dead within a month of being released. Sad part is, I can't even remember her name."

"Everything gets harder to remember with age."

Stacey ignored the comment and cleared her throat. "Nate told me that he was with Odin Rowe the night Mary Spears was killed."

Dan tried not to look surprised.

"Did Nate murder her?" Dan asked.

"No. But he was involved. Odin Rowe really was her killer. Nate left no room for doubt about that."

"Nate admitted this?"

Stacey nodded. "He did. Part of me wishes he hadn't. A big part of me. He was whacked out of his mind at the time he told me. He'd been smoking, drinking, shooting, and snorting. He hadn't slept in a couple of days. And for some reason, out of the blue, he started talking about the evening that Mary Spears went missing. Rambling on like he'd been holding it in for years. He wept. The only time I ever saw him cry. At first, I thought maybe he was hallucinating. But the more he talked, the more I believed him. I asked him questions, and he answered them."

"How long was this conversation?"

"Half an hour? Who knows? I had to take a break and hit the bong at one point just to calm my nerves."

"And then?"

"After that night, he never mentioned it again. And I never brought it up. There were times I wondered if he remembered telling me anything. Back in our heyday, blackouts were pretty common. Hours, days. Even a week could go missing."

"Do you remember what he said?"

"If someone told you they buried a body with a convicted serial killer, would you forget?"

"Probably not," Dan replied.

"Damn right, probably not. Nate told me that on the night Mary Spears went missing, he went over to Odin Rowe's to buy drugs. That was a regular thing at the time. Nate said he went around to the side door of the house and knocked. No one answered, so he peeked through the window of the door and saw Odin Rowe rolling up a girl's body in a painter's tarp. Nate said he froze. He couldn't move. And before he could slip away, Rowe spotted him with his nose pressed to the glass."

"Then what happened?" Dan asked.

"Rowe told Nate he could either join the dead girl or help him get rid of the body."

"And he chose the latter?" Dan confirmed.

"Wasn't much of a choice."

"Why didn't he go to the police the next day?" Dan asked. "Tell them what happened."

"That's what most people would have done. Hell, old man Cardin could have probably kept Nate out of trouble. But Nate was an addict. It was easier to accept free drugs from your dealer as payment for your help."

"I can see that."

"That was the deal. Nate got all the drugs he wanted. And for the next couple of months, until Rowe was arrested for murder, Nate took full advantage of the arrangement."

"What did they do with the body?" Dan asked.

"Rowe forced Nate to help him move Mary Spears's body into Nate's car. Only Nate didn't have his own car. He had totaled his. He was driving the Cardin family car. A station wagon. Rowe figured transporting a dead body in the circuit solicitor's car and having Nate drive was a safe option. If anyone pulled them over and ran the plates, they'd probably see who the car was registered to, and they would be on their way."

"Did they get pulled over?"

"Nope. Nate went with Rowe, and they disposed of the body."

"The circuit solicitor had a dead girl in the back of his family station wagon...," Dan said in disbelief.

"Some stories are hard to make up."

"Where did they bury the body?" Dan asked. "I assume it wasn't in the arboretum."

"Hell no. She was buried down in hunting country. The Cardins have a property near Smoaks. They call it Pine Hall."

"You're sure about this?" Dan asked.

Stacey nodded. "Pine Hall. Nate said she was buried along the property line in a remote corner. Near a creek. They have a few hundred acres. A lot of places to bury a body."

"And the only people who knew this were Rowe and Nate?"

"I figure that's right."

"So, the arboretum story was a cover," Dan said.

"A cover. A lie. A convenience. What have you."

"What happened after they buried the body?"

"They drove back. Nate dropped Rowe off, and then he went home to the house in Lake Katherine. It was probably three or four in the morning by then. Nate parked the family station wagon in the driveway. He checked the car to make sure he wasn't leaving any drugs behind for his parents to find. He didn't find any drugs, but he did come across a red sneaker on the floor behind the driver's seat."

"One of Mary Spears's red sneakers?" Dan asked.

"Yep."

"Uh-oh," Dan said.

"For starters," Stacey replied, lighting a new cigarette with the still-burning old one.

"What did he do with the shoe?"

Stacey sighed and shook her head. She started to answer, choked up, and paused. A few seconds later, she replied, "Nate hid the red shoe in his brother's room."

"In Thomas Cardin's room?" Dan confirmed.

"Yep. Nate snuck into his brother's room and put the shoe under his brother's bed."

"While his brother was sleeping in it?"

"Yes," Stacey replied, a tear running down her face.

"That was not very brotherly," Dan said.

"Nate and his brother never got along. That was no secret. But even Nate realized what he did was wrong. The night Nate told me about Mary Spears, he admitted what he'd done with that red shoe was his greatest regret."

"And then what happened?"

"Nothing."

"How can that be?" Dan replied.

"I can only guess."

"Let's hear it."

"I figure at some point, Mrs. Cardin or maybe even Mr. Cardin found the red shoe. Or maybe Mrs. Cardin found the shoe and gave it to her husband. I mean, from what I know, a few days after Mary disappeared, everyone in town had heard a description of what Mary had been wearing. Right down to her red sneakers. Mrs. or Mr. Cardin probably put two and two together pretty quickly."

"And neither parent confronted Thomas about the shoe?"

"According to Nate, he never heard another word about the shoe. Never saw it again."

"Assuming that Nate's parents found the shoe, they had a dilemma. A real problem."

"You bet your ass they had a problem. And I think the Cardins decided they would have at least one good son. It was obvious Nate was heading in the wrong direction. Mr. Cardin was pissed that his namesake was an addict and a fuck up. I don't think he would've survived if his only other child was a murderer."

Dan sat in silence before breaking it. "So the Cardins got rid of the evidence, thinking they were protecting Thomas. No one ever suspected that Nate was involved, and he never came forward with the truth. Was that the end of it?"

"Just about. At Christmas of that year, Nate misplaced his stash of drugs again. This time, it was heroin. And it was found in a bathroom in the house by one of the younger Cardin cousins. That was the straw that broke the camel's back. Nate was told to get his things and leave the house."

"And he did," Dan confirmed.

"Yep. He moved into a carriage house at a friend's place and then headed to Charleston to work in a restaurant. A year later, I met Nate and we moved back to Columbia. The rest is history."

"I hope you have some good memories of Nate."

"I do. Between the highs and lows, we had our laughs. The night he told me the story about Mary wasn't one of them."

"Maybe something good will come out of it."

"I reckon that depends on you."

CHAPTER 49

FROM THE CREST of the hill, sun setting on the other side of the river, Dan spotted Huff on a chair with a fishing rod in hand. The sound of cicadas and frogs filled the air as Dan wound his way down the wooden stairs toward the riverside deck.

Huff, fishing hat on his head, looked over as Dan rounded the corner near the fishing shed. "Look what the cat dragged in. I didn't expect to see you again."

"I tried to call."

"I was busy dealing with my fishing tackle. It's what retired people do for entertainment. What brings you around?"

"I have news that may interest you."

"Do you?"

"What do you know about a woman named Stacey McSween?"

"Never heard of her. Who is she?"

"Nate Cardin Junior's ex-wife. And she's got a story. A doozy. You're going to want to hear it."

Huff placed his fishing rod on the deck with the line remaining in the water. He looked up at Dan, who was still standing. "Enough foreplay. Lay it on me."

Dan leaned against a dock piling. "Stacey McSween told me that Odin Rowe killed Mary Spears. Just like you've said all along."

Huffs attitude seemed to instantly improve. "Well, thanks for giving me some credit."

"She also said that Nate Cardin Junior helped Odin Rowe bury Mary's body."

"Nate Cardin? Thomas's older brother?"

"That's what she said."

"She's delusional. Nate Cardin wasn't around when Mary disappeared. No one in Mary's group of friends mentioned that Nate Cardin was there the day Mary went missing."

"It was a chance meeting at Odin Rowe's house, after Mary left Lake Katherine."

"How's that?"

"Nate Cardin bought drugs from Odin Rowe. By chance, Nate Cardin showed up as Odin Rowe was wrapping a body in a painting tarp. Mary was already dead. Odin Rowe then forced Nate Cardin to help him bury Mary's body. The two of them transported Mary's body in the Cardin family station wagon."

"Do you have any evidence to support this?'

"It's all hearsay. Nate's been dead a long time. But the story means we have a body out there to find."

"There's always been a body out there."

"This time it's different."

"How?"

"I know where Mary is buried."

Huff squinted. "You'd better not be messing around."

"I wouldn't do that. Not on something important. According to Stacey McSween, Mary Spears is buried at Pine Hall. Near a creek that runs through a back corner of the property."

A long silence ensued.

"You'd better be fucking right," Huff said.

"It's time to reopen the investigation into Mary Spears and search the Cardin family's property," Dan said.

Huff brushed his white mustache with his fingers. "We're going to need a warrant. Depending on how receptive the Cardin family is to the search of their property, it may take a day or two to find a judge willing to sign it."

"I'm flying back to DC later tonight. Let me know when the warrant is good to go. I want to be on site when the digging starts."

CHAPTER 50

DAN ZIGZAGGED BEFORE finding a spot on a side street near the National Cathedral. He crossed Wisconsin Avenue, stepped into the foyer of a century-old building, and pressed the button for apartment 501.

"I'll buzz you in," Grace's voice echoed in the foyer.

Dan walked in the direction of the elevators, passing a large bank of mailboxes on the wall. The dated elevator shimmied its way to the fifth floor and, moments later, Dan found himself face-to-face with Dr. Joffee standing in Grace's doorway.

"A doorman with a medical degree," Dan said. "Times must be hard."

"Come in. Grace had to take a call. She'll be right with us."

Dan followed Joffee past the kitchen and entered the living room. A woman seated on the sofa stood up.

"Dan, this is Dr. Fabrizio. She is the one who performed the hypnosis session with Grace."

The two exchanged pleasantries as Grace returned to the room. "Sorry about that," Grace said. "Work's been in a tizzy."

"No worries," Dan replied, sitting down and pulling out his laptop. Seconds later, the screen came to life.

"I can't wait to hear about your trip to Cedar Falls," Joffee said.

"First things first. You were wrong about Iowa. It turned out to be very interesting." Dan produced a single-page document from his bag and handed it to Grace. Grace read the page and passed it to Joffee, who in turn passed it to Dr. Fabrizio.

"As you can see, that's the official death certificate for Mary Martin. She died from blood loss after being accidentally shot."

"Who shot her?" Joffee asked.

"Probably a boy named Pierce," Grace guessed, referring to the name she provided during her second hypnosis session.

"Bingo. Pierce Lamont was his full name. He went to high school with Mary Martin. According to the story, a large group of kids were at a park near the river when the accidental shooting occurred."

"That's similar to the scene I described in my session under hypnosis."

"It is. Pierce Lamont died the next year in a boating accident."

"That's sad," Grace replied.

"Are you ready for the kicker?" Dan asked.

"Absolutely," Grace answered.

Dan clicked on the keyboard of his computer and spun the laptop around. "That's a picture of Mary Martin from the 1967 Cedar Falls High School yearbook."

Grace leaned forward and gasped.

Dr. Fabrizio pulled the computer closer. "What the hell?"

"Looks familiar, no?" Dan asked.

Joffee did a double take on the image before his eyes danced back and forth between the screen and Grace's face.

"How is that possible?" Grace asked.

"The best scientific explanation is that 'it happens,'" Dan answered. "Do you want to see a picture of Pierce Lamont?"

"I'm still trying to digest how Mary Martin could look like my twin sister," Grace said.

Dan clicked to the next photograph. "Any thoughts on who Pierce Lamont resembles?"

"No way," Grace said. "Are you effing kidding me? That's the spitting image of Thomas Cardin."

"Whoa," Joffee added.

Dr. Fabrizio sat in stunned silence.

"Welcome to the world of soul groups. People who have lived, died, and been reincarnated with other souls over multiple lifetimes."

"You're saying that I was Mary Martin in a previous life?"

"That's what you revealed during your second hypnosis session. The photographs are evidence based on that revelation."

"I'm going to need a few minutes to process what you've presented."

"Me too," Fabrizio said.

"Take all the time you need. But fair warning, I've been digesting it for forty-eight hours and it hasn't gotten any easier."

"Can you show the photographs side by side?" Dr. Fabrizio asked.

Dan rubbed his fingertip across the laptop's touch pad and the two images appeared side by side.

Grace stared at the photos on the screen in silence for several long seconds.

"I want to back this conversation up a little. I'm still trying to wrap my head around what's going on," Grace said.

"Sure," Dan said.

"The first time I went under hypnosis, I identified myself as Mary. I also mentioned that a boy I liked was named Thomas. But he wasn't a judge yet. And that boy was present when Mary was killed."

Dan nodded.

"Based on that first session of hypnosis, Dr. Joffee researched Judge Cardin's background and discovered that someone Cardin knew, a girl also named Mary, disappeared in the 1980s when the judge was in high school."

"Yes," Fabrizio said.

"After discovering the similarities between what I disclosed in my first hypnotic session and Judge Cardin's missing classmate, Dr. Joffee hired you, Dan, to investigate more thoroughly."

"So far, so good," Dan answered.

"Fast forward a couple of weeks and my anxiety spirals out of control, eventually reaching the point where I check myself into a psychiatric inpatient unit. This trip into the abyss was highlighted by vomiting and passing out in the lobby of the emergency room, near the registration desk."

"After that unwanted experience, I agreed to a second hypnosis session. This second session went much along the lines as the first session. Under hypnosis I described being near water, with a boy I liked who wanted to show me a gun. This time I identified the boy as Pierce."

"Correct."

"Pierce showed off the gun, which accidentally discharged, and I was mortally wounded. The name I used to identify myself during this second hypnotic session was Mary Martin. We have verification from her death certificate."

"We do," Dan replied. "We also confirmed that a boy named Pierce was present when Mary Martin was shot."

"We have two issues to figure out. The first hinges upon my initial hypnotherapy session where I identified the boy I was with as Thomas. I further added that he was not a judge yet."

Dan and Joffee nodded.

"So, how did I identify a boy named Pierce as 'Thomas who-was-not-a-judge-yet?'"

"I don't know," Dan said.

"Logically speaking, during both hypnotic sessions, I was describing the same scene, the same occurrence. But in the first session, the person who killed me was 'Thomas who-was-not-a-judge-yet,' and in the second session, I identified that same person as Pierce."

"That's the logic."

"If we agree that's correct, then Pierce died in 1967 and was reborn in 1970 as Thomas Cardin."

"Yes."

"How could I know that Thomas Cardin would become a judge? That wouldn't occur until three decades later. Which means I could see Thomas across multiple lives."

"Or your brain connected the visual similarities between Pierce and Thomas, and it was simply a mental hiccup," Fabrizio stated. "Hypnosis isn't always error free."

"I'm going to need a drink or a Xanax," Grace said.

"I'll take one, too," Joffee said. "One of each."

"The second issue I have is in regard to the name Mary."

Dan nodded, sensing where Grace was headed with the conversation.

"What are the chances that a girl who died in 1986 and a girl who died in 1967, were both named Mary? I don't want to oversimplify things, but isn't that what we're talking about? Isn't this where the rubber meets the road?"

Dan responded. "I've considered the same line of reasoning. We have two Marys. Twenty-one years apart. Both of whom were friends with Thomas Cardin. Mary Spears from his current lifetime. Mary Martin from his previous life."

"What are the odds of that?" Grace asked, half rhetorically. "I mean, logically speaking, it sounds like a statistical problem that can be solved."

"I don't disagree. I'll have someone dig into it," Dan replied. "Changing topics, do you guys want to know what happened to Mary Spears?"

"I thought we already knew. She was murdered by a serial killer and buried somewhere," Grace said.

"That still remains true. But the devil is in the details. Mary Spears was murdered by Odin Rowe. That is known. But what's unknown is that Thomas Cardin's older brother, Nate, may have helped Rowe bury Mary's body. And that body may be buried on a property owned and used by the Cardin family. The same property where Thomas Cardin's father's body was recently found."

"And no one knows about this?" Grace asked.

"As of now, only a handful of people. But if it's true, the world's going to find out."

CHAPTER 51

FOUR MEMBERS OF the South Carolina Law Enforcement Division, colloquially known as SLED, unloaded the ground penetrating radar equipment from the back of a silver police van. The workhorse of buried object investigations resembled a large lawnmower without an engine, blades, or bagger. Once on the ground, a lanky technician checked the settings on the four-wheeled yellow block and performed a series of test maneuvers.

Another half-dozen forensic investigators marked a search grid through a series of small colored flags. A female officer sat at a folding table, open laptop in front of her, a camera with a large lens to her right. The lanky technician began pushing the GPR in the direction of the search grid near the property line marked by a dilapidated barbed wire fence.

Dan and Huff stood near each other, swatting at mosquitos, as the proceedings got underway.

"I've never seen one of these devices in action," Dan said as the technician rolled by.

"The GPR? During my career, I only saw it used a few times. The machine looked a lot different back in the day. And they were very expensive. South Carolina didn't get its first GPR until the mid-90s."

For the better part of an hour, Dan and Huff watched as the forensic technician guided the GPR through the search grid. To the untrained eye, it looked as if the technician was attempting to cut shin-high grass without any efficacy. Intermittently, the woman with the laptop seated at the portable table yelled out directions, and the technician would adjust the machine's route. When the technician finished running the machine through the search grid, the group of forensic investigators gathered at the table. After a brief discussion, the SLED members grabbed shovels, rakes, brooms, and brushes from the back of the forensic van.

"Looks like they're going to hand dig," Dan said.

"The GPR probably indicated the depth of whatever they've found. And if we keep in mind there's a buried body, it was put there by two guys at night using a shovel. It shouldn't take forensic investigators long to accomplish the same task in reverse."

❧

A pause in the digging effort was the first indication that a body had been located. One of the technicians dropped his shovel and fetched the camera off the portable table and returned. As the technician took photos of the dig site, he relayed information to the woman at the table, who entered data into the laptop.

The group of investigators exchanged their shovels for smaller tools and dropped to their hands and knees. Fifteen minutes later, the team of investigators unearthed the corner of a blue painter's tarp.

"We have a tarp," one of the investigators chirped.

As a flurry of hands moved dirt, inch-by-inch the length of the tarp was exposed. Holes riddled the material. Thick dirt caked the surface. The photographer continued taking pictures, undisturbed by the heat or flying insects. Moving cautiously, the investigators located the seam where the blue tarp overlapped itself.

Dan and Huff slowly approached for a closer look.

"We have a body," an investigator announced.

Dan and Huff watched as the tarp was painstakingly unearthed and the remains of Mary Spears's body was exposed to air for the first time in nearly forty years. The group of investigators gently moved the tarp and remains into an oversized body bag.

Among the bones, tarp, and tattered remains of clothing, a red sneaker was plainly visible. Dan nudged Huff. "It's her. It's Mary Spears."

Huff stared straight ahead. "Damn you for coming down here and stirring up this mess."

"Sometimes the truth isn't pretty."

"I need to call Mary's mother," the retired detective said as he somberly stepped away from the dig site.

Dan began the walk back to the house at Pine Hall, the commotion of the forensic team's search fading as he covered acres of flat terrain. With the house in sight, Dan noticed a long black car parked among the multitude of police vehicles.

As Dan reached the clearing near the home, Thomas Cardin climbed from the back of the long car.

"Mr. Lord."

"Judge Cardin. I didn't expect you to be here."

"Why wouldn't I come? My friend, my family's land, my reputation."

"It's easier to play ignorant from a distance."

"I heard they found a body."

"They did. I believe it's Mary Spears."

Judge Cardin nodded. "I'm going to head over to the dig site and take a look."

"Not much to see."

Cardin shrugged. "Are you going to be around this evening?"

"Yeah. I'll fly back to DC in the morning."

"Why don't you stop by the house on Lake Katherine. Tonight. Seven. We have unfinished business to discuss."

"What kind of business?"

"The rest of the story."

CHAPTER 52

DAN STEPPED ONTO the columned front porch of the Cardin family home in the Lake Katherine subdivision. Before he could ring the bell, Judge Cardin appeared at the door.

"Mr. Lord. Please come inside. I'm glad you could make it."

"Thank you for the invitation. It was unexpected."

"As I said, we have unfinished business to discuss."

"If you say so."

Dan followed Thomas Cardin as he walked through the foyer and a short hallway that led to the kitchen. Stepping into the rear of the house, Dan admired the lake view from the back of the house.

"This must have been a fun house to grow up in," Dan said.

Cardin pulled the sliding door open and stepped onto the back deck. "It wasn't bad. We had friends, we had a lake in our backyard. It was safe. For the most part."

Dan followed Cardin outside and said, "Until Odin Rowe met Mary Spears."

Cardin dipped his head and glanced out at the water. "I assume you realize what finding Mary's body at Pine Hall means."

"You're not going to be a Supreme Court justice."

"Finding the body of a missing classmate on family property changes things."

"Without a doubt."

"That's an interesting choice of words. Doubt."

"I don't follow, Judge."

"People are going to doubt my innocence in Mary's disappearance. Regardless of Odin Rowe's confession. Regardless of who has been in prison. Regardless of what is said or what happens next. It is a stain I will not be able to remove."

"That's a strong possibility," Dan agreed. The two men stared at each other, neither blinking.

"I have a question for you, Judge."

"Please."

"I was on site when Mary's body was discovered. Her remains were found with only one red shoe. That's one shoe short of a pair."

"I heard that detail."

"Did that come as a surprise to you?"

"Sounds like you're implying something," Cardin responded.

"I met with Stacey McSween a couple of days ago. She used to go by the name of Stacey Cardin. She provided insight into the location of Mary's remains."

Judge Cardin furled his eyebrows. "Stacey?"

"Yes. Your ex-sister-in-law."

"Would I be correct in assuming that she was the anonymous source that led the investigation to Pine Hall?" Cardin surmised.

Dan nodded. "Detective Huff organized the search based on her testimony."

"I heard Stacey showed up drunk to my father's viewing."

"She did. But I met her in the double-wide trailer that your father had purchased and given to her."

"I wasn't aware my father had been in touch with Stacey. I certainly wasn't aware of any trailer."

"Do you know why he bought Stacey a trailer?"

"I don't."

"According to Stacey, your father paid her to change her name. He didn't feel that she lived up to Cardin standards."

"That sounds like something my father would have done. But I didn't know anything about it."

"I believe you."

"What else did Stacey say?"

"She provided a reason why only one shoe was found with the discovery of Mary's body."

Dan could feel the impact of the statement on Cardin as the judge's shoulders slumped. "In a normal situation, this would be the point where someone says it may be better to take a seat," Dan added.

"I'll remain standing."

"Suit yourself. Stacey knew where Mary's body was buried because your brother told her. And your brother knew because he helped Odin Rowe bury Mary's body at Pine Hall."

"I believe you are mistaken. My brother had issues, but he wasn't a killer."

"No, he wasn't. Odin Rowe killed Mary. Your brother helped him bury the body."

"My brother wasn't around the night Mary went missing."

"You're right. He wasn't with you near Lake Katherine. But your brother happened to pay a visit to Odin Rowe to score some drugs the same night Mary went missing. As bad luck would have it, he caught Rowe in the act of wrapping Mary's body in a tarp. Odin Rowe then forced Nate to drive to Pine Hall and help him bury her. He also forced your brother to transport the body in the Cardin family station wagon."

"That seems improbable."

"Stacey also told me why Mary was only buried with one shoe. She knew where the other shoe ended up the night Mary went missing. I think you may know as well."

Cardin seemed to grind his teeth, the muscles in his jaws stiffening.

"Stacey said your brother, Nate, put one of Mary's shoes under your bed."

Cardin's shook his head in disbelief. "Nate wouldn't have done that."

"I'm relaying what Stacey said. The evidence seems to support it. According to Stacey, your brother found the red shoe in the car when he got home in the early morning hours. He put the shoe in your room under your bed while you were asleep."

Cardin grunted. "You don't believe in sugar-coating things, do you?"

"There's a time and a place for everything. At this juncture, what's the point?"

"Damn you, Nate," Cardin whispered.

"You want to tell me what happened? Your version."

Cardin remained silent.

"Judge?"

After several long seconds, Cardin answered, "The truth is, I don't know what happened. I never knew."

"What about your witness statement testimony to the police?"

"It wasn't unusual for me to walk Mary to the edge of the neighborhood when it was time for her to go home. I assumed that's what happened. So that was my testimony. I was three sheets to the wind. Drunk as a skunk. I vaguely recall walking Mary down the street. The next thing I remember was my father waking me up the following morning. I've spent the last forty years scared about what could have happened in between."

"Are you saying that you thought you were responsible for Mary's disappearance?"

"Responsible. Involved. I've considered the possibility nearly every day of my life since."

"That's quite a burden to carry."

"It was. And now I can exchange the burden of wondering what I may have done with the burden of knowing that my brother tried to frame me."

"I apologize for being the bearer of bad tidings."

"On the contrary, you're the bearer of liberation."

"I've read all the police and court files but there are still holes in the story. I would like to have them filled in. Out of her friends, I know you were the last one to see Mary alive. You must have something to add."

"I'm not sure where to begin. Or end."

"It ends with the red shoe."

Cardin gazed at the water. "I found Mary's shoe the following morning. My father came into my room to wake me up for a baseball game. During the night, I had vomited in the trashcan and on the carpet. My father immediately recognized the smell in the room and, without any sympathy, told me to get ready for the game. Needless to say, I was in no condition to move, much less play baseball. Sometime later, he came back into my room for a second time and again told me to get ready. My baseball bag was on the floor, half under my bed. My father grabbed the bag and dragged it out. I sat up, I looked down at my equipment and noticed a red sneaker on the carpet next to the bag."

"What did your dad say?"

"Nothing. Before either of us acknowledged the shoe, I grabbed my trashcan and vomited again."

"A memorable first-time drinking experience."

"I'm happy to report it was my first and last hangover. At any rate, my father berated me for several minutes, telling me how disappointed he was in me. He said it was the type of behavior he expected from my brother but not from me. All the while, this red shoe was on the floor staring up at me. Staring up at us. Of course, at that moment in time, it was just a red shoe. It wasn't a clue."

"And when did you find out that Mary had gone missing?"

"By late morning, the phone was ringing off the hook. By that evening, a description of Mary was broadcast statewide. Missing posters were printed and posted all over the city."

"Did the description of Mary include her shoes?"

"It did."

"What happened to the shoe in your room?"

"I have no idea. I went back to my room for it, but it was gone. And that was the end of it. My father and I never spoke of the shoe. Not the day Mary went missing, nor at any time after that."

"You must've known he'd taken it."

"I didn't know for sure. As time passed, I also considered the possibility that I had misremembered seeing the shoe. Maybe even imagined it."

"That sounds naive on your part."

"It was. Regardless, I spent almost forty years wondering what could have happened. Forty years of silence. Until I received a letter from my father a few days ago."

"What letter?"

"A handwritten letter from my father, written days before his death."

"What did the letter say?"

Cardin rubbed his chin. "Let's make a deal."

"I'm listening."

"I'll share my father's letter with you. And in return, you tell me how a forty-year-old murder, one that had been solved long ago, ended up on your radar."

"Deal."

"Stay here. I'll be right back."

Thomas Cardin stepped inside the house and returned with an envelope. He handed the envelope to Dan, who noted Thomas Cardin's name handwritten across the front.

"Are you sure this is something you want me to read?" Dan asked.

"Why not? As you alluded to, we're neck deep in it now."

Dan opened the envelope, unfolded the letter, and began reading.

Dear Thomas,

I apologize for this letter, which is now in your possession. More specifically, I apologize for the circumstances which have resulted in this letter finding its way to your hands. Your hands. The same hands I marveled at when they were small enough to fit in my own with room to spare. The same hands that cast your first line in the lake outside the window from the house where you grew up. The same hands that helped me recover from the accident that took your dear mother's life. Hands that have undoubtably flipped through millions of pages of legal briefings, rulings, and cases. Without a doubt, you have been the highlight of my life. It has been my honor and privilege to be your father. Your recent nomination to the Supreme Court is a wonderful blessing and acknowledgment of all of your hard work and dedication.

But alas, I will not be around to see the full fruition of your success. While my body continues to put up the good fight, my mind is unquestionably faltering. The filter between my thoughts and words no longer exists. With so much on the line regarding your nomination, I cannot afford to be a potential liability. The Cardin name deserves and demands more than I can provide. As you are aware, life can change in an instant, whether it be the result of squealing brakes, an indiscretion involving drugs, or the unexplainable presence of a single red shoe. Given my mental deterioration, I can add my mind to the list of potential catalysts that could ultimately result in your demise.

Do not cry for me.
Do your best.
Don't look back.

Your father.

Dan folded the letter, slipped it into the envelope, and handed it back to Cardin.

"One thing is for certain. Your father loved you."

"He did. But all for naught." Cardin looked as if he were holding back tears.

"Are you okay, Judge?"

"I'm processing."

"That's fair, given the circumstances."

"Now it's time for your half of the deal. How did you get involved with Mary Spears's case?"

"I was hired by a doctor in Washington, DC, who had a patient who claimed they had knowledge of who killed Mary Spears."

"Odin Rowe killed Mary."

"As it turns out, he did," Dan replied. He pulled his phone from his pocket and began swiping through saved images. After several seconds, Dan held the phone up for Judge Cardin to see.

"Do you recognize that person?"

"May I hold the phone?" Judge Cardin asked.

Dan handed the phone to Judge Cardin and waited for a reaction.

"Obviously, I recognize who is in the photo, but I don't recognize the photograph. I have no idea where or when it was taken," Cardin said.

"That's because it was taken before you were born. That's a school photograph of a boy named Pierce Lamont. I found it in the yearbook for Cedar Falls High School. Class of 1967."

"Or you used AI to generate it."

"I could have had that done. But I didn't."

"You need to walk me from A to B to C. I'm not following."

"Someone claiming to be a girl named Mary in a previous life reported that you killed her. A simple search of your name and a missing girl from your neighborhood led us to Mary Spears. Turns out, that in all likelihood, the person in question was referring to a different Mary. Mary Martin. Born in 1949. Died in 1967. She was a friend of Pierce Lamont. The boy whose image you're looking at."

Judge Cardin rolled his eyes. "Are you serious?"

"Yes."

"That's one of the most implausible things I've ever heard."

"What can I tell you?" Dan said with a shrug.

"Do you have a yearbook photo of the girl, the second Mary, who was Pierce Lamont's friend?"

"Swipe left."

Judge Cardin did as he was instructed and immediately recognized Mary Martin from her yearbook photo. "Grace Homan?"

"Yes. But the Grace Homan you know had nothing to do with the revelation. Not consciously. She was under hypnosis when she experienced what is referred to as a past-life regression. Grace has no recollection of anything she said or divulged while under hypnosis."

"Part of me wants to call that convenient amnesia."

"I can understand that, but she didn't have ulterior motives. She was terrified that you would find out. She was afraid of losing her career."

"The legal profession can be unforgiving."

"Among other adjectives."

"I can't help but think that if Stacey McSween had spoken up sooner about what my brother had done, and where Mary's body had been buried, my father would still be alive."

"That's a what-if game that cannot be won. Some would say it shouldn't even be played."

"So where does that leave us, Mr. Lord?"

"We're done. Unless you have something else."

"Should I anticipate further legal repercussions?"

"I told you, I was only interested in finding out what happened to Mary Spears. The rest of it is noise. I hope you get to remain in your current position. I hope everyone gets to move on with their lives."

"What about the accusation that my father paid to have Odin Rowe murdered?"

"Lack of evidence would make that impossible to prove. And honestly, who cares about Rowe?"

"The press."

"I'll make sure it's something you don't have to worry about."

"How is that?"

"I'll handle it," Dan said simply, not wanting to go into detail.

"Maybe we'll see each other again back in DC. It's a small town in many ways."

"Yes, it is. I hope it's big enough for the both of us."

"I believe it is," Cardin assured him.

"One more thing I wanted to say about Odin Rowe. And it will be the last time I say his name."

"What's that?"

"I have to give him a little credit. He outfoxed everyone. The detective on his case and your father weren't fully convinced he was responsible for Mary's murder. And Odin Rowe smelled opportunity. Your father had the power to work out a deal with Rowe. With the missing shoe found under your bed in mind, your father told Rowe he could save his own life by confessing to all three murders or face the death penalty. Your father came up with a script and they all followed it. Little did he know, Rowe was actually responsible for everything he confessed to."

"I hope that's the end of the story," Cardin said quietly.

"So do I."

After a long pause, Cardin broke the silence. "When do you head back?"

"First thing in the morning."

Dan sat at the bar in The Happy Cock, listening to a group of white kids speaking to each other in Chinese. He finished his third beer, splitting his attention between a soccer game and CNN on competing screens.

As he ordered another drink, a photograph of Thomas Cardin flashed on the screen, the image framed by a red, white, and blue flag.

Closed captions ran across the bottom of the screen and Dan read words as they passed by.

> "...After much deliberation, I have decided to remove myself from consideration as a nominee to the Supreme Court. I am honored and flattered by the nomination. That said, given extenuating circumstances, I believe it is in the best interest of the country to withdraw my nomination. I hold the Supreme Court and the laws of this land in the highest regard. Our legal system requires fairness, transparency, and truthfulness. Anything less is unacceptable. Anything less is a distraction. I refuse to allow myself to be a distraction to the process of confirming a new Supreme Court justice. Thank you for your time. I will not be taking further questions at this juncture."

CHAPTER 53

FROM THE SIDEWALK, Dan spotted Detectives Fields and Wallace at a table inside Bistrot Du Coin. The French restaurant was a mainstay on Connecticut Avenue, the decor emulating a street-side Parisienne café. Dan walked past the hostess stand, pointing in the direction of his waiting party. Seconds later, he sat down at a circular table with a granite top.

"This is certainly an improvement over the Irish bar."

"We ordered mussels and frites," Detective Fields said.

"I call them clams and fries," Wallace added.

"Sounds good."

"What's on the agenda besides French food?" Wallace asked.

"I wanted to follow up with you. The last time we spoke I mentioned that I might need your help, and that your lack of jurisdiction in South Carolina may be useful to what I had in mind."

"I recall."

"Turns out, I didn't need your help after all."

"Now I really want to know what the favor was going to be," Wallace said.

"At the time I mentioned it, I was considering asking you to perform a polygraph exam on Judge Thomas Cardin."

"And why in God's name would I say yes to that?"

"Because I'm charming. And you can be bought with expensive

cigars. And it would have been a patriotic gesture for this country to identify a killer before they became a Supreme Court justice. But it's irrelevant now. Judge Cardin declined the invitation to a polygraph. Since then, the case has concluded."

"We saw that Thomas Cardin withdrew his nomination for the Supreme Court," Fields said.

"I assume you had something to do with that," Wallace added.

"I don't think I did."

"Why don't you tell us and let us decide?"

"Can I get a beer first?"

∽

Dan returned his beer glass to the table and wiped the small foam mustache off his upper lip.

"What are my rules regarding the types of cases I refuse to work?"

"No Mafia and no spies," Wallace answered. "But since we've met, you've broken both of those rules."

"I'm adding one more to the list. The reincarnated."

"Oh boy, this should be good," Fields said.

"Here's the Cardin case, from soup to nuts. It started with a woman who moved to DC about eight months ago after taking a job with Judge Thomas Cardin. Cardin serves on one of the most important courts in the US. The woman in question is a highly intelligent type A workaholic with impeccable credentials.

"Shortly after beginning to work with Judge Thomas, this woman began experiencing debilitating anxiety attacks. As the attacks worsened, she sought help with a psychiatrist in town by the name of Dr. Joffee. After months of traditional treatments without any improvement in the patient's symptoms, Dr. Joffee suggested alternative therapy options. The woman in question agreed to try hypnosis, which was ultimately performed by another doctor with extensive experience in hypnosis therapy—Dr. Fabrizio. Basically, Dr. Fabrizio puts patients into a hypnotic trance and tries to uncover things in the past that may explain their current anxiety.

"During the hypnosis session, much to everyone's surprise, the female patient referred to herself as a high school–aged girl named Mary. This is different from the clerk's real name. Also, during the hypnosis session, the woman indicated that Thomas Cardin had killed her while she was this person named Mary. Dr. Fabrizio, given her expertise, quickly realized the session had gone beyond simple hypnosis, and what the patient was actually describing was past-life regression.

"Out of curiosity, Dr. Joffee then poked around online and discovered that a girl named Mary Spears, who was friends with Judge Thomas Cardin in the 1980s, had disappeared. Her body was never found. Dr. Joffee then hired yours truly to investigate further.

"I soon learned that the girl, Mary Spears, who went missing in 1986 was murdered by a serial killer, Odin Rowe. But on the day leading to the evening that Mary went missing, she had spent time with her friends in a neighboring subdivision. Among her friends was a teenager named Thomas Cardin."

"Uh-oh," Fields said.

"Save that," Dan said. "I read through the legal and law enforcement files regarding Mary's disappearance and learned that Thomas Cardin was actually the last person to have seen Mary alive. On top of that, Thomas Cardin's father was the district attorney at the time and the prosecutor on the case. In South Carolina, district attorneys are actually called circuit solicitors. Regardless, you have a son who was the last person to see a girl alive before she went missing, and a father who was prosecuting the case against a serial killer."

"Sounds fishy," Wallace said.

"The serial killer signed a confession and was sentenced to life in prison for the murder of three girls in Columbia, South Carolina, in 1986."

"So the serial killer actually murdered this girl named Mary?"

"That's the legal version of the story. Then I discovered some details of the confession were not factually accurate. And that got me thinking."

"Let me guess, it got you thinking it was all smoke and mirrors. That Thomas Cardin did kill this girl and that the confession was a convenient way for the district attorney to clear his son."

"Yes. South Carolina wasn't afraid of the death penalty in the eighties, and a guy who killed three girls was prime death row material. But he got a life sentence instead. I also stumbled upon the fact that the lead detective on the case was the missing girl's cousin."

"You have a nose for finding a good shitshow," Wallace said.

"Fast forward a couple of weeks after the initial hypnotherapy session, and the female patient continued to have anxiety attacks. Eventually her symptoms became so extreme that she agreed to another session of hypnotherapy. During this second session, the patient again expressed the belief that she was killed while she was in high school. This time, however, she said her name was Mary Martin, not Mary Spears, and that she was a student in Cedar Falls, not Columbia. She stated that the boy who killed her was named Pierce, not Thomas."

"Sounds like she was playing with you."

"The thought occurred to me, but I no longer think that's the case. Through vital records, I was able to identify a girl from Cedar Falls named Mary Martin who was indeed killed by a male friend named Pierce. This occurred in 1967. Incidentally, Thomas Cardin was not born until 1970.

"Out of a plethora of data mining and AI good fortune, I was able to identify and meet with Thomas Cardin's ex-sister-in-law. She and Thomas Cardin's brother had been in and out of rehab numerous times. After Thomas Cardin's brother died, the sister-in-law was paid to change her name back to her maiden name."

"They chased her out of the family?" Wallace asked.

"They did. But she walked away with some cash and a place to live. She also took a secret with her. She claimed that in 1986, Thomas Cardin's brother helped bury Mary's body. To make matters worse, he helped bury it on a property owned by the Cardins. And even worse still, Thomas Cardin's brother placed one of the missing girl's shoes under Thomas Cardin's bed."

"That's not cool," Fields chimed in.

"To say the least."

"And then what happened?" she asked.

"Then things get murky. It seems that Thomas Cardin and his father both saw the shoe in Thomas Cardin's bedroom the morning after the girl went missing. At the time, no one knew Mary Spears was missing. A couple of hours later, the community and town was abuzz with news of the missing girl. Thomas Cardin remembered the shoe. When he went back to his room, the shoe was gone. He never mentioned it and his father never brought up the topic."

"They just acted like it was never there?"

"That's right. Thomas Cardin said he'd been blackout drunk the night before and he wondered if he'd had anything to do with Mary's disappearance. His father, it seems, was going to make sure that no suspicion was cast on his son. In 1986, the father buried evidence of the shoe and got a serial killer to confess to the missing girl's murder. Forty years later, the father paid two other inmates to eliminate the serial killer in prison. The father then burned all the legal files as a last-ditch effort to protect his son's reputation. For the final nail in the coffin, his father killed himself and took his side of the story to his grave."

Wallace interjected, "And once they found the girl's body on the Cardin property, that was the end of Thomas Cardin's nomination."

"It was."

Dan pulled out his phone, swiped at the screen, and then placed his phone on the table, screen facing up.

"Can one of you search on your phone for a picture of Thomas Cardin when he was younger?" Dan asked. "Quite a few have been in the press recently."

Wallace found a photograph of Cardin from his first year of law school at Duke. He placed his phone on the table next to Dan's.

"The photograph on my phone is from the 1967 Cedar Falls High School Yearbook. It's an image of a young man named Pierce Lamont. He was identified in the patient's second hypnotherapy session as the boy who shot her."

"Holy shit. It looks like Thomas Cardin," Fields said. "The resemblance is uncanny."

"I just got goosebumps," Wallace added.

A waiter in a bow tie interrupted the conversation with a bowl of mussels in a white wine sauce. He returned a moment later with two large baskets of frites.

Fields bit into a French french fry, swallowed, and spoke. "For the life of me, I can't get over the coincidence of the name Mary," she said. "This patient claimed to be Mary in a past life, and then claimed to be a different Mary in a different past life?"

"Perhaps. Everyone thought that during the woman's first hypnotherapy session she was referring to herself as Mary Spears, the missing girl. But in hindsight, the patient was identifying herself as Mary Martin, who died in 1967. The fact that a girl named Mary, who was friends with Thomas Cardin, went missing in 1986 was an old-fashioned coincidence."

"Seems too coincidental."

"I'm working on that."

CHAPTER 54

DRESSED IN BLACK, Dan began walking toward the silhouette of a large group on the horizon. Stepping through the parallel rows of tombstones, Dan approached the back of the gathering as the pastor finished his eulogy with an Our Father. One by one, attendees stood in line, grabbed a rose from a basket near the front row of chairs, and placed it on the casket.

Dan stood at a distance until the last person in line had placed a rose on the coffin and the crowd began to disperse. In the midst of the somberness, Mary Spears's mother doled out quiet hugs and kisses through streams of tears.

Dan waited for an opening and stepped forward to pay his final respects to a girl he'd never met. Taking one of the remaining roses from the graveside basket, he placed it on the coffin. He prayed in silence, crossed himself, and turned away. As he parted the row of chairs near the gravesite, Mary's mother greeted him.

"I was hoping you would make it," Mary's mother said before Dan spoke. "LeRoy tells me you had a hand in bringing my daughter back. I want to thank you."

"It was a group effort."

"Well, the group, as you call them, couldn't bring my daughter home for all those years. And then you showed up."

"Sometimes you get lucky."

"I think we both know it wasn't luck, Mr. Lord. You may have improved my opinion of attorneys just a little."

"Don't go overboard."

"Thank you for what you did," Mary's mother said as she embraced Dan in a long, tight hug. "Here comes LeRoy," she warned, patting Dan on the shoulder before she turned to talk to the pastor.

"I owe you an apology," Huff said, arriving with an extended hand.

"You owe me more than one."

"I was wrong. You were right. You did good. It wouldn't have happened if you didn't come down here and start raising hell."

Dan shrugged. "Maybe."

"Did you hear that Thomas Cardin withdrew his nomination for the Supreme Court?"

"I did. I feel bad for him. It doesn't seem like he had anything to do with Mary's disappearance."

"No, it doesn't."

"I hope the press goes easy on him."

"When did the press do that for anyone?'

"Never."

"I assume you're heading back to DC, and you won't be showing your face around these parts anymore."

"Not on a regular basis, no."

"If you're ever back in town, give me a ring. We can try our hand at fishing again."

"The next time I come to Columbia, it won't be in the summer."

"Fair enough. Take care, Dan."

CHAPTER 55

FOUR PEOPLE IN Dr. Joffee's office made a full house. Dan and Dr. Joffee grabbed chairs on opposite ends of the coffee table while Grace Homan and Dr. Fabrizio filled the sofa. A laptop on the desk was pointed at the seating area.

Dr. Joffee spoke. "I think we can get started. The gang's all here. We also have Dr. Pando from the University of Virginia DOPS program on Zoom. Thanks for joining so late in the evening."

"I wouldn't miss it."

"Without further ado, Dan has something to he wants to share."

Dan took a minute to summarize the case before reaching the crux of the meeting. "Several times during this investigation, the question of probability has come to the forefront. I've spent some time considering that question. Distilled to its simplest form, the question is how likely is it for one person to know two people named Mary, one born in 1949 and the other born in 1970. Ultimately, that's what this investigation comes down to. Thomas Cardin knew a girl named Mary who was born in 1970. Thomas Cardin in a previous life knew a girl named Mary who was born in 1949."

Grace Homan nodded at Dan with laser-like focus.

"Does anyone want to guess how popular the name Mary was in 1949?"

"Popular," Grace said.

"That's right. In the year 1949, Mary was the most popular girl's name. In fact, for every single year between 1880 and 1955, Mary was the most popular girl's name. At its peak, Mary was four times as popular as the next three names combined. Think about that. For seventy-five years straight, Mary was the most popular girl's name. In 1949, if you were a grade school student in an average-size class, there was a 90 percent chance you would have a classmate named Mary."

"What happened in the fifties?" Dr. Pando asked.

"In the fifties, Linda overtook Mary for the top spot for several years, but Mary remained popular. In fact, Mary remained in the top five names for two more decades."

"That's a lot of Marys," Grace said aloud.

"It is. An almost unimaginable number of Marys. No name in the last fifty years came close to the dominance of Mary for the preceding seventy-five years. Not all the Michelles, Emilys, and Sophias combined.

"Because of the name's popularity, the real anomaly in this investigation is the name Mary in 1970, the year Mary Spears was born. For that year, Mary was the ninth most popular name. That equates to somewhere between 2 and 3 percent of all girls. In the first half of the last century, Mary was between 6 and 8 percent of all girl names.

"What does this mean? It means the likelihood of knowing two Marys, one born in 1949 and one born in 1970, was much higher than any of us would have thought."

Heads in the room nodded.

"Of course, this analysis doesn't take into account the likelihood of reincarnation, group reincarnation, or the likelihood of someone under hypnosis recalling a past life. Those are unknown variables. But for knowing two people named Mary, it is not rare."

"I feel better," Grace stated.

"Why is that?" Dr. Joffee asked.

"It means, statistically speaking, what I revealed under hypnosis doesn't make me crazy. I'm within the normal distribution."

"I don't think the doctors in the room are ready to embrace a normal distribution as an assessment," Dan said, smiling.

"Dan, would you mind coming back to UVA and giving us a presentation on this investigation?" Dr. Pando asked. "We can sign NDAs and redact names. It would be a good case study."

Dan looked at Joffee, and Joffee gave a nod of approval. "I think that can be arranged," Dan agreed.

"Good."

"Anything else, anyone?"

"I say we all go out for drinks," Grace said, noticeably perkier.

CHAPTER 56

DAN PRESSED THE buzzer on the gate and waited for Tobias to reply. Horses on the neighbor's farm were grazing in the field. The morning sun crept over the Blue Ridge Mountains, beginning its effort to burn away the morning clouds. Without a response from Tobias, the gate opened and Dan drove up to the house. Peso was waiting on the front porch as Dan approached, and the large dog began licking his hand.

Dan knocked on the door and heard Tobias yell. "Come on down."

With Peso by his side, Dan entered the house, traversed the first floor, and descended into the basement. Tobias was seated in front of his wall of monitors, bottles of medication and a glass of green juice off to the side of the desktop. Tobias moved close to the screen, read several lines of code to himself, and then leaned back in his chair.

"Sorry, I had to finish something."

"I can wait."

"I'm done."

"I had a favor to ask. Can you delete all evidence of the payment that was made to the prison accounts?"

"The anonymous, untraceable payments made via prepaid cards?"

"That's them."

"Those payments are already untraceable."

"Can you make the transactions disappear?"

"I can, if you tell me why."

"Because I promised Thomas Cardin I would make them disappear. I know they're anonymous, but, in theory, someone could stumble their way onto those payments."

"Done. I'll make them disappear," Tobias replied. "By the way, this is the second time you've asked me to clean up after one of your cases."

"Thanks. I appreciate it."

"Anything else you need?"

"No."

"Then I have something I want to show you. I've been working on a profiling database."

"Who are you profiling?"

"I started with the worst of the worst. Murderers, rapists, and pedophiles. But I've moved on to everyone."

"How are you managing that? Sounds like you've been poking around in places you shouldn't have been. No one has access to enough data to profile everyone. With the exception of the NSA."

"That's not entirely accurate. Do you want me to give you a demo?"

"No. I'm going to pretend I never heard you mention anything of the sort. I'd prefer to remain ignorant so I can maintain plausible deniability."

"Let me know if you change your mind."

"I will," Dan replied, sighing. "And I'd be remiss if I didn't warn you to be careful."

"I'm being careful."

"I hope so."

"On the topic of being careful, I have a favor to ask."

"Sure."

"If something were to happen to me, I want you to make sure that Peso is taken care of."

"Sounds like you're planning something."

"Just promise me you'll take care of the dog."

"No problem. I'll handle it."

"Good. The dog likes you better, anyway."

Dan knew Tobias was withholding additional information. "I want a promise from you. Before you go and do anything crazy, promise that you'll check with me."

"I promise I'll try. But you know what they say about crazy…"

"Yeah. Crazy people are usually the last to know they're acting crazy."

AUTHOR'S NOTE

For the record, I began writing this book long before I ever heard the name Alex Murdaugh.